"Haven't you heard about the infamous Haynes brothers?"

Jordan asked.

Holly shrugged. "Only rumors."

"Four generations of heartbreakers. Three generations of philandering men and bitter women. Unfortunately, we have a natural ability to attract women."

She raised her chin slightly. "I hadn't noticed. Oh, what I meant was—" She paused.

He waited, wondering what she would say. Would she claim to be completely unaffected by him, and if she did, would be believe her?

"I'm sorry," she finally said. "I really should be going."

He turned slightly. It would be easy to pull her close. Easy to draw her into his arms an kiss her until she forgot where and who she was. He might hate that part of himself, but like his brothers, he was every inch a Haynes. He knew how to seduce a woman....

SUSAN MALLERY is the *USA TODAY* best-selling and award-winning author of over fifty books for Harlequin and Silhouette Books. She makes her home in the Los Angeles area with her handsome prince of a husband and her two adorable-but-not-bright cats.

Susan Mallery

HOLLY AND Mistletoe

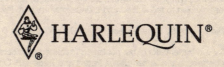

TORONTO • NEW YORK • LONDON
AMSTERDAM • PARIS • SYDNEY • HAMBURG
STOCKHOLM • ATHENS • TOKYO • MILAN • MADRID
PRAGUE • WARSAW • BUDAPEST • AUCKLAND

ISBN 0-373-81129-2

HOLLY AND MISTLETOE

This edition published by arrangement with Harlequin Books S.A.

® and TM are trademarks of the publisher. Trademarks indicated with
® are registered in the United States Patent and Trademark Office, the
Canadian Trade Marks Office and in other countries.

www.eHarlequin.com

Printed in U.S.A.

To Barbara Zeiger.
I was determined to give you a second firefighter
to fall in love with, and here he is. Enjoy!
With love and thanks, for the years of friendship.

Chapter One

The woman sitting next to him clung to his hand as if she were afraid he would bolt. Her eyes were closed, and her lips moved in silent conversation. Long blond hair tumbled over her shoulders and brushed against their joined fingers.

Jordan Haynes recognized the sights and smells of the hospital. He recognized that the faint blurring at the edges of his mind meant he'd been given a strong painkiller. But he didn't recognize the woman. Still, it was damn nice of her to be so concerned, whoever she was.

She dropped her head slightly, and her hair slipped onto his wrist. Cool silk, he thought, wishing he had the strength to raise his free hand and touch the pale strands. His arm felt as if it had been pinned down by an elephant, although he knew it was just weakness that made him unable to move. So instead of touching her hair, he turned his attention to her face.

She had freckles across the tops of her cheeks and on

her nose. Freckles. He grimaced. Her wide mouth tilted up at the corners. Except for the mascara darkening her lashes, she didn't wear makeup. He would bet fifty bucks that her eyes were blue and that she'd been a cheerleader in high school. She looked wholesome enough to be in a milk commercial. So what was she doing in his hospital room?

Her hair continued to stroke his skin. The soft, erotic touch had his mind producing fantasies his weakened body had no chance of fulfilling. At least not any time in the near future.

He tugged his hand free of her grasp. Instantly her eyes opened. Yup. Dark blue. He owed himself fifty bucks. As soon as he got out of here, he would pay up.

The woman smiled. Her pink lips parted, exposing white teeth and a smile so pleased, she might have just won the lottery.

"You're awake," she said, then took hold of his fingers again. The smile broadened. "I'm thrilled. The nurse said you were going to be fine, but I was worried. How do you feel? Any pain? Do you want some water?"

He tried to speak and realized his throat was scratchy. He coughed. Before he was done, the woman had stood up, reached for a small plastic pitcher and poured some water into a glass. She slipped one arm behind his shoulders, then raised the glass to his lips.

"Sip slowly," she said.

He obliged. When he'd finished half the cup, he nodded to indicate he was done. She set the glass on the table beside his bed, then returned to her seat. This time she clasped his hand in both of hers. Before he could extricate himself, she leaned forward and pressed their joined hands against her chest.

That got his attention. While she'd been standing, he'd gathered a quick impression of curves. Awe-inspiring curves. She had the kind of breasts that made up every adolescent boy's fantasies. Right now his wrist nestled between them while the knuckle of his index finger brushed against the base of her throat. It didn't matter that her loose sweatshirt was hardly seductive. As far as he was concerned, they could spend the rest of the day in this position.

Then he noticed her blue eyes darkening with emotion, and he had the uncomfortable feeling she might be fighting tears. Dear God, anything but that.

"Who *are* you?" he asked gruffly.

The woman stopped blinking and smiled again. "I'm Holly Garrett." She made the announcement as if that cleared up everything.

He didn't know any Holly Garrett, although judging by the way she was staring at him—as if he'd single-handedly saved the world—she obviously knew him.

Great. Either the painkillers were doing strange things to him, or he was losing his mind.

"And?" he prompted.

She stared blankly for a moment, then laughed. He felt the vibration of the sound against the back of his hand, which was still pressed against her chest. Friendly, he thought. A charming trait in an attractive woman.

"There was a storm," she said. "You saved my cat."

The memories flooded him, and he groaned. The high winds had blown over a tree, sending it crashing through a single apartment above a detached garage. Not only had the unit been partially crushed, but the pipes had broken and flooded the place. When his men had arrived, there hadn't been much left to save. He recalled a frantic woman trying to get through a stuck door. Water had been everywhere. The two-story structure looked as if it was about to collapse. Jordan had grabbed her around the waist and hauled her to safety. She'd been screaming about her damn cat.

Like a fool he'd gone after the animal. And look what it had gotten him. He'd been back in Glenwood less than six months, and already he was in the hospital. Damn.

"You were wonderful," Holly said, her voice thick with emotion. "I don't know what I would have done if something had happened t-to…" Her voice gave out.

"Ah, yeah, well, nothing did, right?"

She sniffed. "Thank you," she murmured, and squeezed his fingers.

"Just doing my job," he muttered. And a poor job at that. He was going to take some well-deserved teasing when he went back to the station.

Judging from the throbbing in his legs and back, he wouldn't be returning to work any time soon. Everyone had seen what had happened, too. He'd found the cat and had made it safely out of the apartment, clutching the squirming furball under his coat. Once they were out on the balcony, the cat had tried to get away. Jordan had been afraid the animal would be injured by the fire trucks or lost in the crowd, so he'd hung on to the cat from hell. They'd wrestled each other, and the cat had nearly won. But in the end Jordan had prevailed and grabbed it by the scruff of its neck. Unfortunately in the process he'd lost his footing on the wet wooden balcony above the garage and had fallen off the side.

In front of everyone. He swore silently.

"Anything broken?" he asked, eyeing his leg under the sheet and blanket. He couldn't tell if he was in a cast or not.

Holly shook her head. "No. I took Mistletoe to the vet, and she's just fine."

"I wasn't asking about the cat," he said dryly.

She stared at him a moment, then blushed. Color climbed

from her neck to her face, covering her cheeks, then moving up to her hairline. Her mouth formed a perfect circle. "Oh."

She glanced down, seemed to realize she was clutching his hand to her bosom and released him. "Oh, sorry. You meant *your* injuries. I don't have specifics. The nurse said you would be going home tomorrow, if that helps." She gave him a quick glance. "I'm sorry we were so much trouble."

The hand she'd abandoned felt cold. He missed her heat and the faint thudding of her heartbeat. Not to mention the close proximity to her impressive breasts.

"Just doing my job," he said again.

She shook her head. "No, you did more than that. One of the other fire fighters told me it was dangerous for you to go back for Mistletoe. There was some question about the structural integrity of the apartment. And now you're injured. I feel so horrible. If there's anything I can do, please tell me."

He thought about asking her to hold his hand again, but before he could form the question, the door opened and a half-dozen people poured into the room.

His younger brother, Kyle, was first. "Heard you fell off a building," Kyle said, grinning. "Anything to be a hero."

Two of his sisters-in-law pushed Kyle out of the way. Elizabeth and Rebecca rushed to his side. "How do you feel?" Elizabeth asked.

"You can stay with us," Rebecca offered. "There's plenty of room."

His third sister-in-law, Sandy, asked, "Anything broken?"

"I'm still not sure," he said, but was drowned out by his older brothers, Travis and Craig, who offered their expert medical opinions on his condition.

Austin Lucas, a friend of the family, stepped to the other side of the bed and shook hands with him. "Glad you're going to be okay."

"Me, too," Jordan answered, then realized Holly was gone. Somehow she'd slipped out of the room as his family had entered.

He looked at the concerned group of people surrounding him. They talked to each other about his condition and argued over who was going to have him stay with them while he convalesced. The conversation washed over him, a warm, loving blanket of concern. He knew everyone in the room cared just as he cared about them. He loved them, but he wasn't always one of them. Like Austin, Jordan spent much of his life on the fringes, watching the rest of the world connect in a way he couldn't understand.

So he let them argue, because he knew in the end he would do what he wanted. He would go home and be alone, because that was the way he preferred it.

"Yes, yes, it's very macho, but I'm not impressed." Elizabeth Haynes stood with her hands on her hips. Although her husband wasn't the oldest of the Haynes brothers, Travis had been the first of them to marry, so Elizabeth was the leader of the women. Right now she was speaking for all of them, and Jordan didn't like what she was saying.

"I'm staying in my house," he said, and glared at her defiantly. The fact that he was flat on his back diluted some of his power, but he wasn't going to acknowledge that.

"Fine. Stay here. Just not alone."

He raised his hand to his face and rubbed his eyes. Everything hurt. His legs, his chest, his back, even his hair. He'd stopped taking painkillers that morning. Maybe it had been a mistake.

Elizabeth sat on the edge of the bed and took one of his

hands. It reminded him of another woman who had recently done the same.

He couldn't get Holly Garrett out of his mind. As a rule he avoided romantic entanglements. This time he was tempted to break his rule. Fortunately his physical limitations prevented him from acting on impulse. With a little luck, by the time he was healed, he would have forgotten all about her. In the meantime he had to get everyone to stop treating him like an invalid.

"You have two choices," Elizabeth said. "Come home with one of us, or…"

"I'll take the 'or,'" he said.

She ignored him. "Or have Louise stay here and look after you."

He scowled.

"I know," she said. "You hate Louise. No one knows why. Not even Louise. Over the years you've made your feelings about her very clear. However, you're out of options. The doctor said you have to stay in bed for two weeks. So someone has to be here to look after you. It's up to you, Jordan. Stay here with Louise or come home with one of your brothers."

Jordan turned his head toward the window. He could see bright blue sky and a few puffy clouds. Late fall in northern California could be rainy, but today the weather welcomed him home.

Stay here with Louise or go live with one of his brothers. The latter wasn't a problem. He got along with all of them. But it was only about a month until the holidays. Everyone would be busy with preparations. He would be in the way.

Louise. He swore silently. No one understood why he didn't like her. But he knew the truth. Her guilty secret. He'd carried it around with him for seventeen years. Everyone accepted her as a de facto member of the Haynes family. Everyone but Jordan. He questioned her motives for getting close to the brothers.

"Well?" Elizabeth prompted.

"You're not leaving me with much of a choice."

"That's the point."

He drew in a deep breath. He'd bought the old Victorian mansion less than two months ago. So far, he hadn't made much of a dent in restoration. Maybe he could get some work done while he was convalescing. He wouldn't be allowed back at the fire station until after the first of the year.

"I want to stay here," he said, then regretted his decision.

"If you're sure." Elizabeth leaned close and kissed his cheek. "Be nice to her, okay? She's doing you a favor."

"No problem."

She smiled. "Liar. You're going to make her life hell. I'd better go warn her." She rose and started out of the room. When she reached the doorway, she glanced back at him. "None of this would be a problem if you'd found yourself a wife."

He smiled at the familiarity of this conversation. Elizabeth was forever trying to get him married off. "I like being single."

She didn't return his smile. "That's twice you've lied to me, Jordan. It's a good thing I love you as much as I do. Maybe I'll have my husband beat some sense into you."

"I could take him."

She raised her eyebrows.

"Well, maybe not today, but by the end of the week, for sure."

She stared at him for a moment. "Maybe this is a good thing—lying flat on your back will give you time to think about your life."

"I like my life just fine."

"You've got your brothers fooled, but we females know better. You need a woman."

"I'm a wounded hero. Leave me in peace."

"You're a stubborn pain in the rear, but I still adore you. Take care of yourself and be nice to Louise."

She gave a quick wave and disappeared into the hallway. Jordan listened to the sound of her footsteps on the hardwood floor until they faded into silence. Then he was alone.

It was how he preferred to spend his life. Alone. He was used to the solitude. But for the next few days he was going to have company. Louise. Elizabeth had admonished him to be nice. He grimaced. If she knew the truth, she wouldn't be so eager to have Louise around. But Elizabeth didn't know. No one did. He wasn't sure why he'd been so diligent in guarding Louise's secret. Probably some useless sense of honor. It didn't matter that he owed her nothing or that she'd destroyed his family. He couldn't bring himself to betray her.

He heard footsteps again, but these weren't his sister-in-law's. Louise Carberry entered the room and stared at him. She was of average height with short blond hair and blue eyes. He guessed she had to be in her midforties, although she looked younger. A bright, long-sleeved fuchsia blouse hung loosely over purple pants. Louise dressed as if she were color-blind. She folded her arms over her chest and stared at him. He stared back.

The moment reminded him of wrestling with the damn cat on the landing. He'd won the battle but lost the war when he'd gone over the side of the balcony and fallen to the hard ground below. His gaze narrowed, and he wondered if he would end this encounter equally battered.

Holly parked her car in front of the large Victorian mansion. It was barely after six in the evening, but already it was dark. The sun set before five in the late fall. She could see the faint outline of the beautiful old house. The peaked roof, the oddly shaped windows.

Years ago this part of Glenwood had been home to the rich and powerful families who made their fortunes in timber, mining and the railroads. By the Second World War most of them had left the small community for San Francisco or Los Angeles, but their houses remained. Some had been torn down, and some had been converted to offices. A few were being restored.

Holly stared up at the building and wished she had the money to buy one herself. She would turn the downstairs into a showroom and live upstairs. She smiled. It was a lovely dream but had no basis in reality. Still, her fingers itched to feel the original wood molding and trace the shape of the stained-glass windows above the double-wide front door.

She opened the car door, collected the pink bakery box, then got out. The early evening was still. Only the faint call of a night bird disturbed the silence. She drew in a deep breath and inhaled the scent of trees and the faint hint of some distant fire. The homey scent reminded her she'd lost *her* home three days ago. Everything she owned had either been crushed or soaked beyond repair. At least Mistletoe was safe.

Holly clutched the bakery box firmly and started up the stairs. Store-bought cookies wouldn't begin to repay the debt she owed Fire Captain Jordan Haynes, but they were the best she could do right now. She didn't have access to a kitchen. As soon as she could afford to get a new place, she would bake something wonderful.

She climbed the three stairs leading to the front porch. The wide wooden deck was bare. A single light burned by the front door. It wasn't difficult to imagine what the porch would look like in the summer with sunlight spilling onto the refinished floor. There would be a swing at one end, by the large window on her right. Maybe a white wrought-iron table-and-chair set at the other end. She could see ladies in long dresses and gentlemen in tall hats. Children would play on the lawn, their laughter a happy background noise to the adults' polite conversation.

"You are the most stubborn man it's ever been my misfortune to know."

The loud voice startled Holly, and she jumped back. She stared at the front door. She'd been about to knock, but obviously this wasn't a good time.

A low male voice rumbled, answering the woman's claim, but Holly couldn't make out the words.

"If I didn't care about the rest of your family, I'd leave you here to starve," the woman continued. "It would serve you right, too. Even my Alfred, God rest his soul, wasn't this fussy about his food."

More male rumbling.

"Fine. Be insulted. You don't like anything else about me, why should I be surprised that you resent being compared to a dog? Oh, and Alfred was better looking than you, too."

Before Holly could step back, the front door flew open. A woman stood in the doorway and stared at her. "I thought I heard a car pull up."

Holly didn't know what to do. She was poised awkwardly on the porch, with one foot behind her as she tried to make her escape.

"I..." she said, then paused. "I've come to see Captain Haynes, but I'll come back. This obviously isn't a good time."

The woman grimaced. "There's never a good time with that one. He's the most stubborn, pigheaded, difficult man

I've ever met.'' She paused and shook her head. "Why you'd want to see him is beyond me, but you might as well come in. Maybe you can talk some sense into him. Oh, by the way, I'm Louise.''

She held the door open. Holly forced herself to walk forward. Once in the house, she shifted her weight from foot to foot and stared at her hostess.

The woman wore a bright yellow long-sleeved shirt tucked into cobalt blue slacks. The silver belt around her trim waist matched the moon-and-star silver earrings she wore. The two women were about the same height, although Holly had come straight from work and still wore two-inch heels.

"What are you doing now?" a male voice inquired. The tone of the question implied the woman was doing something he wouldn't like.

"Answering the door. Quit being such a baby. You don't want me in the room with you, but you yell at me if I go away. Make up your mind, Jordan.''

"Who is it?" he asked.

Louise rolled her eyes. "One of your women.''

"Oh, no,'' Holly said quickly. "I'm not—''

"Which one?''

Louise glanced at her. "What's your name?''

"Holly, but I'm not—''

"Holly,'' she yelled toward the back of the house.

Jordan was silent. Holly figured he was trying to place her.

"I'm not one of Captain Haynes's women,'' she said.

Louise smiled. "Then that makes you a smart girl. That boy is nothing but a difficult toad.'' She shouted the last part of the sentence, aiming the words in the direction of what must be his room. After drawing in a deep breath, she released it slowly. "I'm real sorry I ever agreed to this.

He's going to be the death of me. And Lord knows I'm far too young to die.'' She paused and drew her eyebrows together. "Who are you, then?"

"I'm Holly Garrett." Holly shifted her package to the other arm and held out her hand. "My apartment was destroyed in that big storm earlier in the week. Captain Haynes went back inside to save my cat." She shook Louise's hand. "I'm the reason he was injured. Actually Mistletoe is, but I feel responsible."

"Mistletoe?"

"My cat. She got scared once they were out of the apartment and tried to get away. Captain Haynes managed to hold on to her, but in the process he lost his footing on the balcony and fell over the side. I feel terrible about what happened."

Louise's lips started to twitch. She chuckled for a moment. "Felled by a cat. Serves him right."

"I brought cookies," Holly said, holding out the box. "They're not much. I couldn't make them myself. I don't have a kitchen right now. I wish I did. I really like to cook and bake."

"Louise!" Jordan yelled.

"Wait a minute," she yelled back, then lowered her voice. "He's going to be flat on his back for two weeks. I don't think I'm going to last here."

"You're his…?"

"Housekeeper. It's a temporary job. Very temporary. You want some coffee?" Louise didn't wait for an answer. She just headed for the rear of the house.

Holly trailed after her. As they passed through the foyer, she noticed the stunning chandelier hanging down from the ceiling two stories up. The tiny crystal teardrops were original. They caught light and created rainbows. The banister was hand carved, the floors in great shape. In her mind's eye she saw the house as it had once been and what it would be like again, given enough time, money and love.

"He's through there," Louise said, pointing to a half-closed door.

Holly saw a library and beyond that the foot of a bed in what had once probably been the study.

"How is he?"

Louise snorted. "If his foul temper is anything to go by, he's improving every hour."

They entered the large kitchen. A tray sat on the table in the center of the room. Louise motioned to it. "Says he won't eat it. Can you imagine? I've been cooking all my life, but Mr. High-and-Mighty doesn't like it."

Holly glanced at the plate filled with meat loaf, mashed potatoes and vegetables. It smelled wonderful. Her stomach growled. She hadn't had anything since breakfast, and suddenly she was starving.

Louise smiled. "Help yourself."

"Oh, I couldn't."

"Louise!" Jordan called again. He sounded furious.

Holly looked at the tray, then in the direction of the makeshift bedroom. She owed Jordan Haynes a big debt. He'd saved her cat. Mistletoe had been her mother's gift to her the Christmas before she died. A single dinner wouldn't do much to repay what she owed him, but it could be a start. She didn't know much about men, but she was intimately familiar with a sick room.

"Maybe I could help," she said cautiously.

Louise planted her hands on her hips. "Honey, you're welcome to try." She glanced at the clock over the stove. "My evening college class starts in forty minutes. I don't have the time to fix Jordan something else. Why don't you go introduce yourself and if he takes to you, then be my guest."

"Thank you," Holly said, then headed back the way she'd come. She knew several dishes specially designed to tempt an invalid's appetite. She'd taken care of her mother for years.

"Oh, and Holly?"

She paused, then glanced over her shoulder. "Yes?"

"Tell the boy to put some clothes on."

Chapter Two

Tell Jordan to put some clothes on? Holly blinked several times. "You mean he's—" She couldn't even say the word, but she could sure think it loudly. Naked?

Louise winked. "You'll just have to go see for yourself, won't you? Don't worry. He hasn't got anything you haven't seen a dozen times before."

Holly gave a weak smile, then headed for the study. Actually Louise was wrong. Jordan *did* have something she had never seen before. At least he did if he was naked.

As she walked through the library, one part of her mind noted the hand-fitted floor-to-ceiling bookshelves and the large crystal light fixtures hanging in each corner. In front of her she could see the bottom of a bed. Her steps slowed. Naked? No, Louise wouldn't do that to her.

She stopped on the library side of the doorway and cleared her throat. Maybe she should warn him that she was about to enter his room. So if he was, well, naked, he could cover up.

Still, she hesitated before speaking. She didn't know what to say. Just thinking about the handsome fire fighter made her nervous. At the hospital she'd been so concerned about his condition, she'd barely had time to notice his looks at all. But once he woke up and they spoke, she hadn't been able to think about anything else. Her stomach had gotten all sort of quivery, and she'd barely been able to form whole sentences. Thank goodness his family had shown up and she'd been able to escape before she made a complete fool of herself.

Now here she was, about to enter his bedroom. Well, not *really* his bedroom. He had been put downstairs because it was more convenient and would make it easier for him to get around without having to worry about stairs. She remembered when they'd first moved her mother to the downstairs family room. Holly sighed at the memory. She might not know a single thing about men, but she knew how to take care of someone. That's why she was here. Because Jordan Haynes was injured. If she remembered that and forgot how he looked, then everything would be fine.

"Captain Haynes?" she said softly as she stared at the scarred hardwood floors. "Hi, I'm Holly Garrett. We met in the hospital. May I come in?"

"Sure."

She paused, waiting to hear the rustle of bed sheets as he covered himself. There was only silence. She reminded herself that sick and injured people had a lot of similarities. They got frustrated, bored, tired of the pain and isolation. And if she was worried about him being naked, she wouldn't look at anything below his neck.

She drew in a deep breath, smiled broadly and stepped into the converted study.

Thick drapes had been pulled over two sets of windows. In the daylight the room would get morning sun. A hospital bed had been set up in the center of the room. She was familiar with the model. The electric motor allowed the occupant to raise and lower both the head and the foot to find the most comfortable position. A low table had been pushed to one side, and there was a straight-back chair nearby.

Holly ignored the patient for as long as she could, then gave a quick prayer for courage and turned her attention to him.

He wasn't naked. Not completely. Still, her breath caught in her throat, her heart started pounding and she had the uncomfortable feeling that she was turning bright red.

Jordan had raised the back of the bed so he was in a nearly sitting position. Dark hair tumbled onto his forehead. Equally dark eyes studied her in return. She wasn't sure if it was the shape of his masculine features, the set of his jaw or just a perception problem on her part, but she knew he was the best-looking man she'd ever seen. The muscles in her legs felt funny. It took her a moment to figure out they were shaking.

Her gaze dipped to his bare chest and the sheet bunched around his waist. She swallowed, resisting the urge to run for cover. Sculpted muscles defined his shoulders, arms and the hard, flat region of his belly. He looked as if he were posing for a provocative calendar.

"Searching for visible proof of my injuries?" he asked.

Holly realized she'd been staring at him for several seconds. This time she didn't have to guess about blushing. The heat climbed quickly from the edge of her collar to her cheeks. She ducked her head.

"I…" What was she supposed to say?

"Have a seat."

She sank into the straight-back chair and folded her hands on her lap.

"You're the lady with the cat," he said.

She risked a glance. He didn't look annoyed. "Yes. You saved her. I stopped by to see how you were doing. I don't mean to intrude."

He studied her as intently as she had studied him. His attention made her uncomfortable, but she didn't feel she had the right to protest. Fair was fair.

She smoothed a hand over her skirt and wondered what he saw when he looked at her. Blond hair and blue eyes, which sounded more exciting than they were. Curves, she thought grimly, knowing her five-year battle against an extra fifteen pounds had ended in an uneasy truce. The pounds didn't multiply, and she stopped trying to make them go away. So her breasts and hips were a little larger than fashion dictated. She would survive.

"Did you bring the cat to finish me off?" he asked at last.

It took her a moment to realize he was teasing. She smiled. "Mistletoe is very sweet. I'm sure she didn't mean to hurt you. She was just scared."

"Yeah, right. I saw the look in her eyes. She was glad I went over the side." His gaze brushed across her face. "What happened to your hair?"

"My hair?" She reached behind her head and touched her braid. "Nothing. I'm wearing it back."

"Let me see."

She half turned in her seat and tilted her head so he could see the French braid. She'd pinned the end up by the nape of her neck to form a loop.

"I like it loose," he said. "You've got beautiful hair."

"Oh." She blinked. "Ah, thank you."

Had he just paid her a compliment? Holly figured he had. Why? Is that what men and women did? Was he flirting? No. Not with her. She wasn't his type. Actually she didn't know what his type would be, but she was pretty sure she was the furthest female from it. He was injured, that was all. Or possibly delirious.

She cleared her throat and wished she'd had more experience with this kind of situation. The problem was she'd never spent any time with a man and his bare chest before.

"I brought cookies," she said. "They're from the bakery. I don't have a working kitchen yet, but when I do, I'll make something from scratch. That is, if it wouldn't be too inconvenient."

"I think I can handle the inconvenience of you baking me something," he said, then smiled.

The smile caught her unaware. Lines crinkled by his dark eyes. His teeth were white, and his handsome face became almost painfully beautiful. Everything inside her bubbled so much, she thought she might start floating around the room. Wow. She needed to get out more.

"I'm pretty hungry," he said. "Would you mind bringing me a couple of those cookies now? I'd get them myself, but I'm—" He motioned to the sheets.

"Naked," she said without thinking.

"What? No. I'm not supposed to get up for a couple of days. I'm not naked."

Naked? Had she actually said *naked*? Holly covered her face with her hands and made a whimpering noise. "No," she said. "I didn't mean… That is, I…"

"Holly?"

He said her name softly. She thought about just running from the room, but her legs were too shaky to cooperate. "I didn't mean that," she murmured. "Louise said for me to tell you to put some clothes on, so I just sort of thought—''

''It's okay.''

She risked sliding her hands down so they just covered her mouth, then she glanced at him. He wasn't smiling, but he didn't look mad. She breathed a sigh of relief and dropped her hands to her lap. ''Sorry. Look, I'll go get those cookies for you.''

She rose to her feet and reminded herself of his injuries, which were, indirectly, her fault. Act like a nurse, she told herself. She knew how.

''Are you on any medication?'' she asked. ''Pills you have to take with food?''

''Nope.''

She thought about testing for fever but knew she couldn't disconnect enough to touch his forehead without swooning. She consoled herself with the thought that he didn't look hot.

She fought a giggle. Okay, yes, he looked hot, but sexy hot, not fever hot.

Her body continued to tremble, but she tried to ignore it. After taking a couple of steps toward the door, she paused. ''I'm a pretty good cook,'' she said, not looking at him but instead staring at the library in front of her. ''If you don't like what Louise prepared for dinner, I could make something else.'' She swallowed. ''No, it's a dumb idea. Never mind.''

Just as well. She had to get out of his house before she embarrassed herself again. She wanted to tell Jordan it wasn't her fault. Except for a couple of her mother's doctors, she'd never spent any time around men. They were as foreign to her as space aliens.

''I'd like that very much,'' he said.

She whirled around to face him. ''You would?''

"Sounds great. But only if you keep me company. I've been home for two days without anyone to talk to. I'm about to go crazy." Then he gave her that smile again.

Despite the shaking and the way her heart was slamming against her ribs, she forced herself to smile back. "Okay. I'll make something fast."

"I can't wait."

Holly didn't remember leaving the room or walking through the library and down the hall. The next thing she knew, she practically floated into the kitchen. Louise was leaning against the sink. She raised her blond eyebrows.

"Well?" the older woman asked.

"I offered to cook him something, and he said yes."

Louise shook her head. "He's the most stubborn man I've ever met. You're welcome to him." She walked over to the refrigerator and pulled out two steaks.

Holly eyed the meat. "Can he really eat that much?"

Louise grinned. "Only one of them is for him. The other is for you. I heard your stomach growling. You've been at work all day, haven't you? Barely stopped for lunch."

Holly thought of the half sandwich she'd never had time to get back to. It had been a busy afternoon. Still, she would much rather be busy and go without food than sit alone in an empty store, wishing for customers.

Before she could comment, Louise continued, "I know what it's like to be young. Thinking about everything but being healthy." She opened the refrigerator and pointed to the bottom bin. "There's plenty of fresh vegetables. He likes them steamed. Of course, not when I steam them."

"Why doesn't he like *you?*" Holly asked.

The housekeeper shrugged. She crossed the worn linoleum floor and grabbed a denim jacket hanging from a hook by the back door. "I don't know. He's always been this way. I've been working on and off for the Haynes family for years. There's four brothers, five if you count Austin, who isn't technically family but might as well be. I've helped when they've had new babies, cooked for the bachelors, nursed them through illness—'' she tilted her head toward the study ''—and injury.'' She smiled. ''They're a wonderful group of people. Except that one.''

''Then why are you here?''

Louise slipped on her jacket. There was a backpack on a second hook. She reached for that and slung it over her shoulder. ''Because I care about the family. I told them I would look after him, and the good Lord willing, I'll survive. But that Jordan has a chip on his shoulder. Don't ask me why. He's never said, and I haven't bothered to ask. Maybe I will one of these days.''

Louise opened the back door. ''My class starts at seven. I'll be home around ten-thirty.''

''Oh, I'll be long gone,'' Holly said. ''I'm just going to cook his dinner, then leave.''

''I appreciate this. I would have gone to my class no matter what, but I would have spent the whole time feeling guilty.'' Louise gave a quick grin, then left.

Holly turned to the old-fashioned kitchen and realized she hadn't asked where anything was. She was going to have to fumble around to find pots and pans. She didn't really mind. She was in one of the beautiful Victorian mansions she'd admired since coming to town. Jordan Haynes might not get along with his housekeeper, but Holly thought he was nice. Best of all, she was taking the first step in repaying her debt to him.

Jordan watched Holly carrying in a laden tray. She'd found an apron and slipped it over the white frilly blouse and long, soft-looking blue skirt she wore. Her wide eyes shone with excitement, and her mouth quivered on the verge of smiling.

"Are you hungry?" she asked.

He inhaled the savory aroma of steak, baked potato and broccoli. "Starved."

She set the tray on the table he'd pulled next to the bed. Like the bed, the table had been rented from a hospital-supply center. He'd figured if he had to be restricted for a couple of weeks, he might as well be comfortable. The table slid around easily and could be raised and lowered to fit across his bed.

Holly reached for the bed controls. "Can you sit up a little more? It will be easier to eat."

"Sure."

She worked the controls like an expert. Next she raised the table two inches and slid it close. She unfolded a napkin and handed it to him. She played nurse very well. Interesting.

He glanced at the tray and saw it was set with two plates. "Thanks for joining me," he said. "Sometimes I get tired of eating alone."

Holly sank into the chair next to him. "I'm glad you don't mind. Louise suggested I join you. I was going to ask, but..." Her voice trailed off.

The all-business persona faded as quickly as it had arrived. She looked at him out of the corner of her eye, as if she didn't dare stare directly. Quite a contrast of personalities. Deliberate or unconscious? Then he reminded himself he'd spent nearly three days staring at the same four walls. His family had stopped by to visit, but it wasn't enough to fill the hours. He didn't care if Holly was a serial killer. He was grateful for her company, whatever her motives.

She took her plate and set it on her lap. He cut a piece of steak and tasted it. The meat was cooked perfectly.

"Great," he said when he'd swallowed, then leaned back. "So, Holly Garrett, cat owner, how'd you find me?"

"I went to the fire station. I thought I could leave the cookies with one of the men there and they would deliver them."

"Fat chance. They would have been devoured in thirty seconds."

She smiled. "That's what the captain on duty told me. He gave me your address. I hope you don't mind."

"It's fine. Glenwood is a small town. Everyone knows everyone. That's why I moved back."

"Where did you move from?"

"Sacramento. I'd grown up in Glenwood. When I decided to become a fire fighter, I left."

She cut some broccoli and speared it with her fork. "Don't they have a training academy here?"

"The county does. But that wasn't the problem. My father was the sheriff. His father was a cop, all my uncles are cops. I'm one of four boys, and the other three are all cops."

"You were expected to be a policeman, too." It wasn't a question.

"Exactly." He remembered the fights he'd had with his old man. His brothers had teased him about his choice, but they'd supported his decision. Not Earl Haynes. His father had threatened to disown him. By that time Jordan hadn't cared much about his father's opinion. Not after everything the old man had done.

Holly tilted her head slightly. "Are you happy with what you do?"

"Yes. But I didn't like being away from my brothers and their families. So I put in an application here. When a position for fire captain opened up, I got the job.'' He grinned. ''One of my brothers, Travis, is the sheriff. He never said anything, but I suspect he put in a good word for me.''

Holly laughed softly. The sweet sound penetrated his chest and, for a moment, thawed some of the cold he felt there. Then the laughter faded, and her eyes darkened with an emotion he could only label as sadness.

Don't be a fool, Haynes, he told himself. He didn't know this woman well enough to be reading her emotions.

''Your family sounds wonderful,'' Holly said, the tone of her voice confirming his guess. ''I can understand why you would move back to be near them. How long have you been here?''

''About six months.''

''That's when I got here, too.''

''What brought you to Glenwood? It's not exactly a bustling metropolis.''

''My mother and I inherited a store.''

So she wasn't a nurse. ''Which one?''

''An antique store across from the park. Now it's called A Victorian Parlor.''

He remembered seeing the shop after it had opened. ''When I'm feeling better, I'm going to be working on restoring this old place. Maybe I should come by.''

''Definitely.'' She leaned forward. ''The store specializes in Victorian pieces, with a whole section on restoration. There are books of wallpaper, both reproductions of old prints, as well as Victorian inspired. I can order fixtures, faucets, even disguised switch covers. As far as the restoration books go, a few are for sale, but mostly I loan them out. That's one of the things I like about Glenwood. There are so many old homes that people are restoring.''

She hung on to her plate with one hand and gestured with the other. Enthusiasm filled her voice.

"You like your work," he said.

"I love it."

"Then I'll come into the store and get your help."

"I'd like that."

Their eyes met. She bit her lower lip and turned away. Jordan studied her. Part of him wanted her to be as shy and innocent as she seemed; another part of him hoped it was an act. If she was playing a role, then he wouldn't like her—and that would be easier for him. Mostly because he didn't want to admit being attracted to Holly Garrett.

"I remember that place being empty for a long time. When did you and your mother inherit the store?"

"My mom's aunt passed away about five years ago. She's the one who left it to us." She toyed with the last piece of steak, then pushed it away and set the plate on the floor. "My mother was ill for several years. She had breast cancer that kept coming back. We talked about the antique store. It was our joint dream." Holly leaned back in the chair and folded her hands on her lap. "After she died three years ago, I paid off the rest of the medical bills, then saved money. When I had enough, I moved up here."

She told the story simply. Jordan knew there were many details she'd left out. He wondered about family. Was she an only child? Where was her father in all this? But he didn't like questions, and he wasn't about to force her to answer his. At least part of the mystery was explained. If her mother had been ill for a long time, Holly would have become familiar with hospitals. No wonder she could do a great nurse imitation.

"Do you like owning your own business?" he asked.

"I love it. When I was still in high school, I had a part-time job working in an antique store. After I graduated, I worked there full-time. I know a lot about antiques, restoration. One day I want to buy an old place like this and restore it from the ground up.''

"Two of my brothers have houses like this. Travis has finished his. Kyle and Sandy are still wrestling with plumbing upgrades. When I'm up and around, I can show you the houses if you'd like.''

"That would be wonderful. What are you going to do with this house?''

"I'm not sure. In some of the rooms I'm stripping paint off the original molding. You wouldn't believe what people do to beautiful wood.''

"Tell me about it. I've seen some horrible things. It should be illegal.'' She moved her chair a little closer to his bed. "Once I went to an estate sale. A woman had covered every piece of furniture with gold paint. It was appalling.''

Holly continued with her story, but Jordan was having trouble concentrating. He stared at her face. When she'd visited him in the hospital, he'd noticed her freckles and the fact that she didn't wear much makeup. Today was the same. Her lashes were darkened with mascara, but other than that, she was as clean scrubbed as a ten-year-old.

He watched her full lips move as she spoke. Enthusiasm made her eyes sparkle. Her arms moved, and with them, her body. His gaze was drawn to her chest. She was definitely this side of curvy. Her breasts would spill out of his hands, but he didn't think he would mind all that much.

He fought down a grin. His family and friends considered him reclusive and brooding. Occasionally he bordered on surly. So what the hell was this woman doing in his house? And why was he so pleased to be in her company?

"When you're ready to strip wallpaper, let me know,'' she said. "I have a steamer that works like magic.'' She glanced at the high ceilings. "Even with that, in some of the rooms it's going to take days."

"I'll get my brothers to help me," he said. "I've helped them enough times."

"You're one of four, right?"

He nodded.

"That's nice." She sighed. "I always wanted a big family, but it was just my mom and me."

Holly was alone. Jordan didn't know what that felt like. Many times he found himself standing on the outside of family activities. Watching rather than participating. But that was about him, not about the family. He always had a place to go where he was welcome. He couldn't imagine a world where no one cared about him.

"There's no husband lurking in the background? Or a jealous boyfriend? I'm not in a position to have to defend myself."

She blushed. "Hardly. I haven't really had time for that sort of thing."

What sort of thing had she had time for?

Leave it alone, Haynes, he told himself. She wasn't the woman for him. He'd wondered if the innocent act was real. Now he had a bad feeling it was. Wholesome. Just as he'd first thought.

"How old are you?" he asked.

"Twenty-eight."

Twenty-eight and never been kissed. He pushed the rolling table to one side. That was unlikely. Holly had been kissed. How could she look the way she did and not have been kissed? She probably had a trail of men drooling after her everywhere she went.

"Have you met a lot of people in Glenwood?" he asked. He meant men, of course, but asking that directly would be rude. Not to mention the fact that it would imply an interest he didn't have.

Liar, a voice in his head yelled. He ignored it.

"Some. People who come into my store are nice. I know my landlord, of course. I've made a couple of friends."

She looked away from him as he spoke, and he knew in that instant she was lying. She hadn't made a lot of friends, but she didn't want him feeling sorry for her.

He thought about the women his brothers had married. All of them were terrific and friendly. He had a feeling if he mentioned Holly to them, they would take her under their wings and draw her into the group. Or at least help her feel less alone. But Holly might not want him interfering.

Before he could ask or offer, she rose and collected their dinner plates. "Would you like some coffee?" she asked.

"That would be great. Oh, and some of those cookies you brought."

She gave him a quick smile, then headed out of the room. He watched the sway of her hips as she walked, and felt a stirring deep inside. He ignored it, just as he ignored the flicker of interest and the sensation of being intrigued. It had been a long time since a woman had caught his attention.

He reminded himself there was a price to be paid for getting involved. A price for caring. He wasn't willing to pay that again. But that wasn't what this was about. Holly was keeping him company. Nothing more. Soon she would leave, and he wouldn't have to see her again. Bad enough to risk getting involved with any woman. Worse to risk the heart of an innocent.

Chapter Three

Holly brought in coffee and a plate of cookies. While she'd been in the kitchen, she'd removed her apron. Jordan tried to ignore her curves and his body's natural reaction to them. Aside from the fact that they were strangers, he was in no condition to act on any impulses, however pleasant the fantasy.

"I didn't know how you liked it," she said as she set the tray on the table across his bed. "There's milk and sugar." She motioned to the small containers next to the plate of cookies.

"Black is fine."

She picked up her cup, added milk, stirred, then took her seat. "How do you feel?" she asked.

He shrugged, then grimaced as muscles in his back protested. "Like I was thrown off the side of a building."

Instead of smiling, she grew solemn with concern. "I'm so sorry."

"It's not your fault."

"Yes, it is." She leaned toward him and placed her cup on the table. "I shouldn't have asked you to go back and rescue Mistletoe. When I think about it now…" She swallowed. Her blue eyes darkened with an emotion he couldn't read. "You could have been killed."

"I wouldn't have gone in if I'd been in that much danger."

"Really?"

He nodded. "I like what I do for a living, but I don't have a death wish."

She gave him a faint smile. "She's all I have left from my mother. Mistletoe was a gift to me the Christmas before Mom died. I'm very grateful for what you did." Her voice was husky.

Somehow, in all the moving around, her chair had slid closer to the bed. Now, if she leaned forward as she was doing now, her hands rested on the edge of the mattress. A single strand of blond hair hung down by her cheek. The wisp brushed against her skin, but she didn't seem to notice. His gut clenched as he wondered if she was going to cry. He freely admitted he was a typical male, completely knocked off balance by female tears.

"Just doing my job," he said lightly.

She responded with a smile. "What made you want to do that rather than become a police officer like the rest of your family?"

He pushed the controls and lowered the bed a little, then tucked one hand behind his head. "When I was about eight or nine, a house in the neighborhood caught fire. I watched the fire department at work. I'd never really understood what my father and uncles did. I knew from television they were supposed to catch the bad guys, but Glenwood isn't a hotbed of criminal activity. The sheriff's department acts more as a deterrent than a crime-solving organization. But I could see what the fire fighters did, and I was impressed. That stayed with me.''

He reached for his coffee. That wasn't the only reason. Growing up, he'd also watched his old man. By the time he was twelve, he knew he didn't want to be anything like his father. Earl Haynes had a reputation for being a ladies' man.

Jordan swore silently. It wasn't just the women his father flaunted. It was the disrespect for everyone else. No one mattered, and nothing was important but Earl's pleasures. He often hit the boys for no reason, then told them to consider themselves punished in advance of their next mistake. Jordan's brothers had been able to look past the man and carry on the family tradition of law enforcement, but not Jordan.

He could feel his anger building. Even after all this time, his father still got to him. He wondered if that would ever change.

''Jordan? Are you feeling all right?'' Holly's voice was concerned. She rose and touched her palm to his forehead. With her other hand she took his wrist and felt his pulse. ''Slightly elevated,'' she murmured, ''but you don't feel hot.''

She pressed the back of her hand against his cheek, then touched his earlobe. He figured if she kept that up much longer, he could really show her an elevated pulse.

''Do you want a painkiller or are you due for some other medication?''

''I'm fine,'' he said. ''Relax.''

He *was* fine. Since getting out of the hospital, he'd grown used to the dull ache in his body. He'd wanted to give up his prescriptions altogether, but he needed the medication to sleep at night. During the day he did without.

She released his hand, sank back in her chair and continued to study him. Gone was the blushing innocent. He liked the contrast of competence and shyness almost as much as he liked her freckles.

She gave him a half smile. "I should leave so you can get some rest."

"I'd prefer that you kept me company. It gets pretty boring lying here all day."

"You've got Louise."

Rather than answer that, he reached for his coffee.

Holly opened her mouth to speak, but before she could say anything, there was a noise from the kitchen. She stood up and turned toward the sound.

"I'm back," Louise called.

Figures, Jordan grumbled to himself.

Holly glanced at her watch. "Goodness. I didn't realize how long I'd been here. You must be exhausted. I'm so sorry. You should have said something." She twisted her fingers together. "My only excuse is that I've been spending too much time on my own. Mistletoe is a sweetie, but she's not much for conversation."

She was babbling. He liked it. It meant she was nervous and unsure of herself. Better than that, it meant she liked him. He wanted her to like him.

He heard footsteps in the hallway, then Louise stepped into the room. Her eyebrows arched in surprise.

"You two seem to be getting along. Everything all right?"

"It's my fault," Holly said quickly. "After dinner I—"

Jordan didn't know how else to shut her up. He reached out and grabbed her hand. She turned and stared at him. He ignored her.

"Everything is fine," he told the housekeeper. "How was your class?"

Now both women were staring at him. He figured he had Holly's attention because of the incredibly hot sparks arcing between their clasped hands. He'd never felt anything like it before, and he sure as hell didn't know what it meant. He also wasn't going to let go, because he had a feeling if he did, she would bolt. He wanted to make sure she was going to come back and see him again.

Louise stared at him because his question was the first civil comment he'd spoken since she arrived. For a moment he wondered if it was really so necessary to be such a bastard around her. Then he reminded himself of all she'd done and how many lives she'd torn apart, and he knew she deserved all that and more. The fact that she was doing a nice thing by looking after him was something he would have to learn to ignore.

"The professor barely looks old enough to have to shave every day, but he lectures real nice," Louise said cautiously.

"I should go," Holly said, tugging her fingers free.

Jordan didn't want to let her go. For one incredibly stupid moment he wished he could stand up and kiss her. If he'd been on medication, he would have said it was the drugs talking, but he hadn't had anything since the previous evening. So it was the boredom or the pain. Or maybe it was the fact that outside his family, he didn't have many friends. He liked Holly. She was someone he could be friends with.

Even as he thought the statement, he half expected to be zapped by lightning. Sure, he wanted to be friends with her. That's why he'd spent half the evening staring at her curves.

"Come back tomorrow," he said without thinking.

Holly's full lips turned up at the corners. "I'd like that," she said softly.

He smiled. Her reaction was instant. Her mouth parted, and her breathing increased. He saw the faint tremor that rippled through her body. He'd never much wanted it, but apparently he still had it. The infamous whatever that made Haynes men popular with the ladies. Years before he'd used it to get whatever he wanted, but he'd grown up and the game had lost its appeal.

He turned off the smile, and Holly blinked, as if she were awakening from a spell. She gave him a quick wave and walked from the room. Louise followed. Jordan was left alone in the silence.

He would have to be careful. Despite his preoccupation with her curves, he liked Holly and he would be grateful for her company. But only as his friend. He didn't want anything more. He knew the truth about romantic entanglements. He'd learned it from an expert. Despite all the songs and movies about the joys of falling in love, the truth was that love hurt.

Holly walked into the kitchen to collect her purse.

"I'm impressed," Louise said, strolling behind her. "You worked a miracle."

"It wasn't very difficult." Holly smiled at the housekeeper and hoped her trembling wasn't obvious. Touching Jordan to see if he had a fever was one thing. She could ignore the fact that he was handsome, charming and very close to naked. But when he'd taken her hand and smiled at her, she'd thought she was going to faint.

She drew in a deep breath. It wasn't fair that one man should have so many good qualities. They should be spread around among several men. Then she wouldn't have to worry about making a fool of herself in his presence.

"Maybe it wasn't hard for you," Louise said, "but I can't get a lick of cooperation out of that boy. I don't suppose you'd consider coming here full-time until he's healed.''

Holly grinned. "Sorry, I've got a business to run."

"Just my luck. Guess I'm stuck with him." She rolled her eyes. "He forgot himself and was nearly pleasant to me tonight. I'm sure I'll pay for that in the morning."

"I don't understand why he acts like that."

Louise touched her right earring, separating the dangling silver moon and stars. "Could be any number of things. He's never come out and said. Glenwood is a small town. People know each other's business. But he's carried his anger for a long time. I suppose one day I'll have to have it out with him, but not tonight." She smiled brightly. "You coming back tomorrow?"

"You really think I should?"

"Of course. If nothing else, I could use a break from his bad temper."

"I know it's difficult. My mother was sick for nearly ten years. When she was feeling good, she was fun and easy to be around, but after days of being in pain she got—" Holly hesitated.

"Cranky?" Louise offered.

Holly smiled. "That's as good a word as any."

She glanced back toward the study. Jordan *had* asked her to come back, and she really would like to spend some more time with him. Tonight had been great fun. Talking with another person was much better than spending the evening alone.

"So you'll be here?" Louise asked.

Holly started toward the front door with the housekeeper following behind. "Yes. I'd like that very much."

"Good. I look forward to it, and I'm sure Jordan does, too." She held the door open.

Holly stepped onto the porch and waved. "Good night."

It was just dinner and conversation, she reasoned as she started her car and backed down the driveway. It wasn't really like a date. So what if Jordan was funny, charming and handsome? She was being neighborly. Besides, she'd been so busy getting her business started, she hadn't had time to meet anyone. Jordan could be her first friend. And Louise, too, although the thought of seeing Louise again wasn't quite as exciting.

If nothing else, the visit would get her out of the store. Since she'd lost her apartment, she'd been sleeping in the shop. There were plenty of sofas to bunk on. They weren't that comfortable—but it was only for a few weeks. Stocking her store with inventory for Christmas had taken every last penny she had. When the storm had struck, she'd lost all her furniture and most of her clothes. She couldn't afford to replace everything, let alone come up with first and last months' rent. But if she had a good holiday season, she would be fine come January first. Then she would find a new apartment and buy a few things. In the meantime she had the store, and that was enough.

That night, as she stretched out in her sleeping bag on one of the more comfortable sofas, she thought about her evening with Jordan and smiled in the darkness. Her pleasure wasn't just about how he looked, even though his smile took her breath away. It was that he really took the time to listen to her. No one had ever done that before. She shifted, and Mistletoe meowed in protest. The cat was using her feet as a pillow. Holly could feel the vibration of Mistletoe's purring through the sleeping bag. The familiar sensation relaxed her.

"Maybe I'll take you to meet him," she murmured. "Then you can thank him in person."

Mistletoe yawned, obviously not impressed.

* * *

Three days later Louise opened the front door as Holly climbed the stairs.

"Right on time," Louise said.

"There weren't any customers in the store, so I closed exactly at five." She stepped inside, then set the large basket she was carrying on the floor. "I hope you don't mind, but I brought Mistletoe."

Louise eyed the basket. "Is she the cat responsible for Jordan's injuries?"

"Yes. She's really very sweet, but she got scared by everything going on."

"Don't make excuses. I like her already." Louise bent down and opened the basket. Mistletoe was curled up inside. Her long gray fur fluffed out around her. Big green eyes stared at Louise. The housekeeper let Mistletoe smell her hand, then scratched behind her ears. The cat purred in ecstasy.

"She's beautiful," Louise said.

"A purebred Persian, and she doesn't hesitate to remind people that she's special."

Louise stood up. Mistletoe sniffed the air, then stepped out of the basket. Her round belly hung low.

"Has she been eating too many table scraps or is she pregnant?"

"Pregnant," Holly said. "It's only a couple of weeks until she's due. I've been coming here every night, and I didn't want to keep leaving her alone. You're not allergic, are you?"

"Not at all." Louise bent over and petted the cat. "Aren't you a pretty girl? Now, you go bother Jordan. There's a sweet cat. Yes, you go shed cat hair all over his sheets." Mistletoe arched into the caresses. When Louise straightened, the animal began to explore the foyer.

Holly took a deep breath. "Something smells wonderful. What is it tonight?"

"Spaghetti. I had some frozen sauce. I just defrosted it in the refrigerator, then started heating it about twenty minutes ago."

In the past three days they'd settled into a routine. For some reason Jordan continued to complain about Louise's cooking. So Holly took credit for the evening meal, even though she didn't prepare it. It made Jordan happy, and Louise didn't mind.

The housekeeper disappeared each evening. Some nights she was at the local college taking courses. Other times she was baby-sitting or studying in the library. Holly privately thought she simply left to get away from Jordan.

"I don't understand why he's so stubborn," Holly said as she followed Louise into the kitchen.

As usual the housekeeper dressed to attract attention. This evening she wore a brilliant orange long-sleeved silk blouse tucked into black jeans. A gold belt circled her small waist. Her dangling earrings—a teapot twirling from one ear, a cup and saucer hanging from the other—swayed with her movements.

Holly admired her sense of style even if it wasn't what she would have chosen for herself. For the shop Holly favored ruffly blouses and long, flowing skirts. They reflected the era of the store but allowed her to be mobile. Fortunately she'd kept her work clothes at the store, preferring to change into jeans before she went home. She'd lost a lot of casual wear but could still be dressed appropriately at work.

"You really don't think he's caught on?" she asked as she leaned against the kitchen counter. The old-fashioned room hadn't been updated since the early fifties. The counter tiles were alternating light and dark green. The big stove had rounded corners and a storage area on one side. The only modern appliance was the microwave on the counter.

"Even if he has, why would he want to admit it?" Louise bent over and pulled out a large pot. "This should do for the pasta. The sauce is simmering on that back burner. Just give it a stir every fifteen minutes or so. The longer it cooks, the tastier it will be."

She motioned to a loaf of bread by the sink. "I picked that up fresh this afternoon." She winked at Holly. "I think he suspects I'm doing the cooking, but he likes pretending you're doing it instead. He gets to growl at me and have you keep him company every night. What's not to like?"

"I suppose. I guess I feel a little guilty claiming credit for all your wonderful meals."

"If it makes him feel better to think he's eating your food and not mine, let him. The faster he's feeling better, the quicker I can get out of here."

"How's he doing today?"

Louise grimaced. "Pretty bad. The fool got up this morning. The doctor told him to relax. Anyway, he overdid it and spiked a fever this afternoon. I finally convinced him to take an over-the-counter painkiller, and last time I checked, he was sleeping. You might want to look in on him. I think he'll wake up on his own in an hour or so."

"That's fine." Holly brushed her hands against her skirt, then stared at Louise. "I have another favor to ask."

"Sure, what?"

She cleared her throat. "Could I use the shower?" She felt her cheeks getting hot, but plunged on before she lost her nerve. "I've been living at the store since the fire. There's a bathroom with a sink but no shower. I've been bathing piecemeal, and I really want to be able to wash my hair without having to bend over that tiny sink."

Louise stared at her for several seconds. "Child, you don't even have to ask. Why didn't you say something sooner? There's five bathrooms in this house, and Jordan's only using one of them. Come right this way."

Louise marched out of the kitchen. Holly followed on her heels. She was quickly shown the downstairs bathroom, the closet with fresh towels, then handed a thick terry-cloth robe.

"The boy never uses it, so it's practically new."

Holly hugged the robe to her chest. She'd brought shampoo and other toiletries, but she hadn't thought of a robe. "Thanks. I appreciate this."

Louise shook her blond head. "I'm the one in your debt. You're giving me a break by staying with him." She glanced at her watch. "I've got to get going or I'll be late. I can't have a tardy on my attendance record. I've never been late once this whole semester. Oh, and I might not get home right on time. Several of us are going out to coffee with the professor after class."

Holly stared at her. "The one so young he doesn't have to shave every day?"

Louise shrugged. "Oh, Richard isn't all that young. He's nearly thirty-five. He just looks young."

"You call him Richard?"

Louise cleared her throat. "Did I say Richard? I meant Professor Wilson. That's his name. I'm out of here. Have fun."

With that, the housekeeper left the bathroom and walked down the hall. Holly stared after her and shook her head. Too much had happened too fast.

She set the robe on a hook behind the bathroom door, then went to collect her toiletries. Once in the foyer, she moved Mistletoe's basket to one side and picked up her oversize purse. Her cat raced down the stairs and came over to be petted.

"Are you enjoying all this new stuff to sniff?" Holly asked.

Mistletoe purred in response.

When Holly straightened, the cat took off to explore another part of the house. Holly moved through the library, then tiptoed into the study.

Jordan was sprawled out on the rented hospital bed. One dark lock of hair tumbled across his forehead. While he was asleep, he appeared a little younger, although just as good-looking. Her heart did its usual rapid patter against her ribs, but she was learning to accept the fluttery sensation. It was just part of the price she paid to spend time with him.

She reached out and touched his face. He was warm but not hot. If he'd spiked a fever, it seemed to have faded. Also, he was sleeping soundly without the restlessness that accompanies fever.

She studied him for a few minutes, examining the strong line of his jaw, his straight nose, the faint stubble on his chin. Sometimes while they were talking, she had the oddest sensation of being part of a play or a movie. It didn't feel real. What was she doing here?

But she didn't dare question her good fortune. Even though she'd never had much opportunity to spend time with men, she'd always dreamed about what it would be like to know one. Jordan was everything she'd imagined the perfect man would be. He was kind, funny, charming and when he looked at her a certain way, she could feel her bones melting. It would be easy to have a crush on him...or worse.

But she wouldn't. First of all, she'd heard a little about the Haynes brothers from people in town. They had a reputation for being heartbreakers. She might as well try to learn ice skating at a U.S. Olympic team workout. She was completely out of her league. Not only was she a virgin, but she hadn't kissed a single male since she was fifteen. Talk about being out of the loop.

The second reason she wouldn't dare fall for Jordan Haynes was that as much as she might daydream about a man, even marriage, she knew it wasn't in the cards for her. Not because no one would love her. She liked to think that one or two people might think she was special. The real reason was that love required trust, and she'd been let down too many times. She couldn't imagine ever trusting anyone again.

She pulled the sheet higher up his bare chest, then left the room and hurried down the hallway toward the bathroom. She'd spent the past three days longing for a shower and she was going to enjoy every minute of this one.

A hideous howling broke through Jordan's dream and jerked him into consciousness. He sat up in bed, then groaned as pain ripped through his muscles. He shouldn't have gotten up earlier, as Louise had told him gleefully.

He shook his head and tried to figure out what was wrong. His brain was fuzzy, and he couldn't focus on anything. There'd been a sound. A—

The howling came again. Someone or some *thing* was being tortured. He threw back the sheet and tried to rise to his feet. The floor shifted. Or maybe it was him. He gripped the nightstand with one hand and the table by his bed with the other, then pushed up. As he locked his muscles, he realized he'd made one fatal error of judgment. He'd forgotten the hospital table had wheels.

It shot out from under him and went flying across the room. Jordan lost his balance and tumbled toward the floor.

He braced one arm to save himself, but it gave way and he hit the hardwood on his already bruised shoulder.

Footsteps sounded in the hallway.

"Jordan?"

It was Holly. She would be relieved to find out he wasn't naked under his sheet but instead wore shorts over his briefs. Then his eyes closed, and he couldn't think about anything but the pain.

"Jordan, what happened?"

"I heard something. Howling. Tried to get up."

"You fell. Are you hurt?"

He hurt like a son of a bitch. She raised his head to her lap, then stroked his face. He opened his eyes.

For a moment he stared at her, then he blinked, certain he must have hit his head when he fell. She was wearing a white robe and nothing underneath. He knew because the robe had parted, exposing the curve of one breast and the first hint of the rosy skin around her nipple.

He sucked in a breath. Her hair was wet and tumbling around her shoulders. Her eyes darkened with concern, and the fingers on his face were gentle and comforting.

Maybe he was dead. If this was heaven, who was he to complain?

Chapter Four

"Jordan?" Holly said, her voice laced with concern. "Please say something. Are you hurt?"

"I'm okay." He forced the words through the pain and awareness battling in his body. He couldn't remember hurting this bad before, nor could he remember being this instantly aroused. It was an odd combination that again made him wonder if he *had* clipped his head on his way down.

"Do you think you can get back into bed?" she asked, then glanced from him to the mattress. "I doubt I can lift you by myself."

"I can manage. Just give me a minute." He continued to stare up at her face. She smelled like shampoo and soap. Her pale skin almost glowed in the early-evening lamplight. Her chest rose and fell with each breath, and the edge of the robe slipped open a little more, exposing a taut nipple and the underside of her breast.

Heat coiled low in his belly. The pain from his injuries

and the ache from his groin set up a low-frequency hum that had him holding in a moan. He couldn't continue to torture himself this way, he thought grimly.

He rolled to his side, then started to push himself up to his knees. Holly scrambled to her feet and bent over, grabbing him around his chest and adding her strength to his. Together they moved slowly to the bed. Jordan dragged himself onto the mattress. Holly lifted his legs into place, then bent over and smoothed the sheet over him.

"Better?" she asked. "Do you want a painkiller?"

He shook his head, which surprisingly only hurt a little. "I'll be fine."

"You sure?" She sat on the bed next to him. Her hip bumped his.

"Yeah," he murmured, trying not to notice that now he could see her other breast.

She bent close and touched his forehead. "You feel a little warm."

"I'm sure it will pass."

She frowned. "I hope you're not spiking another fever."

He glanced at the deep V exposed by the oversize robe. "I'm sure that's not it."

She was so intent on his condition, she didn't notice she was flashing him. He wasn't sure if he should be pleased or insulted. While he appreciated the concern, no man wanted to be considered as sexually interesting as a eunuch.

"How did you end up on the floor?" she asked.

He'd almost forgotten the circumstances that had brought Holly rushing to his side. He rubbed his temple as he tried to remember. "I heard a noise."

"What was it?"

"I can't remember. I was asleep and something woke me. I got up to see what it was."

"Maybe you were dreaming."

"Maybe." He stared at her for a moment, for the first time really taking in the oversize robe and her wet hair. He reached out and fingered a damp strand. "What have you been up to?"

Holly blushed, then turned her head away. "I, ah, was sort of using your shower. I hope you don't mind."

He wanted to say she could use it anytime, but only on the condition he got to watch. Though he figured she wouldn't know he was kidding. Then he realized he wasn't kidding. Had it been that long since he'd been with a woman, or was it specifically that Holly Garrett intrigued him?

Dangerous question, Haynes, he told himself, and decided to ignore it.

"I don't mind," he said. "Is there a problem with the plumbing at your new apartment?"

She drew in a deep breath. The edges of the robe trembled slightly but didn't part any more. Staring at them was screwing up his concentration, so he lowered his gaze to her lap, where she rested her hands.

"Plumbing? Oh!" She seemed to realize how she was dressed. She touched her wet hair, then pulled the collar of the robe together and held it tight. "I, um, I don't really have an apartment."

He drew his eyebrows together and stared at her. "Where are you living?"

"At the shop." She gave him a quick smile. "It's really very nice. There's plenty of furniture. Some of the sofas are very comfy. I have a sleeping bag, a hot plate and a small refrigerator. There's even a bathroom, but it doesn't have a shower. So I asked Louise if it was all right for me to use the shower here. You were sleeping, or I would have asked you."

"You can't live there," he said.

"Why not? It's perfectly safe. I didn't have renter's insurance, and right now I can't afford to replace everything I lost, let alone come up with first and last months' rent. But right after the holidays everything should be fine. It's only for a few weeks."

She was talking quickly, and he wondered if it was to cover her nervousness. He figured it was. Now that she was no longer acting as his nurse, she was shy and embarrassed.

As he watched, the fingers at her collar tightened. "Go get dressed," he said gruffly, then closed his eyes as she scurried from the room.

When she was gone, he raised his arm to cover his eyes. He didn't want to think about Holly Garrett living alone in her store. After six the shopping district was deserted. She could get into trouble, and no one would be around to call for help. To make matters worse, thinking about her living there made him think about her not having access to a shower and instead using his.

She'd been so soft and tempting in his robe. His mind filled with a hundred different ways he could take them both to breathlessness and back. But he wasn't going to act on any of them. He was too old and cynical for a woman like her.

For a moment a flicker of regret raced through him. Regret for all he'd never experienced and for all he would never have. If he were someone else, if circumstances were different, he could pursue his interest in Holly. He could woo her slowly, risk caring about her and being cared about in return.

A fantasy, he told himself, even as he acknowledged the fantasy was a hell of a lot better than reality. It wasn't that he didn't believe in love; he just didn't like the consequences.

Seconds later the noise that had awakened him returned.

It was a low-pitched yowl. Before he could make up his mind about the risk of trying to get out of bed again, Holly returned carrying a large gray cat.

He eyed the beast distastefully. He recognized the face. That cat was responsible for him being laid up. He thought about grabbing the creature and expressing his feelings, but in his weakened condition he didn't dare. The cat stared back at him, dislike gleaming from its bright green eyes. He figured the cat had gotten the best of him once, and that had been while he was healthy. God knows what it could do to him now.

Holly shifted the massive feline in her arms and smiled. "This is Mistletoe. Mistletoe, this is the brave man who saved your life."

Man and cat glared at each other. Neither was impressed.

"Mistletoe is a pedigreed Persian," Holly said, then set the animal on the floor. "I hope you don't mind that I brought her over. She's very special to me."

At the sound of her name, the cat glanced up at Holly, then purred and rubbed against her legs. When the feline completed the circle, she looked at Jordan and flattened her ears.

He stared back. "She's pretty fat."

"She's pregnant."

He had a moment of guilt for thinking evil thoughts about an expectant mother, then realized Mistletoe would probably pass her bad temper on to her offspring.

"I don't like to leave her alone at night," Holly said. "She's very well behaved. She won't be any trouble."

"Yeah, right," he muttered.

Holly picked up the cat and walked toward the bed. "Maybe you should pet her and get acquainted."

Mistletoe began to squirm. Holly set her on the foot of the bed. The cat glared at him. He glared back. She arched her back, gave a sharp *pftt,* then jumped down and stalked away.

Holly stared after her. "I don't understand. She's really very sweet and loves everyone."

"Uh-huh," Jordan said, knowing he'd just been insulted by a twenty-pound monster.

"I'm sure she'll adore you once she gets to know you."

Mistletoe had already sent him off the balcony of a building. He would hate to see what the cat was capable of when she put her mind to something.

Holly curled up in the chair Louise had brought into Jordan's temporary bedroom. The overhead light was off. The only illumination came from two floor lamps in opposite corners.

Jordan sat up in bed with the sheet bunched around his waist. They'd finished dinner and were sipping coffee. Holly was pleased with how far she'd come. Despite being in the same room with a good-looking man *and* his handsome chest, she was able to talk like a normal person. Definitely an improvement over the first day. Jordan still had the power to make her blush, but that was getting better, too.

She studied his face and eyes, searching for signs of fever or pain. "How do you feel?"

"That's the third time you've asked me, Holly. I'm fine." Then he smiled.

She bit back a sigh. Okay, she was able to survive the bare chest and witty conversation, but the smile... That smile could still reduce her legs to the consistency of whipped cream. She leaned forward and set her coffee mug on the nightstand before she did something stupid like dropping it.

"I'm concerned about that fever coming back." She rose

to her feet and leaned over the bed. She touched his forehead, then his cheeks. "You're cool to the touch."

"You do that very well." He raised his eyebrows. "Lots of practice?"

"With my mom."

"How long was she sick?"

Holly settled back in her chair. "Ten years. I was fifteen when she found a lump in her breast. It was cancer. At first they just took the lump out, but then the cancer came back." She closed her eyes, recalling the terror of that time. Her mother had been her only parent. Because it was just the two of them, they were very close. She'd tried to be strong, but all she could think about was what was going to happen to her when her mother died.

"That's a lot to handle when you're fifteen," he said.

She nodded. "She had the usual treatments, but she was really sick. I guess some people tolerate them better. There were a lot of times I missed school to be with her."

"What else did you miss?" he asked, his voice low and concerned.

She opened her eyes and stared at him. "What do you mean?"

"You were a teenager. Most kids have a hard enough time dealing with school and growing up. You had your mother to worry about. You must have missed out on a lot."

Her eyes burned, and for a brief second she was afraid she was going to cry. Then she sat up straighter and blinked several times until the burning went away.

"Thank you," she said.

"For what?"

"For saying that. No one really noticed before. I was just a teenager, but I was expected to act like an adult. There wasn't anyone else to take charge. My mom couldn't do it. The doctors and nurses were busy. Mom had a few friends, but she didn't want them to know how sick she was. And my friends were young like me."

His dark gaze met hers. "You must have been scared."

"I was. I didn't want her to die. It was hard because I'd just started high school and I was involved in a lot of activities. I had to give them up. There was even this boy. Jimmy. We sort of dated. As much as one dates at fifteen." Holly stared down at her hands and realized she was twisting her fingers together. Consciously she stilled the movement. "He dumped me because I had to spend too much time taking care of my mom."

"Tell me his last name. As soon as I'm better, I'll find him and beat him up for you."

She smiled. "That's sweet, but no thanks. It was ages ago. It doesn't matter anymore."

"Sure it does. Some of those hurts never go away."

They stared at each other for a long time. Something in Jordan's eyes convinced her that he really did understand what she was talking about. She wondered what hurts he carried around from his past.

"Did your mother go into remission?" he asked.

"For a couple of years. I got through high school. After I graduated, I went to work full-time. I'd wanted to go to college, but there were medical bills. Then the same week we got the news that we'd inherited the antique shop up here, Mom found a lump in her other breast."

Holly's breath caught in her throat. She remembered hearing the sobs through the thin walls of their bathroom. She'd rushed inside and found her mother crouched down on the floor, crying and rocking. At that moment Holly had known the cancer had returned.

"Mom was strong. She had another remission, but this one was shorter. Then they found the cancer had spread everywhere. She hung on for a couple of years. It was hard on her, but she was very brave.''

''Sounds like you were, too.''

''I didn't do anything.''

''You took care of her, didn't you?''

''I was her daughter. What else was I going to do? I was all she had.''

She shifted in the chair and pulled her knees up to her chest. ''Enough about this. I'm supposed to be entertaining you, not getting your spirits down. Let's talk about something more lighthearted.''

Jordan thought for a moment. ''If you could have gone to college, what would you have studied?''

''That's easy. Business. I want to do a good job running the shop, but I don't have all the education I need. I admire Louise for going back to school. That's what I want to do. Next question.''

''You never mention your father.''

''I don't have any contact with him.'' She thought about the single conversation she'd shared with her father six years ago. She could remember everything about it, right down to the sound of the rain on the windows. ''He had an affair with my mother. When she got pregnant, he disappeared.''

She said the words matter-of-factly. Jordan stared at her and wondered how she'd managed to stay so giving and innocent in the face of so much tragedy.

Holly had been abandoned by one parent and lost the other, yet she'd survived. More than that, she was happy and successful.

''I know about fathers like that,'' he said. ''My dad stuck around, but I often think it would have been better if he'd left.''

''Why?''

She looked at him intently. After her shower she'd dressed in jeans and a dark blue sweatshirt. The soft fabric deepened the color of her eyes. Her hair was long and loose over her shoulders. He wanted to pull her close and bury his hands in the long silky strands. He wanted to kiss her and make love to her until she forgot the past and its pain. He could make her forget. He could even seduce her. But if he did, he would break her heart, and that was one thing he wouldn't allow himself to do. So instead, he told the truth. If that didn't drive her away, nothing would.

"Haven't you heard about the infamous Haynes brothers?" he asked.

She shrugged. "Rumors, really. Nothing specific."

"Four generations of heartbreakers. Four generations of boys born into the family. Three generations of philandering men and bitter women."

"You and your brothers are the fourth generation?"

"Yeah. We saw what our uncles did and how our father treated our mother. He was out with women several times a week. Earl Haynes believed everything he did was fine as long as he actually slept in his bed. Everyone in town knew about his affairs, including my mother."

She sucked in a breath. "You and your brothers knew, too?"

He nodded.

"How awful." She shook her head. "I don't understand how someone could act like that."

"It was easy."

"What do you mean?"

"The men in my family have a natural ability to attract women."

She raised her chin slightly. "I hadn't noticed."

"Gee, thanks."

She looked startled, then laughed. "Oh, I didn't mean that the way it sounded. What I meant was—" She paused.

He waited, wondering what she was going to say. Would she claim to be completely unaffected by him, and if she did, would he believe her? He knew all the tricks, but he didn't use them anymore. But he'd caught Holly staring at him a couple of times. She might not be swooning, but he doubted she was immune.

Finally she flipped her hair off her shoulder and smiled. "What was the question?"

"I'll give you a break," he said. "You don't have to answer it."

"What happened with your parents?"

"They're divorced. My dad's living in Florida with wife number five. I only met numbers two and three, but if she's anything like them, she's about twenty-five with an IQ smaller than her waist. Dad was never much into substance."

"And your mother?"

Jordan didn't want to think about that. "She left when I was in high school. No one knows where she is."

Despite his best efforts, the day came back to him. It had been an afternoon in the spring. Sunny, warm, perfect. He had been there, although neither parent had known. He'd seen everything. He knew the truth.

He shook his head, and memories were banished to a dark place he preferred not to explore.

Holly leaned forward and touched the back of his hand. "I'm sorry," she said. "I didn't mean to bring up painful memories."

She was the nurse again. Comforting and impersonal. For reasons he didn't understand, he wanted more. He turned his hand so her fingers grazed his palm. Instantly sparks arced between them. She stiffened. His blood heated. Before she could pull away, he captured her palm in his.

Her eyes widened, and she swallowed. "I, ah, it's really late. I should probably go."

"Thanks for dinner," he said. "It was great." He brushed his thumb against the back of her hand. Her skin was soft and warm.

She rose, but before she could pull away, he gave a quick tug. She resisted for a moment, then settled on the edge of the bed. Her long hair swung around her shoulders, shielding then exposing her face.

He turned his hand slightly and rubbed his thumb against the inside of her wrist. Her pulse was rapid. Her lips parted, and he wondered if she was having trouble breathing. His gaze dipped lower, to her full breasts. He wanted her.

Color rose to her cheeks, blending with the freckles. Her pupils dilated. He inhaled the sweet essence of her body. It would be easy to pull her close. Easy to draw her into his arms and kiss her until she forgot where and who she was. He might hate that part of him, but like his brothers, he was every inch a Haynes. He knew how to seduce a woman.

But not Holly, he thought as he gave her hand one last squeeze before releasing her. Not because he didn't like her, but because he did. And because he wanted her to come back again.

She stared dreamily at him, swaying as if propelled by a secret breeze. Then consciousness returned, and she stiffened.

"I should head home," she said again.

"I'll see you tomorrow."

She smiled, then was gone.

After the sound of her car disappearing down the driveway had faded, Jordan stared at the ceiling. Something had happened tonight. Something he didn't want to think about.

Somehow he and Holly had connected. He didn't tell many people about his past, and he suspected she felt the same way. But they'd both shared. He wasn't sure what that meant, but he knew it was dangerous. So was his thinking that she was special and sweet.

He shifted under the sheet, and a tuft of cat hair floated to the floor. Too sweet for that damn cat, he thought. And too trusting to be staying alone in the business district at night. Glenwood might not be a hotbed of crime, but bad things had happened here. He would call the sheriff's station and make sure they patrolled the area.

Before he could get up and walk to the phone, Louise returned. As she did every night, she came in and checked on him.

"Holly already gone?" she asked as she leaned against the door frame. She brushed her blond bangs out of her eyes.

"About ten minutes ago."

Louise started to leave.

"Wait," he said. "Holly asked you if she could use the shower."

"Is that a problem?"

"No. I didn't know she was living in her store. I don't think it's safe."

Louise folded her arms over her chest. "I'm sure if she had somewhere else to go, she would."

"She said she couldn't afford an apartment."

Louise reached for her right earring and toyed with the small cup and saucer. "I know what you're thinking Jordan. Your heart is in the right place, but Holly isn't going to accept money from you. Probably not even a loan."

"I figured that."

She gave him a tentative smile. "It was nice of you to be concerned."

He looked away from the older woman. His instinct was to say something rude. The problem was he was warming to her. It didn't matter how much trouble he was, Louise still took care of him. He knew it was about his family and not about him, but that didn't change much. He was torn between feeling guilty for acting like a complete bastard and anger for what she'd done.

When he reminded himself it was a long time ago, a voice in his head said if it hadn't been for her, everything might have been different. He remembered the lies and the secrets, then he got mad and it was easy not to be polite.

Life was hell sometimes.

"You think she'd let me pay her for keeping me company in the evening?" he asked.

"Lord knows I take money for putting up with you, but Holly seems to like you. No accounting for taste."

He turned away so Louise wouldn't see his smile. He liked Holly, too.

"I'll figure out something," he said. "She can't stay there indefinitely. In the meantime would you bring me the portable phone? I want to call the sheriff's office and ask them to patrol that part of town at night."

Louise slowly shook her head. "Mostly you're a pain in the butt, Jordan, but sometimes you can be a real nice guy."

"Don't let it get out."

She grinned. "Who would believe me?"

Chapter Five

When Holly arrived the next day, Louise was already gone. The housekeeper had left a note on the front door explaining she was baby-sitting for one of the "friendly" Haynes brothers and for Holly to come on in and make herself comfortable.

Holly tested the front door and found it open, then she stepped inside. The house was silent, and there weren't any smells of cooking. After letting Mistletoe out of her basket, Holly walked into the kitchen, where she found another note telling her that Louise had prepared a casserole for dinner. It was in the refrigerator and would require forty-five minutes at three hundred and fifty degrees to heat. There was also a salad and a loaf of French bread.

"I could get used to this," Holly said softly, and smiled. Mistletoe strolled into the kitchen and wrapped herself around Holly's legs.

"She even left you some chicken."

Mistletoe purred.

"You like Louise, don't you?" Holly said, bending over and stroking her cat. Mistletoe raised her head to have it scratched between her ears. Her purr rumbled louder.

"I like her, too," Holly said. "And I like Jordan." She crouched down and rubbed under Mistletoe's chin.

"I have a confession," she continued. "I feel badly that Jordan got hurt saving your life, but I'm not completely sorry that he's having to rest for a while, if that makes sense."

Mistletoe looked at her with bright green, knowing eyes.

"I like coming here to visit him," Holly whispered.

Mistletoe's gaze never wavered. She seemed to figure out the topic of conversation, because her eyes narrowed and she gave a short, sharp *pftt* before walking off.

Holly followed her into the hallway, then made her way through the library. At the door to the study, she paused.

Jordan sat up in his hospital bed. Today he wore a cobalt blue T-shirt. While she missed his bare chest, the man sure knew how to fill out clothes. The shoulders were pulled tight, and the much-washed fabric molded itself against his chest.

Dark hair hung over his forehead, and his brow was furrowed in concentration. As always he took her breath away. Her legs began to tremble, and she wondered if she would be able to get out a coherent thought. After so many days she would have thought she would get over her attraction or befuddlement, but she hadn't. Briefly she wondered if it would always be like this.

She smiled. Always. As if they were going to continue to see each other. No doubt as soon as he was up and around, Jordan would be delighted to see the last of her. He only bothered with her because he was bored by spending so much time in his own company. Once he could resume his life, he wouldn't have time for a slightly overweight, shy, twenty-eight-year-old virgin.

She raised her hand and knocked on the door frame. Jordan looked up.

"I've been waiting for you," he said, deepening his voice until it sounded like thick dark chocolate blending with rich cream.

"I was delayed at the store. A couple of women came in wanting to buy wreaths. I have so many to choose from, they had trouble making up their minds. In the end they bought six."

Jordan set down the papers he'd been studying. "Far be it from me to interfere with your business." He motioned to the chair next to him. "Have a seat. I want to talk to you about something."

She settled down next to him, and he handed her an old photograph. She studied it for several seconds before recognizing the structure in the picture.

"This is your house," she said.

"Yeah. Right after it was completed. Check out the old cars in front."

Although the mansions in Glenwood had been constructed in the Victorian style, most of them had been built around the turn of the century or a few years later. They'd been the first in the area to have complete indoor plumbing and that newfangled invention: electric lights.

Holly noted the beautiful lines of the house, then realized the just-planted saplings all around the yard had grown to be the majestic oaks and pines she'd parked under today.

"Can I make it look like it used to?" Jordan asked.

"Sure. With enough time and money, anything is possible. Some original fixtures, switches and that sort of thing might be hard to find, but practically it's often better to use reproductions. If the structure is sound, you can do anything. I assume you had that checked before you bought the place.''

He nodded.

''Then the rest of it isn't that bad.''

She stared at the photo and wondered what it would be like to own something as wonderful as this house. Maybe Jordan would let her help him with some of the work. She would be thrilled to give him the benefit of her experience.

She held the picture, but instead of seeing the image, she saw Jordan laughing. Her mouth curved up in response. He was so good-looking he would be dangerous to be around for any length of time. But she would try to muddle through.

A part of her wondered why he was being so nice to her. She knew some of it was because she was keeping him company. Foolishly she wanted him to act that way because he liked her.

What a silly dream, she told herself, and knew it came from her loneliness. While her mother had been ill, especially the last couple of years before her death, Holly hadn't had time to make and keep friends. If she wasn't working to pay the bills, she was home caring for her mother.

After her mother's death, she'd been too numb to think about anything but surviving. Since moving to Glenwood, she'd finally been able to acknowledge the emptiness she carried around inside. However, she hadn't had a chance to do anything about it. Being with Jordan was both perfect pleasure and penetrating pain. He made her laugh and feel as if she finally fit in somewhere. He also pointed out the silence of her days and coldness of her nights. He made her want things she'd never had. He made her dream again.

While she didn't mind the dreaming, sometimes she found the process uncomfortable. Since meeting him, he had been the focal point of her dreams. Silly and pointless, she reminded herself. Jordan Haynes was—

A large hand moved up and down in front of her face. "Holly, are you still in there?"

She blinked several times and stared at him. "What?"

"I'm talking and talking, but you're a million miles away."

She laughed to cover up her rush of embarrassment. Thank goodness he couldn't know what she was thinking.

"Sorry. This photograph set me off." She handed it to him, then folded her hands in her lap. "You have my complete attention. What were you saying?"

"I have a proposition for you."

"P-proposition?" Her mind went blank for a split second. Her body filled with that mysterious heat Jordan was forever setting off in her.

She was reasonably sure she was attracted to him. Her body was always tingling, burning, humming and shaking when they were together. But she didn't know what any of that meant. Was it normal? Would she get over it? Was it specifically about him, or would it have happened if she spent time with any good-looking man?

If only she had more experience with the male gender. If only she could know what to do.

He picked up a couple of photographs showing the interior of the house as it had been seventy years earlier. "I've wanted to start work, but I haven't had the time. And now with this—" he motioned to his hospital bed "—it's going to be a while until I can get going."

Holly bit her lower lip. She wasn't sure where he was going with this. Did he want her to offer to help? She would be happy to.

"That's where you come in," he said, and gave her a winning smile. She was relieved that she was sitting down.

If she'd been standing, she would have been concerned her knees would give out.

"I want to hire you," he said.

"Really?"

He nodded.

"I've never done anything like that before," she said slowly. "Although I don't know why I couldn't." She thought for a moment. "I would love to work on the house. It's wonderful. Just the dining room alone, with those high ceilings and the beautiful chair-rail molding. I do have the store, though. That would be my first priority."

"No problem. The store's closed Sunday and Monday, right?"

"Yes."

"What about working Monday and two evenings?"

Holly twisted her fingers together and hoped she wasn't grinning too broadly. Jordan didn't want to get rid of her. He wanted to see her again. So what if it was just about restoring the house? He would still be here, and they could talk. Maybe—

"I'd like to pay you with cash, and room and board."

Her head snapped up, and she stared at him. "What?"

He leaned back against the bed and met her gaze. "You're surprised."

"I don't know what to say." She didn't know what to feel, either. Room and board? He expected her to live here? With him?

Then she remembered what had happened the previous day. She'd admitted she was living in the store and had used his shower. He thought she was homeless and destitute.

"I don't need your charity," she said, and rose to her feet.

He grabbed her hand before she could leave the room.

"It's not charity," he said, tugging her close until she was standing next to the bed. "Please don't be angry."

His dark eyes widened slightly. She tried to read what he was thinking. She didn't think she saw pity, but how would she know?

When he pulled on her hand again, she had no choice but to sink onto the mattress beside him. Her breathing increased slightly as she noticed he continued to hold her fingers in his. This wasn't a medicinal touch. This was...well, she wasn't sure what it was. Her heart pounded rapidly, thudding against her ribs. She was having trouble thinking.

"The house needs work," he said quietly. "You're the town expert."

"I'm sure there are other people just as qualified as me."

"None that I know."

"This is all an elaborate ploy," she told him. "You're offering me a place to stay because you feel sorry for me."

His thumb stroked her palm, disturbing the last few remaining connections in her brain. She stared at him, at the square shape of his jaw and his firm mouth. Faint stubble darkened his cheeks. She was close enough to see the laugh lines around his eyes and the slight bump on the bridge of his nose.

His skin was tanned, different from her paleness. Everything about him was different. The way he talked, his scent, the shape of his body. The differences both frightened and intrigued her.

"I'm offering you a place to stay for two reasons. First I like your company. Second I don't think it's safe for you to live at your shop. The business district is deserted at night. If something were to happen, you would be in that part of town alone."

But she barely heard what he was saying. He liked her company. Wasn't that the same as liking her?

The offer was tempting. Not just because of Jordan, although he was the biggest temptation of all, but also because she missed living in a real home. She could take a shower every day and cook in a kitchen with more than a hot plate. She could sleep in a regular bed and not in a sleeping bag on an uncomfortable antique sofa.

"Say yes," he commanded.

She pulled her hand free of his fingers so she could think. There were merits to his plan. "Mistletoe would have to come with me. I couldn't leave her in the store."

Despite the animal's sweet nature, the Persian and Jordan didn't get along. Holly had tried explaining that Jordan had saved Mistletoe's life, but the cat remained unimpressed.

Jordan exhaled deeply. "I figured that. Mistletoe can stay here, too."

"She really is grateful to you," Holly said.

"Oh, yeah, I can tell. So what's it going to be? Are you going to help me out here or callously abandon me?"

He made it sound as if she would be doing *him* a favor when it was really the other way around. She was tempted. Very tempted. She'd never lived with a man before and would probably never again live with one like Jordan. Should she just take the opportunity and be grateful?

"Louise will still be here," he said.

"That's nice. I like Louise."

He ignored that. "I meant, so you wouldn't have to worry. She'll be here to act as chaperon."

Holly stared at him. He thought she was worried he might try something? Before she could stop herself, she laughed.

He didn't share her amusement. "I think I've just been insulted," he muttered.

"No," she said quickly to reassure him. "I wasn't laughing at you. While I appreciate your concern, I wasn't worried that—" Her throat closed. "Well, that you would, you know." He still looked confused and vaguely put out. She drew in a deep breath. "I know you would never be interested in someone like me."

"Why not?"

She opened her mouth, but couldn't find any words. Why not? It was so obvious. Because he was Jordan Haynes and she was just a silly woman who didn't know diddly about men. "Because, well, I don't know much about men, but there must be a hundred reasons."

"Name one."

She could have named ten, but they were all too embarrassing. She wasn't pretty enough, she wasn't skinny enough, she wasn't anything enough.

His gaze narrowed and seemed to focus on her face. "You're right about one thing, Holly. You don't know anything about men."

He reached for her hand. She let him take it, not expecting him to tug her forward. She found herself falling toward him. She put out her right hand to keep herself from landing on his chest. She was leaning toward him, embarrassingly close to his face. His eyes darkened to the color of the night sky. His sweet breath fanned her face.

Deep inside, that unexplainable heat flared to life. She told herself to run away, but she couldn't move. Something was going to happen; she could sense it. And no matter what it was, she wanted to experience it fully.

She expected a quick, witty retort or maybe a hug, but she didn't expect him to kiss her. In that heart-stopping moment, when he moved closer and his attention focused on her mouth, she realized his intentions. And then it was too late.

His lips brushed against hers. She jerked awkwardly, and he wrapped his free arm around her back, drawing her closer. She sat stiffly, one hand captured in his, the other braced on the bed.

Jordan lifted his head slightly and smiled. ''Relax. This isn't going to hurt.'' Then he raised the bed until they were eye to eye. He released her hand and put both arms around her. Not having anything else to do, her hands fluttered nervously.

''Put them on my shoulders,'' he murmured, and it was the last thing he said for a long time.

As she followed his instructions and rested the tips of her fingers on his broad shoulders, his mouth once again brushed hers. Holly had been kissed once, years before. It had been the chaste, innocent kiss of inexperienced teenagers. It had not prepared her for Jordan.

He claimed her mouth. His lips moved back and forth, exploring her lips, discovering every millimeter of skin. She was too stunned to respond. She could feel the warmth of him radiating toward her like a heater. Through the tips of her fingers, she sensed his strength. He drew her closer, and powerful muscles shifted.

One of his hands pressed against her spine between her shoulder blades. He kneaded her slightly. Perhaps the action was meant to relax her, but she was too overwhelmed by sensation. Her mind flitted from place to place, receiving all the sensory input and trying to sort it out. His other hand cupped her hip. The intimacy embarrassed her. She felt awkward, all large curves and stiff muscles. She couldn't flow with the moment.

He moved his mouth away from her lips and planted a kiss by her chin. An electric jolt rippled through her. Another kiss caressed her jawline. He slipped toward her ear, ending up by her neck. Sizzling impulse leapt just under her skin, and she fought against the need to sag against him. Holding herself stiff and straight took so much energy.

Then Jordan licked the sensitive skin just under her ear. Heat exploded inside her. The unfamiliar fire whipped through her, fanned by needs she didn't understand. Her breasts ached as if they'd swollen. For the first time in her life, she could actually feel the inside of her soft cotton bra pressing against her nipples. It was uncomfortable.

Between her legs the first flicker of awareness sparked to life. A heaviness filled her, and she pressed her thighs tightly together to hold all the feelings inside.

He returned his attention to her mouth again. This time she kissed him back. She moved her lips against his. Oddly enough it was getting more difficult to breathe. She relaxed her fingers and held on to his shoulders. The hand on her back began to stroke up and down, while the one on her hip squeezed and kneaded.

Then he did the most amazing thing. He touched her lower lip with his tongue. Her breath caught in her throat, and all her attention focused on that tiny damp spot on her sensitized skin.

She didn't know what to do. She'd read about that kind of kissing in books, of course. She knew that other people did it. But she'd never imagined she would have the chance to experience it herself. There was something faintly wicked about the thought. Delightfully wicked.

When he stroked her a third time, she knew he wanted her to open her mouth. She wanted it, but it seemed too bold and flagrant. As if she were begging him to kiss her. Confusion settled on her like a blanket. She didn't know what to do. She couldn't think.

"You're thinking too much," Jordan murmured.

She jerked back in shock and stared at him. "How can you read my mind?"

He opened his eyes, exposing dilated pupils and a hungry expression. "I don't have to. Your body gives you away. You're too scared to relax. It's just a kiss, Holly. It can't be your first one." He smiled at the thought.

"Of course not," she said, reminding herself technically it wasn't a lie. There *had* been that kiss when she was fifteen. Even if it hadn't been anything like this, it still counted.

He cupped her face in his hands. "You're lovely," he said, then slid his fingers into her hair. She wore it in a loose French braid, and he wove through the strands, massaging her scalp and making her want to moan with pleasure.

"I'm not at all lovely," she said. "I'm—"

She never got to finish her sentence. He swooped down and kissed her. Before she could press her lips primly together, he'd slipped inside.

At the first touch of his tongue on the inside of her lower lip, her body froze. As he brushed the tip of her tongue with his, her heart stopped. She'd expected to like kissing him; she hadn't expected to be moved to another dimension.

He circled her, stroked her, teased her. Sensations filled her being. The feel of him, the textures, the sweet taste, the heat, the closeness. One hand continued to stroke her hair and scalp. The other dropped back to her hip. But this time, instead of staying still, it slipped around and cupped her behind.

There was too much to think about, too much to experience. She would perish from sensory overload. She would perish if he ever stopped.

He continued to kiss her, so she continued to live. Gradually he withdrew his tongue. She waited for him to return. When he did, it was just to tease, then escape. They played that game several times before she realized he wanted her to follow him.

The concept should have overwhelmed her. Instead, she found herself eager for the experience. This was her first adult kiss, and she was determined to enjoy every minute of it.

She did to him as he'd done to her. She slipped into his mouth, pausing to taste his bottom lip. He felt unfamiliar but exciting. She wanted more. She continued forward and touched his tongue with hers. They began a sensual dance that made her skin burn and her blood heat.

Before, her mind had raced as she tried to figure out what she should be focusing on. Now she couldn't think at all. She could only drift along on a current of need and excitement.

So this was passion, she thought as he drew her closer and her breasts flattened against the hard plane of his chest. This was desire. This was sex.

Jordan moaned low in his throat. She wondered if everything felt as good to him as it did to her. He must have kissed hundreds of women. She probably didn't measure up at all. But she couldn't find it in herself to care. All she wanted was for the moment to go on forever.

But eventually it had to stop. Jordan broke away, then rested his forehead against hers and stared into her eyes. They were both breathing heavily.

He gave her a crooked smile, then brushed a strand of hair from her face. "Amazing," he murmured, his voice thick and husky.

"You think so?" she asked, hoping he wasn't just being kind. The kiss had been a miracle for her, but she didn't have anything to compare it to.

"I know it was." Some of the light faded from his eyes. "I'm sorry, Holly. I shouldn't have done that."

Sorry? Because it was so hideous? She straightened and tried to pull away. His left arm was still around her, and he didn't release her.

"Wait a minute," he said. "I'm not sorry I kissed you, I'm sorry that it might have scared you away. I want you to come stay here. If you agree, I don't want you worried that I'm going to be attacking you. I can control myself."

She blinked several times, but none of it made sense. "You didn't scare me," she said finally. "I know you wouldn't, well, you know, do anything bad." She could feel the heat creeping up her cheeks, and she ducked her head. "I trust you."

Damn. Jordan stared at Holly and didn't know if he should be flattered or take off in the opposite direction. She trusted him. Great. Right now he was hard and hot from wanting her, and he didn't feel like being noble. But he would be because she was innocent. It was unlikely that Holly was actually a virgin, but she was the next-closest thing. He hadn't been sure before, but he was now. Her kiss had been tentative. At least at first.

Just thinking about her shy foray into his mouth made him want to bed her right here. If he'd had the strength, he might have hauled her next to him. But he was battered and sore, so she was going to escape unscathed. Just as well for both of them. He liked Holly. He didn't want to screw up her life. Or worse, destroy it. And that's what would happen. He knew the dangers of getting involved. He knew the price everyone paid. He didn't want that for her, and he wouldn't risk it again for himself.

He released her, and she half turned away from him. Her spine was straight, and her hands rested neatly in her lap. But he knew she was still aroused. He could see it in the outline of her nipples through her bra and blouse, and hear it in her still-rapid breathing. She'd wanted him. The thought both frustrated and aroused him.

"You never agreed to stay," he said.

She glanced at him. Her blue eyes darkened with confusion. "Jordan, I—"

The front door opened, and the sound of familiar voices filled the house.

"Where do you think he's keeping himself?" a man asked.

"In the study," a woman answered. "He didn't want to deal with the stairs."

Holly stood up. "Who are those people?"

"My family. At least part of them." He leaned back and grinned. "This will teach you to keep the front door locked."

She looked around, as if searching for an escape. It was too late. Kyle Haynes, Jordan's younger brother, walked in. He had that damn cat in his arms.

Kyle glanced from Jordan to Holly and back. He raised his eyebrows and grinned. "In here, guys. I found something very interesting."

Chapter Six

Holly stared at the man in front of her. He looked a lot like Jordan, but there were subtle differences. The stranger had similar features, and he was nearly as good-looking, but his smile was all wrong. Jordan's made her feel as if she were on a roller coaster, while this man's didn't make her feel anything.

"You might as well take a seat," Jordan told her. "They're going to be here for a while."

"They're staying? Then I should leave."

"No. Don't do that. You're going to have to meet them eventually." If you stay here. That was the unspoken part of the sentence.

Her head was spinning. Too much had happened too quickly. His offer, their kiss.

The kiss. The kiss that had filled her body with an incredible need she still didn't understand. Jordan had changed her with just his touch. It was as if he'd disassembled her being, then put her back together, but with everything in a slightly different place. She felt confused and unable to deal with what was happening.

"Holly," he said quietly, "come here for a second." He patted the side of the bed.

She moved closer but didn't sit down. She could hear more voices in the hallway. How many of them were there and what were they going to say when they found her in Jordan's bedroom? She couldn't even rely on the truth to see her through. They *had* been doing something. Something very intimate. What if their visitors could tell?

She took a step back and bumped into the nightstand. As she turned to steady the lamp, Jordan grabbed her hand and tugged her until she was right next to his bed.

"Your fingers are freezing," he murmured.

"I know. I'm terrified."

"Picture them in their underwear if it helps."

She glanced at the stranger who was still petting Mistletoe. Her cat was vibrating in ecstasy, rubbing her head against the man's chest and demanding more attention.

Jordan's fingers tightened on hers. "Forget about picturing anyone in his underwear. It was a bad idea."

She looked down at Jordan. He shrugged as if to say it didn't matter, then he gave her a wink. She tried to relax.

"You going to introduce me?" the man holding her cat asked.

Jordan grinned. "Maybe I don't want to."

"I can see why."

The man glanced at her, and Holly had to fight embarrassment.

"I might as well get it over with," Jordan said. "Holly, this is my younger brother, Kyle. He's married to Sandy, who is too smart to have connected up with someone like him, but there's no accounting for taste."

"Hey, wait a minute," Kyle said, and moved farther into the room. He put Mistletoe on the bed. Instantly the cat began spitting. Kyle grinned. "I see the lady doesn't care for you, Jordan. Can't say that I blame her. What with you being the homely brother and all."

Holly was stunned. Kyle had called Jordan homely? Was he crazy?

Jordan ignored the insult. "The cat knows you're the baby, so she's practicing with you until she has her own."

Kyle picked up the cat again, and Mistletoe snuggled in his arms. Holly sank into the chair next to the bed.

"I told you she was friendly," she said, pointing at the purring feline. Mistletoe seemed like the safest topic of conversation.

"Yeah, right," Jordan muttered as the bedroom door pushed open more.

Two women and one more man entered the converted study. They stared from Jordan to Holly and back. The man glanced at Kyle. "Where'd you get the cat?"

"She's mine," Holly said as she stared at him. He looked just like Jordan. Oh, not exactly. The shape of the mouth was different. They weren't twins, but they were obviously brothers, as was Kyle. Tall, dark and handsome. Apparently it was a Haynes cliché. She could have picked any of the three out of a crowd.

Then she realized everyone's attention had focused on her. She swallowed and wondered if they would think her rude if she ran out of the room screaming.

"This is Holly Garrett," Jordan said, giving her fingers a slight squeeze. "She's been in town about six months. She owns that antique store, A Victorian Parlor. She's an expert at restoration and is going to help me with the house."

Everyone started talking at once.

"I hate the wallpaper in the upstairs hall," the woman with long brown hair said. "It's too modern. Do you have sample books at your store?"

"The exterior of our house needs painting," the second woman said. "I just can't decide on the color. I want it to be authentic. Do you have any suggestions?"

The man who had come in last glanced at his brother holding the cat. "You know this is going to mean more work for us."

"I know."

Holly shrank in her chair, glancing from face to face, not sure which question to answer first. She leaned toward Jordan. "Who are these people, and what do they want from me?"

"It's perfectly safe," he told her. "I know we're a little overwhelming at first, but you'll grow to like us."

Holly wasn't so sure.

Jordan held up his free hand. "Let's not scare Holly off in the first few minutes."

There was a moment of silence.

"You're right, Jordan." The woman with long hair stepped forward. She held out her hand to Holly. "I'm Elizabeth. I know this family is terrifying at the beginning. I had it easy. I was the first of the brides. Not counting the failed marriages." She grinned. "The Haynes brothers are starting to get this relationship thing right."

"Oh?" Holly licked her lips and searched the other woman's face, trying to memorize her features. She hadn't expected to get involved with Jordan's family, but if she was going to be living here, she might have contact with them. Especially at this time of year. "You're Elizabeth."

Elizabeth flicked her long brown hair over her shoulders. "I'm married to Travis." She linked her arm through the crook of her husband's elbow. "He's the second of the four brothers. This is Sandy."

Sandy waved. "I'm married to Kyle, who has obviously made a friend for life." She motioned to Mistletoe still purring in Kyle's arms.

"The wives are easy to separate," Elizabeth said. "I have brown eyes, Sandy has green. Jill is a tiny redhead."

"And Rebecca is tall with long dark hair. She's also really skinny," Sandy said, then sighed. "If she wasn't so nice, I could hate her."

"But I thought there were only four brothers," Holly said, confused. She was just starting to keep everyone straight, but obviously she had it wrong.

Elizabeth plopped on the edge of the bed and patted Jordan's knee. "There are. Travis, Kyle, Craig, whom you haven't met yet, and Jordan."

"Then who is Rebecca married to?"

"Austin," they all said at once.

Jordan brought her hand to his mouth and kissed the back. "You'll figure it out," he promised.

She wasn't so sure. Especially not now, with her arm trembling uncontrollably and her heart pounding with the realization that everyone in the room had seen his kind gesture.

Elizabeth tugged at the sleeve of her sweater. Everyone was dressed casually in jeans topped by sweatshirts for the men and sweaters for the women. It was cozy in the house, but the evening temperature would dip to forty degrees.

"Austin is a friend of the family," Elizabeth said. "Not a brother by birth, but he's been unofficially adopted."

Sandy settled on Jordan's other side and grinned. "Interestingly Austin and Jordan are the most alike. They brood."

"You don't brood," Holly said without thinking.

Jordan smiled. "I like this girl."

Elizabeth eyed him speculatively. "It's been a long time since you've brought anyone home."

"Oh, I'm just a friend," Holly said quickly. Attention focused on her. She cleared her throat. "Jordan isn't interested in... I'm not... We're friends. Really."

Knowing looks were exchanged. Holly realized that she and Jordan were still holding hands. She tried to pull free, but he wouldn't let her. She crossed her legs and attempted to act casual.

"How long have you known Jordan?" Sandy asked.

"Yeah," Kyle said, leaning against the wall. He was still stroking Mistletoe. "Interested minds want to know."

"A couple of weeks," Holly said, stretching the truth a little.

Elizabeth leaned close. "So what do you think of our James Dean?"

"Excuse me?"

Sandy chuckled. "Oh, Jordan's the mysterious brother. Didn't you know?"

Holly shook her head.

"Craig is the oldest," Elizabeth said. "So he's responsible and a little uptight, but Jill is curing him of that."

"And fast," Sandy added.

"I hate this part," Travis interjected. He leaned against the doorjamb and folded his arms over his chest.

"Me, too," Kyle said.

The women ignored them.

"Travis is next. He's the ladies' man." Elizabeth glanced at her husband. "He does a fine job, too, but now it's just for an audience of one."

For a moment they stared at each other. The love between them was as tangible as the floors. It filled the room and made Holly feel as if she were spying on something intimate.

"Next comes Jordan," Sandy said, breaking the spell. "He's the loner."

"Am not," Jordan said mildly.

"Then why are you always on the outside looking in?"

"I'm not. It's a matter of perception."

"Oh, sure. We all believe that." Sandy brushed her bangs out of her eyes and smiled. "Finally we have Kyle. He's the baby and the charmer. My prince who came to rescue me."

"You sure resisted," her husband muttered.

"Not anymore."

Holly shook her head. There was too much to take in. Names, relationships, faces, histories. She would never get it right.

Elizabeth stood up. "I'm going to make coffee."

"I'll help," Sandy said.

The two women started from the room. The men watched them go. Elizabeth came back and physically tugged Travis and Kyle after her.

"Give them a minute alone," she said under her breath, but Holly caught the words. Then everyone was gone.

"You okay?" Jordan asked.

She shook her head. "How do you keep them straight?"

"It's easy for me. I grew up with my brothers, so I'm used to them. I was about ten or twelve when I met Austin. As for the wives, they came along one at a time. I'm sorry you're going to have to meet everyone at once."

She turned in her chair and faced him. "I don't understand. If you're all so close, why aren't you staying with one of them instead of here alone?"

He grimaced. "They argued over who was going to take

me in, but I would rather be in my house. It's the holidays. I didn't want to be in the way."

"They love you very much," Holly said.

"I know. I love them."

"That must be nice. My mom loved me a lot, but there was only her. I used to wish for brothers and sisters." Especially at Christmas. It was the time she most disliked being an only child.

"You can borrow mine," he said. "Then you never have to worry about being alone again."

The idea tempted her. She studied his dark eyes. "Is that the best part of a large family?"

"Sure. Plus I know they're here for me. I can depend on them."

She studied their joined hands. His fingers were long and tanned. Sometimes he made her feel small and delicate, a miracle of sorts. She wondered what it would be like to depend on someone. She'd never been comfortable with the concept. She didn't depend on anyone. Life had taught her it wasn't safe.

"I envy you that," she said.

They shared a smile, then heard noise in the hallway.

"Ready for the next assault?" he asked.

She nodded.

He squeezed her fingers. "I'll be right here," he promised.

For that moment she believed him.

"Hey, gorgeous. Want to run off to the Bahamas?"

Holly glanced up and stared at the man in front of her. Her brain clicked slowly as she assembled the individual features in her mind. Tall, dark hair, good-looking. Haynes brother. One she'd met. Which one? The man grinned, and she had her answer.

"Hi, Kyle. What are you doing here?"

He unzipped his leather jacket, exposing the shirt of his khaki sheriff's uniform and leaned against the counter. "Was that a no?"

"To what?"

He looked hurt. "My illicit offer to run away."

She laughed. "What would Sandy say?"

"Oh, we'd have to bring her with us. Otherwise, she'd get really mad."

"As tempting as that sounds, I'm going to have to pass."

He winked. "Let me know if you change your mind." He glanced around the store. "Great place. Do me a favor. If you see Sandy coming, close up shop. I don't mind spending the money, but I know she's going to talk me into doing work."

Holly laughed. "You could always hire someone."

"Jordan's got the best help already. Where does that leave the rest of us?"

It took her a moment to figure out what he was saying. "Oh, well, I won't be working on his house too long." She felt her smile freeze on her face. Did he know that she was going to be living with Jordan? Well, not exactly living with him. They would be in the same house but not living *together*.

Kyle glanced at his watch. "You close at five, right?"

She nodded. There weren't any customers in the store, so there was no point in staying open late.

"Are you packed?" he asked.

"P-packed?" She had the answer to her question.

"That's why I'm here. Jordan asked me to help you move your things." He glanced down. "There you are, sweet girl. I'd wondered where you'd run off to." He bent over and picked up Mistletoe. "Jordan said you were a miserable excuse for a cat, but you're just picky about who you like, aren't you? You have excellent taste.'' As he spoke, he stroked the cat's gray ears and under her chin. She purred her pleasure.

"It's really not fair,'' Holly said, watching the two of them. "Jordan saved her life, but she doesn't care.''

"It's a personality thing. My brother doesn't have any.''

Holly bristled. "He does, too. Jordan is very nice. Charming, funny, sweet…'' Her voice trailed off when she realized Kyle was staring at her.

He raised his eyebrow, then spoke to Mistletoe. "We think Holly likes Jordan, don't we?''

Mistletoe declined to comment.

"You tricked me,'' Holly muttered, wondering if he thought she was a fool.

"Just doing a background check,'' Kyle said, his voice kind. "Jordan's been out of the mainstream for a while. We were all surprised to hear about you.''

"I'm not… We're just…friends.''

He set Mistletoe on the counter, then leaned close. "It's okay, Holly. You don't have to explain anything to me. And for what it's worth, Jordan likes you, too. Now, go pack your things.''

It only took her about fifteen minutes to gather her few belongings together. Kyle carried them to her car, then put Mistletoe in her basket. He set the cat carefully on the front seat.

"I'll follow you over to Jordan's and help you unload.''

"You don't have to do that,'' she protested.

"I want to.'' He closed the passenger door.

Holly started the engine. Confusion clouded her mind, and she drove automatically.

Kyle had said that Jordan liked her. Was it true? Did he? And if he did, what did it mean? Her stomach tightened with nerves. Oh, my, if he liked her, she couldn't live with him. But she wanted him to like her—didn't she?

"Now what?" she asked aloud.

It didn't matter. So what if they liked each other? They were friends, nothing more. They certainly weren't going to have a relationship. Jordan wouldn't want a woman like her. He would want someone sophisticated and experienced. Besides, she didn't want a relationship, either. People had always let her down. An emotional commitment would require trust, and she wasn't ready for that. She might never be ready.

But he'd kissed her.

That kiss. She couldn't forget it. Last night it had haunted her dreams, awakening her time and again. She'd lain in bed listening to her heart pounding, feeling strange heat in her body, fighting a restlessness she didn't understand.

That kiss had been the most amazing thing she'd ever experienced. However, she didn't have a whole lot of experience. This was the nineties. People kissed all the time. Jordan had probably forgotten that it had happened. She would be foolish to think it made any difference.

By the time she arrived at Jordan's house, she'd nearly convinced herself that was true.

Louise met them at the door. "Jordan's asleep," she said, then pressed her finger to her lips. "He spiked another fever today. He's been grouchy as a grizzly, so I'll thank you to be quiet. The longer he sleeps, the better for me."

She looked at Holly. "I can't tell you how happy I am that you're going to be here. I'll still take care of him, but I'm sure he'll be in a better mood with you around. Your bedroom is through here."

She led the way up the stairs. The third door on the left

was open. Holly stepped inside and gave a start of surprise. The room was beautiful.

Original wallpaper—a pattern of cream background covered with pale blue roses—gave the room a cozy feel. A nineteenth-century four-poster bed stood in the center of the room. The dresser matched. There was a tall wardrobe instead of a closet, and several throw rugs on the hardwood floor. A small table and two chairs provided a conversation area in front of a window.

"It's stunning," she said softly.

"I thought you'd like this better than one of the remodeled bedrooms."

Kyle entered and set her suitcases on the bed. "You really want to sleep with all this old stuff?" he asked.

Louise slapped his arm. "You've always had more charm than sense."

"That's why you love me." He leaned down and kissed Louise's cheek.

She made a *humph* noise in her throat. "Get on back to your family."

Kyle walked over to Holly and gave her a quick hug. "Call me if you need anything."

He left the room.

Holly stared after him, amazed that she'd been accepted as easily as that.

"The bathroom is new," Louise said, pointing to a door on the left side of the room. She crossed to the bed and opened the basket. Mistletoe stuck her head out. "I'll bet you're hungry."

The cat meowed.

"I thought so." Louise patted her head, then started for the door. "You go ahead and unpack. I'll feed Mistletoe, then come up and check on you."

"Thanks."

Holly hung the clothes she wore at the store in the wardrobe. She was still surprised by everything that had happened. Jordan's family was accepting her as if they'd known her for years. She wasn't sure why. Were they like this with everyone? She knew three of the brothers worked in law enforcement. She would have expected them to be suspicious of strangers.

Louise returned with a tray. She set it on the table. "Hot cocoa and cookies. A little snack to tide you over until Jordan wakes up."

"How's he doing?"

Louise shrugged. "His fever seems better, and he's sleeping. It's his own fault. He's been doing too much. His body needs rest."

Holly nibbled on her bottom lip. Was the fever her fault? Yesterday she and Jordan had shared a passionate kiss. Could that have been too much for him?

"Have a seat," Louise said as she took one chair. She was wearing a fire-engine red jumpsuit unbuttoned low enough to show off impressive cleavage. Her earrings were a cascade of crystal and red beads that hung nearly to her shoulders. Makeup accentuated her blue eyes.

Holly sank into the chair and took the offered mug of cocoa. "I'm so confused," she said.

"About?"

"Everything. Jordan's family is being nice to me."

"So?"

"They don't know me. I could be a horrible person."

Louise laughed. "Not if you lived another five hundred years." Her smile faded. "You remember the story of the Three Musketeers?"

Holly nodded.

"That's the Haynes boys. All for one and one for all. They look out for each other. If one of them likes someone, that person is drawn into the family. That's what happened to Austin, and to me.''

"How long have you known the family?"

Louise took a sip of her cocoa. "I knew the boys' father. Earl Haynes was the sheriff when I was growing up. He was as good-looking as his sons. They're good men, but Earl had the devil in him. He liked ladies, and they had a hard time resisting him.''

She was silent, remembering a past Holly didn't share. For a moment Holly wondered if Louise had a connection to Earl Haynes, but realized that was unlikely. Someone would have said something about it.

Louise shook herself, as if tossing off memories. "Anyway, once they got word that Jordan invited you to stay here, they took that to mean you were being accepted. Now you're part of the family.''

"That's impossible. They don't know me."

Louise looked at her a long time. Her blue eyes were sad. "You have any family?"

"No. My mother died three years ago, and she was my last relative.''

"I understand that. I'm alone, too. Sometimes it gets damn ugly. The Haynes boys invited me into their circle, except for Jordan, of course. I don't belong, but they let me pretend. I'm grateful to them. Come Christmas, I'm going to be in a house full of children and laughter. They remember my birthday. It sure beats spending those times alone.''

Without thinking, Holly stretched out her hand. Louise took it and smiled. "Aren't we a sorry pair," the housekeeper said lightly.

"I think we're very lucky. I'm glad you're my friend."

Louise sniffed. "Don't go getting all emotional on me," she said, setting her mug on the tray and standing up. "I'll end up with my mascara under my eyes. I hate it when that happens. I'm going to go start dinner. Then I've got class with Professor Wilson.''

Holly followed her down the stairs, then detoured into Jordan's study. He was asleep with the sheet bunched up around his waist.

Dark hair narrowed as it arrowed down his belly. Where the sheet dipped dangerously low, she saw the first hint of black curls that surrounded his—

Holly jerked her attention to his face. Oh, God, he was *naked!* She'd never seen a naked man before. She had a vague idea of what they would look like down there, but no real practical experience.

Before she started to hyperventilate, she reminded herself this was a sickroom. Jordan needed her care and concern, not her adolescent interest.

There was a bowl of water on the nightstand. She dampened the washcloth Louise had left, then brushed it over Jordan's face. She could feel the heat radiating from him. She sat on the edge of the bed and continued to cool him. She ran the cloth over his chest and his arms.

The familiar ministrations were almost comforting. She'd done this countless times for her mother. The fact that Jordan was a man didn't matter. It was all about healing.

She murmured soothingly, telling him he would soon be better. The fever would break, and his strength would return. Over and over she dipped the cloth in the water, squeezed it dry, then brushed it over his chest and face. After twenty minutes he opened his eyes.

''Holly?''

''I'm right here. How do you feel?''

He squinted at her, then cleared his throat. ''Hot.''

''You've got a fever. Do you want some water?''

''Yeah.''

She raised the bed slightly, then poured a glass from the pitcher. He tilted his head forward. She shifted so she could support his shoulders, then held the glass to his mouth. He sipped slowly.

When he was done, she continued to stroke him with the cloth. With her free hand she touched his face, then his arm. His eyes fluttered closed.

"That's nice," he said.

"You're trying to do too much," she told him. "You've got to concentrate on getting better."

He opened one eye. "And I was about to tell you how glad I was to see you. I take it all back."

She smiled.

"Did Kyle get you moved?"

"Yes. I'm right upstairs." She leaned closer and brushed his hair off his forehead.

His eyes opened, and he stared at her. She was close enough to kiss him. She refused to think about that. Right now he needed a nurse.

"You brought that damn cat, didn't you?"

"Of course." She moved the washcloth across his chest.

"It's good that I know you," he muttered.

"What do you mean?"

"You're the touchingest nurse I've ever met. If I wasn't so sure you were innocent, I would swear you were coming on to me."

Holly froze. In her mind's eye she saw how this must look to him. She was sitting on his bed with her hips pressing intimately against his. One hand caressed his face while the other stroked his chest. Okay, the hand on his chest held a washcloth, but that was just window dressing.

"I..." She closed her mouth and wished she could die.

"Don't stop," he said. "I like the attention. I know you

mean it impersonally, like a nurse, but my body doesn't exactly understand.'' He reached for the sheet.

Holly sprang to her feet. When all he did was draw the material up to his chest, she realized she'd overreacted. She dropped the washcloth and pressed her hand to her face. She was going to die. Absolutely die.

She turned on her heel and raced from the room.

"Holly, wait!'' Jordan called after her.

She ignored him and kept running. When she reached the cool quiet of her room, she threw herself on her bed and shut her eyes.

How could she have been so silly? Why had she made a fool of herself? It was horrible. She was never going to be able to face Jordan again.

She heard a faint meow-purr, then Mistletoe jumped on the bed and sniffed her face.

"Your mother is a fool,'' she said, pulling the soft cat down next to her. Mistletoe settled against her side.

What must Jordan be thinking about her? She so wanted to impress him. It was obvious she didn't have a clue as to how to act around men, and he was the last male she should be practicing on.

She wanted to run away and never face him again. The only problem with that plan was the reality of the situation. She had just moved into Jordan's house. This time there was no escape.

Chapter Seven

Jordan had heard Holly come into the house, but so far she hadn't come looking for him. At first he'd told himself she was busy, but after nearly an hour he knew she was avoiding him. The big question was why?

What had he done or said to offend her? He didn't remember much about the previous evening. As Louise had delighted in informing him when he'd finally awakened from a long and restless sleep, his overactivity had caused him to spike another fever. If he kept this up much longer, he was going to fry his brain.

He'd thanked the housekeeper for her concern and had privately agreed with her assessment. He had to start following the doctor's instructions, or he was never going to get well. That meant staying off his feet most of the time. Which he planned to do, just as soon as he found out what was wrong with Holly.

Moving slowly, he peeled back the sheet and swung his

feet to the floor. There was a pair of jeans tossed casually over the nightstand. He grabbed them and tugged them on. He considered a shirt, but didn't think he had the strength. Besides, Holly had seen him bare chested before and hadn't seemed to notice. He doubted she was going to start now.

He braced himself on the bed and nightstand, then pushed to his feet. The muscles in his legs trembled but didn't give way. After a couple of minutes he felt strong enough to start walking.

Louise had left nearly an hour before. He'd heard her car pull out right after Holly had arrived. The house was huge, and Holly could be anywhere. Once in the hallway, he stopped and listened, then followed the faint scraping sound coming from the dining room.

He grabbed the railing and climbed the three stairs to that level, then rounded the corner. The large crystal chandelier's light filled the room. A radio sat in one corner of the bare floor. Strains of classical music drifted toward him. Holly had pushed a drop cloth close to one wall. A piece of plywood resting on two sawhorses gave her a large work space. There were bottles and brushes, a few cans and a spatula. He took all that in quickly before turning his attention to her.

She stood with her back to him, carefully peeling off strips of wallpaper. She wore jeans that hugged the curves of her hips, rear end and thighs. For a moment he couldn't think about anything but holding her against him. He wanted to trace the curves, cup her softness, touch her, taste her, be with her, in her.

Although he hadn't dated in a while, when he had, he hadn't favored one particular type of woman. He found all their bodies attractive, all their differences intriguing. But looking at Holly, he felt a stirring deep inside, as if she aroused him on a more primal level. He wasn't sure why.

She wasn't fashion-model thin, but in his mind that was the best part. He tried not to think about how she would feel on top of him, her breasts spilling into his hands, her legs brushing against his.

He swallowed hard and ignored the pressure between his legs. Holly raised her hand to test the seam of the wallpaper farther up the wall. Her sweatshirt rose a couple of inches, exposing pale white skin and the curve of her waist. He swore silently. If she could destroy his self-control without even trying, he didn't want to know what she could accomplish when she put her mind to it. Heaven help them both.

"Hi," he said.

She spun toward him. The spatula went clattering to the floor, and she covered her cheeks with her hands. Her blue eyes widened. "I didn't hear you," she said breathlessly.

"Sorry. I didn't mean to scare you." He motioned to the wall. "What are you doing here?"

She turned her attention to the wall, staring at it blankly as if she had no idea what it meant. In the few moments before she spoke, Jordan studied her profile.

She had a small nose and full lips. Freckles dotted her cheeks and nose. Her thick hair had been pulled back into a ponytail that hung to the middle of her back. He did his best not to notice the thrust of her breasts. He didn't want to be in more trouble than he was. Life would be a lot easier if he could remember what he'd said or done to upset her.

"This is the dining room," she said at last. "I'm working on the wallpaper. I use these chemicals instead of a steamer because I don't know what's underneath. They didn't use the same kind of building materials seventy years ago. I brought home some wallpaper books for you to look at. There are two ways to go. There are reprints of original wallpaper or Victorian-inspired prints."

She gave him a quick look, then returned her attention to the wall. "I think you'd be happier with a Victorian-inspired print. The reproductions are often too busy for contemporary tastes. Also, you've got a chair rail running around the room." She touched the molding about three feet off the ground. "You could paint under the chair rail, then use paper above it. That's not how many of the Victorians did things, but it looks nice. I'm not sure how authentic you want the rooms. For most people it's a compromise between the flavor of the period and what they can actually live with."

She paused to take a breath. He realized she was babbling, and hoped that was a good sign. She seemed more nervous than angry. He moved closer, then leaned against the doorjamb to steady himself.

"I don't want to talk about the dining room," he said. "I want to talk about why you're avoiding me."

She gasped softly and ducked her head. He could see the color climbing her cheeks. "You know why."

At least she'd admitted it. That was something. "Holly, I don't—"

She cut him off with a wave of her hand. "I understand."

"No, you don't."

"I do. It's silly, really. My only excuse is that while my mother was ill, I took care of her. One of the nurses told me once that chronically ill people don't have much human contact. Oh, they're bathed and fed, but no one touches them just because. They need that contact. It keeps them connected and feeling alive. I did that for years. I guess it's a habit."

She turned her attention from the wall to him. Her mouth twisted. "Pretty stupid, huh, but I swear it's the truth."

"I appreciate your honesty, but I don't know what the

hell you're talking about. What exactly are you apologizing for?''

Her mouth opened and closed a couple of times before she got the words out. ''You want me to *say it?*''

''If it's not too much trouble.'' At her look of incredulity, he shrugged. ''I had a fever last night. I don't remember what happened.''

''You don't remember?'' Her voice rose in volume and pitch. She spun on her heel and began to pace the room. ''He doesn't remember. I don't sleep the whole night, and he doesn't remember. Great. Just perfect. I knew it. I'm not ready to be out in the world. This proves it. I should have become a nun.''

When she passed in front of him, he grabbed her arm and held her in place. ''Would you please tell me what you're talking about?''

She drew in a deep breath. ''You had a fever. I was trying to cool you off.''

''So?''

''I was…touching you.''

Where? For how long? Had she liked it? He was sure he had. His blood heated on cue and headed south. He released her arm, but she didn't move away. ''And?''

''And, that's it. I used a washcloth and wiped off your face and chest.'' Her gaze lowered to the floor.

''Wish I'd been conscious,'' he muttered.

''What?''

''Nothing. I appreciate the concern and the effort. So what's the problem?''

She linked her fingers together in front of her stomach, then released them. ''You were sort of asleep and then you woke up.''

Now it was Jordan's turn to be embarrassed. Had he

made a pass at her or worse, although he wasn't sure what would be worse. Maybe he'd flashed her.

"And," he prompted.

"And, well, you said I was the touchingest nurse you'd ever been around."

"And?"

"What do you mean 'and?' Isn't that enough? You said if you didn't know better, you would think I was making a pass at you."

He searched his brain for some other meaning to her words. "I don't think I understand."

"I was *touching* you," she shrieked.

"What's the problem? I happen to like you touching me."

She gave a strangled moan and sank slowly to the floor. After drawing her knees to her chest, she lowered her head until he couldn't see her face. "I just want to die."

Jordan tried to crouch next to her, but it hurt too much. Awkwardly he lowered himself to the floor and braced his sore back against the wall.

"I'm really sorry," Holly murmured. "It's really all because of my mom. I was just so used to taking care of her that I—" She paused and looked at him. "I said this already, huh?"

"Yeah."

She nodded. "I just didn't want you to think..." Her voice trailed off.

"Think what?"

She shook her head as if indicating she couldn't speak. Jordan tried to understand her state of mind, but he didn't know what the big deal was. So she'd touched him. So he'd commented on the fact. It was hardly a hanging offense.

He stretched his legs out in front of him, then winced as

the injured muscles protested. He placed his palm on her arm, then slid down until his hand was over hers. That seemed to give her courage.

"I didn't want you to think I was coming on to you," she said. "That never crossed my mind."

"Bummer."

"What?" She stared at him as if he'd grown a second head. "You can't be serious."

"Why not? I'd love to have you come on to me." He tugged on her hand until she relaxed enough to let him lace his fingers with hers, then he rested their joined hands on his left thigh.

She stared at him. "But I'm... But you're..." She shook her head. "You're teasing me, right?"

"Nope."

"But I'm not sexy. I don't even know how to be sexy. I'm inexperienced to the point of being stupid around men, and I'm fifteen pounds overweight."

He forced himself to keep staring at her face when what he really wanted to do was drop his gaze to her breasts. "Don't you dare lose a pound. You're perfect."

Conflicting emotions raced through her eyes. He could see she wanted to believe him but she didn't dare. Jordan frowned. Why didn't Holly know she had the ability to turn him on? Had someone hurt her that badly? Animal rage surged inside him. If a man had caused her to doubt herself, he would find him and punish him.

"Wow," she said. "That was pretty amazing."

"What?"

She shrugged. "Your family mentioned you were the brooding one in the group. I didn't believe them. You've always been so friendly. But just now you got this look on your face."

"Sorry. I was thinking about something else."

"I could tell." She stared at him. "Do you really brood?"

"Sometimes." But not around Holly. When he was with her, he forgot about being on the outside looking in. With her, he belonged.

Warning lights began to flash, but he ignored them. He knew his friendship with Holly was dangerous, but he was willing to risk it. After all, it was just temporary. When she could afford her own place, she would move out and disappear from his life. So it was safe to enjoy the short time they had together.

She shifted and sat cross-legged. His knees hurt just thinking about trying that position.

"Jordan, do you really think I'm sexy?" She shook her head. "Sorry. I shouldn't have asked. I'm not fishing for compliments. I've just never thought of myself that way. I've never been involved with a man, so I don't know how they think."

It took every ounce of self-control not to pull his hand free of hers. Jordan sat very still, trying to absorb what Holly had just said. She'd never been involved with a man. No way could she mean that. He'd suspected she was innocent, but not *that* innocent.

"By 'never,' you mean less than ten or something, right?" he asked desperately.

She stared solemnly. "'Never' as in 'none.' I had a boyfriend when I was fifteen. That lasted for a couple of months. He even kissed me a few times, but it wasn't anything like when you and I did." Her voice got lower and lower. "Then my mom was diagnosed with the cancer, and I didn't have a lot of extra time to spend with him. He didn't understand."

"Teenage boys are notoriously selfish," he said. "I

know. I was one once." He shifted his hand so he could brush his thumb back and forth across her palm.

She smiled at him. "I tried to understand. In my head it made sense. We were both young. He wanted to have fun. There was this dance, and I was supposed to go with him. But my mom was just out of the hospital. I was scared she was going to die. I didn't want to leave her alone, so I told him I couldn't go."

He could hear the pain in her words. Jordan released her hand and draped his arm around her shoulders. At first she stiffened, then slowly she relaxed against him. Her head rested on his chest.

"He took someone else," he said quietly.

She nodded. "This girl. Colette. Can you imagine a fifteen-year-old named Colette? I blamed her because that was easier than facing the truth. After the dance he stopped calling me. We never went out again."

He rested his chin on the top of her head and ignored the heat from her hand resting on his thigh. "Who was next?"

She sniffed. "No one. That's the entire story of my love life. Pretty pathetic, huh?"

"You didn't date?"

"I tried, but not a lot of single guys came into the antique store. I went to the local junior college, but I didn't have extra time to socialize. Just when I thought it was all going to be okay, the cancer came back."

"I'm sorry," he murmured.

"Thanks. I'm fine with most of it. Mom and I never wasted time with each other. We got to say goodbye. A lot of people don't get that chance. I do regret how I grew up. I had to do it fast, and I missed out on a lot of stuff like dating."

It was worse than he'd thought. If she'd only dated one

guy when she was fifteen, then she was a virgin. He winced at the word. So much for a quick affair. He wasn't usually the type, but he would have made an exception for Holly. Now he couldn't. She was too innocent.

"You're twenty-eight?" he asked.

"Twenty-eight and never been kissed." She laughed and glanced up at him. "Well, I've been kissed, but I've never done anything else. I've never even seen a man naked."

She squeezed her eyes shut and ducked her head. "Oh, my, I can't believe I said that."

Jordan was having a little trouble with it, too. He was torn between running for cover and volunteering his services. Between the subject matter of their conversation and her nearness, he could give her an eyeful. Hell of a time to develop a conscience.

"What are your plans?" he asked. "Find some nice guy, get married and have a couple of kids?"

"I'd like to, but I don't think it's going to happen. I haven't had great luck with relationships."

"One relationship isn't enough to judge."

She straightened and looked at him. "That's a kind of luck. Relationships require trust, and I'm not very good at that."

"You had a good one with your mom."

She smiled. "It's hardly the same thing, but yes, we did have fun together. When she was feeling well, she used to take me places. We got great at having a good time with no money. We went to exhibits and parks. The free day at the zoo."

A single strand of hair slipped onto her cheek. Holly brushed it away impatiently. "She used to take all the holidays seriously. Half the garage was filled with decorations. Not just for Christmas, but for all of them. We had painted pumpkins for Halloween, decorated flags for May Day, stuffed hearts for Valentine's. On her last Christmas she gave me Mistletoe.''

It was as if the cat heard her name. The gray, flat-faced spawn of the devil strolled into the dining room. Her belly hung low, and she walked with a rolling gait.

"Hi, sweetie," Holly cooed as she reached out to pet her cat. Mistletoe sat down to accept the attention. As she purred, she glared at Jordan.

"That cat hates me," he muttered.

"I don't know why. She's normally very friendly."

"Sure. That's why she spends the afternoon spitting at me."

"She does not."

"Sure, she does. She knows exactly when I'm nearly asleep, and she comes in and hisses. Once I'm awake, she leaves." He glared back at the cat.

"She really likes Kyle."

"That proves my point."

Holly laughed.

Mistletoe rose to her feet and gave a quick *pftt* before heading out. As she passed by Jordan's feet, she swiped out with her right front paw. He pulled back just in time to avoid being skewered.

Mistletoe raised her tail to a saucy angle and sauntered out of the room.

"She's a miserable animal. I hope she doesn't pass her personality on to her kittens."

"She's sweet," Holly protested. She stared after her cat. "But I have to admit, she doesn't like you much." She smiled at him. "So I'm even more grateful that you let me bring her with me. And thanks for letting me be here, too. I don't want you to think I'm going to be in the way for the holiday stuff."

"You won't be in the way. The family is huge and one more only means more fun."

"Thanks. Work keeps me busy during the day, but nights are hard. Especially at this time of year. Okay, okay, enough emotion. I don't want to get all weird and cry or embarrass you."

"I don't embarrass that easy."

"I do."

"I noticed."

She glanced at him out of the corner of her eye. "So you're not mad at me anymore?"

"I was never mad. Just confused." He leaned over and kissed her forehead. He wanted to do a whole lot more, but that seemed the safest at the moment. "Friends?"

"I'd like that." She scrambled to her feet. "So what do you think about the wallpaper?"

As she discussed his various options, he thought about all she'd told him. She'd been alone for a long time. Even before her mother had died, Holly had been responsible for too much. He couldn't change her past, but he could give her a Christmas to remember. He vowed then to make that dream come true.

Chapter Eight

Holly glanced around her store in amazement. She and her mother had often talked about what they wanted A Victorian Parlor to be. They'd discussed the separate rooms, a formal parlor set up in the front, alcoves of decorative items, paintings, several tables with wallpaper and fabric samples. Furniture was scattered throughout the store, but the majority of it was in the huge room to the rear. As they'd planned, she'd filled the store with soft lighting and homey scents. From the moment she'd put the sign up and opened her doors, business had been good. In the past couple of weeks it had become spectacular, and she knew exactly who was responsible. Jordan.

Even on a Thursday afternoon the shop was crowded. Women clustered together in groups and cooed over the ornaments displayed on several Christmas trees. Her wreath inventory was down by half. If business kept up at this pace, she would sell out before Christmas. She was thrilled about all the sales.

In order to keep prices down, she'd bought in as high a quantity as she could afford. The purchases had drained her financial reserves to zero. When she'd worried about making a wrong decision, she'd consoled herself with the fact that the Christmas items wouldn't spoil. What she didn't sell this year, she would sell next. In fact, part of her plan had been to buy two years' worth of inventory. Instead, she was selling it all in one year.

The front door opened, and a handsome couple walked in. The man was tall, maybe six feet four, with dark hair and an earring glinting from his ear. He looked dangerous, the kind of man who was deadly to women and their hearts. The woman also had dark hair, but hers was curly and long, nearly to her waist. She was slender and dressed in a wool jumper over a long-sleeved white blouse.

Holly studied them for a moment and realized she'd seen them when she'd first visited Jordan in the hospital.

The woman caught her eye and smiled, then started in her direction. She glanced at the tag on Holly's apron.

"You must be Holly. I recognized you from Elizabeth's description," she said. "I'm Rebecca Lucas, and this is my husband, Austin."

The three of them shook hands.

"Thanks for stopping by," Holly said, then motioned around the store. "Are you looking for anything in particular, or do you want to browse?"

Rebecca glanced at her husband. "You want to run for the hills, don't you?"

Austin shifted his weight from foot to foot. "Too much girl stuff. And it smells weird in here."

Holly laughed. "Most men feel that way. If you head toward the back and through the room with the furniture, you'll find an alcove with coffee, a couple of chairs and a TV. Most of the husbands hide out there.''

"Go on," Rebecca urged. "I want to get some decorations for the house and have a chat with Holly."

Austin looked at his wife for a moment. Holly saw a flash of love so bright, it nearly brought tears to her eyes. He touched Rebecca's face. The tender gesture was at odds with his dark and dangerous appearance. Then he turned and headed for the back room.

Rebecca stared after him. "I know what you're thinking. I used to picture him as a pirate and wish he'd kidnap me and hide me on his desert island. But behind that tough exterior is a very gentle man."

"If you say so," Holly murmured, wondering how someone as innocent looking as Rebecca had tamed such a hard man. She pushed the thought from her mind. "Do you want something particular for your house?"

Rebecca tilted her head. "Elizabeth told me your wreaths were beautiful. I'd like a couple for the foyer. And maybe some ornaments for the tree."

"The wreaths are on all the walls. Everything I have is out. Do you have a particular theme? I have angel wreaths, toy wreaths, some with fruit, plain, fancy, whatever you're looking for."

Rebecca laughed. "I'm not organized enough to have a theme. I just want something pretty." She glanced around at the crowded store. "You've got plenty of other customers. Go ahead and help them while I look around."

Holly saw a couple heading for the cash register, so she excused herself. For the next half hour she rang up purchases and wrapped delicate ornaments. Then the crowd faded. Holly saw Rebecca talking to another couple. Even if they hadn't introduced themselves, she would have recognized the man as pure Haynes. He had the tall, dark good looks of all the brothers. There was a bit of gray at his temples, a few more lines, so Holly guessed he was the oldest. She was right. Craig and his petite redheaded wife, Jill, were in town for a few days.

Rebecca saw her and motioned her over. "Have you met these two?"

Holly nodded. "They introduced themselves when they first came in." She smiled at Jill. "When's the baby due?"

Jill touched her rounding belly. "May. I wish it were tomorrow. I remind myself she'll be worth it, but the waiting is hard."

"I remember how that feels," Rebecca said. "Are the boys excited about getting a sister?"

"Very," Jill said. "Danny is so thrilled he won't be the youngest anymore." She leaned against her husband, who wrapped his arm around her shoulders.

Holly ignored the flicker of envy that filled her. Holidays were the worst, she told herself. Since her mother had died, she'd really felt alone at Christmas. But soon it would be the first of the year, and everything would return to normal.

"You had the test to determine gender?" Holly asked.

Craig and his wife exchanged a glance. "Not exactly," Jill said. "It's sort of a family thing."

"There hadn't been a girl born to the Haynes family in four generations," Craig said. "I'm one of four brothers, my father is one of six and so on. We figured we couldn't have girls."

Rebecca brushed her long dark hair off her shoulder and smiled. "Then Travis married Elizabeth, and they had a girl. Everyone was stunned. Next Kyle and Sandy had a daughter. Jordan is the one who came up with the theory."

"What theory?" Holly asked.

Jill sighed. "It's very romantic. Haynes men have a

daughter when they're in love. If they're not, they just have boys.''

"So if you want to have a boy, you have to have a fight first?" Holly asked.

Craig chuckled. "I don't think that would work. We'd still be in love. So Jill's convinced it's a girl. So far, the ultrasound is proving the theory correct. I guess we'll find out in May."

"Not being married to one of the Haynes brothers," Rebecca said, "I'm free to have a child of either gender."

Holly wondered if the theory was true. But that didn't make sense. There were four brothers. Did that mean their father had never loved their mother? She thought about asking, then figured this wasn't the time. Maybe later she would discuss it with Jordan.

Craig and Jill had completed their shopping. Holly rang up their purchases, then wrapped everything. Craig collected the packages.

"Louise has our phone number," he said. "Call us if you need anything."

Jill gave her a quick hug, then laughed when Holly bent to avoid her belly. "I know, I'm getting bigger every day. I'm so pleased Jordan's found you."

Holly didn't know what to say. She walked to the front door and held it open. When they were gone, she turned and saw Rebecca leaning on the counter staring at her.

"Is something wrong?" Holly asked, touching a hand to her hair and hoping she hadn't smudged her cheek.

"No. Everything is exactly right. I had wondered what it was about you that Jordan liked. Now I understand."

Holly felt herself flush. She glanced around the store and was relieved when she realized most of the customers had left. There were a few browsing in the other rooms, but she and Rebecca were the only people up front.

"He doesn't exactly like me." Hmm, that wasn't right. "What I mean is we're just friends. I'm staying with him to help him fix the house."

Rebecca raised her eyebrows. "So you are living together. Elizabeth told me you were, but I didn't believe her. Imagine Jordan letting a woman into his house."

"But it's not like that."

"Then why are you blushing?"

"Because I—" Holly clamped her mouth shut. She was only making it worse.

Rebecca shook her head. "I'm teasing you, Holly, and I shouldn't. I was just as tongue-tied when I was first around Austin. There's something about the men they grow here. I wish I could tell you it gets better, but it doesn't. Austin still has the power to make me feel clumsy and foolish, but he's too sweet to use it. Instead, he makes me feel beautiful and loved."

The sharp jab of envy returned, this time stabbing a little deeper. Holly wouldn't mind feeling that way once in a while. But it wasn't to be. She'd chosen her path a long time ago. Love required trust, and too many people had let her down for her to ever take that leap of faith again.

She glanced out the front window and saw Craig tenderly helping his pregnant wife into the car. Concern and affection filled every gesture. She wished it could have been different for herself. She wanted too much.

"But it's not like that," Holly said as she walked to the counter. "We really are just friends." And sometimes she wasn't sure about that. So many things confused her. The way his kiss had made her feel, the passion—at least, she *thought* it was passion—that had flared between them. Her embarrassment when he'd pointed out how much she touched him while he was ill, then the gentle way he'd tried to make her feel better. She still remembered the feel of his arms around her. She didn't know what to think.

Rebecca stretched out her arm and rested her hand on top of Holly's. "I'm teasing you, and that's not fair. I know how difficult it is in the beginning. The family is overwhelming."

"But wonderful. Everyone has come in to buy things. Even you and Austin." Holly frowned. "He's really not related?"

Rebecca shook her head. "They all met when Austin and Travis were in junior high. Austin was a bully, but the Haynes family gave him a place to belong. It's what those brothers do best."

She glanced around as if checking to make sure they were alone, then lowered her voice conspiratorially. "I'll tell you a secret. They didn't grow up in a very happy home, and they learned early on to depend only on each other. They all wanted a loving wife and family, but it seemed beyond them. They tried relationships and failed. Each of them gave up, resigned to living alone. But they were wrong." Rebecca smiled. "First Travis found Elizabeth, then Kyle courted Sandy. Just last year Jill dropped into Craig's life. It's not that the Haynes brothers didn't know how to love—it's that they hadn't met the right woman."

Holly backed up a step. "I'm not the right woman."

Rebecca studied her for a moment. "Too bad, because you'll never find another man like Jordan or another family like this one. They'll take you in and love you until you never have to be afraid again."

"I'm not afraid," Holly said quickly, then wondered why she bothered to lie. Of course she was afraid. Sometimes she was afraid she would die of the loneliness.

"My mistake," Rebecca said lightly. "I thought you

might want something special with Jordan. It's fine that you don't, but do me a favor. Don't break his heart.''

''He's not interested in me that way.'' Holly glanced down at herself. The long apron she wore only emphasized her wide hips. ''I'm not his type.''

Rebecca's smile widened. ''Aren't you?''

Before Holly could say anything else, Austin came out of the back room and wanted to know if they were going to live there permanently. Rebecca laughed, then pointed to half a dozen wreaths she wanted to buy. Austin got them down, then collected the ornaments she indicated she liked.

As Holly wrote up the order, she had to clench her jaw muscles to keep her mouth from hanging open. Somewhere she'd heard a rumor that Austin and Rebecca were wealthy. They'd just bought more in a few minutes than any three other customers combined. She frowned. That wasn't true. All the Haynes family members had bought a lot.

A warm feeling stole over her. Her stay in Jordan's house was temporary, as was her connection with his relatives. Because she was part of Jordan's life, they were including her. She realized she should enjoy the time while it lasted and give back with the same generous spirit. She had much to be grateful for. It was almost Christmas, and this year she wasn't going to be alone.

Jordan dipped his brush in the can of paint, then straightened. Every muscle in his legs complained.

''I heard that,'' Holly said without looking at him. ''You're doing too much.''

''I'm fine.''

''And a liar.''

He grinned. ''Okay, that too. I'll finish this door frame, then I'll quit for the night.''

"Good. If you have a relapse, your relatives will blame me."

He glanced at her. She was sitting cross-legged on the floor. She wore tight jeans that outlined every generous curve and an old sweatshirt that had faded to a misty gray. Her long blond hair had been pulled back in a braid to protect it from the paint that splattered the front of her clothing.

She wielded a paint brush and roller with the speed and finesse of an expert. In one short week his dining room had been transformed. The floors had been in better shape than either of them had realized. Someone had coated them with wax. Once the buildup was removed, the natural beauty of the hardwood shone through. The old wallpaper was gone. The ceiling had been painted creamy white, and next week Holly would hang the new wallpaper. He had taken her suggestion and used the chair rail as a dividing line in the large room. The bottom would be painted colonial blue. Holly was doing that now. The top would be papered. It wasn't authentic, but it fit the shape and function of the room.

"I called about the furniture," Jordan said. He was in charge of painting door frames to match the ceiling and the chair rails. "It will be here in a week."

She looked at him over her shoulder. "Great. Just in time for Christmas."

The chandelier illuminated her features. She'd gotten into the habit of washing off her makeup when she came home from work. He could see the freckles sprinkled on her nose and the tops of her cheeks.

"Speaking of which," she said, "are you going to get a tree?"

"Sure. Sunday. It's the annual Haynes family Christmas-tree hunt."

Her eyebrows drew together. "How do you hunt Christmas trees? They can't run away."

"It's what we call it. Just the men and the kids. We leave women folk at home."

"Sounds odd, but okay." She ran her roller across the paint pan, then returned her attention to the wall. "I've put aside a few ornaments from the store. I'd like to contribute them to the decorating."

"I'd like that," he said. "I always chop down a big tree, then it looks sort of bare and I have to feel sorry for it."

She shifted until she was on her knees, then worked the roller back and forth, smoothing on paint evenly. "I hope you don't plan to do your own chopping."

It was making him hurt just watching her paint. "Doubtful. I'll get one of my brothers to do it."

"Speaking of them, Craig, Austin and their wives were in the store today. In the last couple of weeks half the town has been by to stock up on Christmas supplies. This is going to be my best month yet." She gave him a shy smile. "I know I have you to thank for that."

He shrugged. "I made a few phone calls. No big deal." There was a light in her eyes that made him feel uncomfortable. He hadn't done anything special.

"It is a big deal, and I appreciate the business. I'm keeping my fingers crossed that they came to the shop as a favor to you, but that they really liked what they saw so they'll come back again because they want to."

Jordan put down the paint brush and stretched.

"How are you feeling?" she asked.

"Sore but better. I'm more mobile. I was up most of yesterday, and there aren't any repercussions today. If I continue to heal, I'll be back at the fire station by the first of the year."

"Do you miss work?"

"Yeah. I like my job."

"Me, too." She smiled.

He bent down and picked up the brush he was using and returned his attention to the door frame. They worked well together. There was just the right amount of conversation, sprinkled with laughter. He didn't have to think when he was with her. He considered telling her that, but didn't think she would appreciate the news or view it as a compliment.

"It will be nice to be here for the holidays," Holly said. "Thanks for including me."

"You're no trouble at all."

Before he could say anything else, Louise walked in with a couple of sodas. "I've got to leave for my class," she said. "I brought you these."

He took the cola drink she offered him. "Thanks."

Her eyebrows arched in surprise. "You're welcome."

"You're the best," Holly said, and popped the top on her diet soda.

"I finished the salad," Louise said. "The steaks are ready to go on any time you want to cook them, and the baked potatoes are washed." She addressed her comments to Holly, but kept glancing at him.

Jordan understood her wariness. Since Holly had moved in, he'd made an effort to be polite to Louise. It was an armed truce. He needed the housekeeper to stay, because she made Holly's presence possible. Louise was their chaperon. If she left, Holly would go, too. He didn't want that. He figured he should probably be smart enough to figure out why, but he didn't want to have to think about it. He only knew that he liked having Holly around. If the price of that was civil conversation with Louise, he would gladly pay.

As much as he hated to admit it, sometimes he forgot he

wasn't supposed to like Louise. The older woman was funny and great at her job. She genuinely cared about his family. He wondered how much of that came from guilt. If he let himself forget the past, he could be friends with her, but he wasn't willing to do that yet.

"Enjoy your class," he said.

Louise gave him another puzzled look, then left.

Jordan finished the door frame about the same time Holly finished the first coat of blue paint. She stood up and surveyed her work.

"It's going to be stunning," she said. "The colonial blue is just the right color." She glanced at her watch. "You hungry?"

"Starved."

"Let's go fix dinner."

He followed her into the kitchen. He liked watching the sway of her hips as she walked. The feminine motion appealed to him on a basic level. It was tough to hang back and be polite when all he really wanted to do was haul her close and have his way with her right there on the hall floor.

When they entered the kitchen, there were stacks of cookie sheets in the sink.

"Louise has started baking," Holly said as she studied the counter. She pointed to a foil-covered dish. "Samples for dessert. I can't wait."

"Louise bakes every year for Christmas. It's a tradition."

She pointed to one of the chairs by the kitchen table. He sank down and relaxed, letting the pain ease out of him. Holly worked quickly. In the past couple of weeks she'd become familiar with the kitchen.

"My Mom used to make cookies, too," she said as she pricked the potatoes with a fork and set them on a dinner plate. "I think they were sugar cookies. You know, the kind you can decorate. I was in charge of the icing.'' She leaned against the tile counter and smiled. ''I used to get more on my clothes and eat more than ever got on the cookies. She always did special stuff like that with me. We had a lot of fun.''

A single strand of blond hair fluttered near her cheek. She brushed it away slowly. Her blue eyes were large and thoughtful, focusing on a past he could only imagine.

''What other traditions did you have?'' he asked.

''She used to fill a stocking for me. I loved it. There wasn't anything expensive. Oranges, those chocolate kisses, pens for school, adhesive tape.'' She looked at him. ''What is it about kids and sticky stuff?''

''I'm not sure, but they do love it.''

''We always had a real tree. It wasn't very big, but it was beautiful, especially at night, with the lights.''

''Did you ever see your father at the holidays?''

Instantly her face changed. All emotion faded, along with her color. Her mouth straightened, and she folded her arms over her chest.

''I met him once,'' she said. ''It was about six years ago. My mother was very ill, and the expenses were enormous. I knew who he was. He has a lot of money. I thought maybe—'' She swallowed. ''I went to see him to ask him if he could help with the medical bills. He said no and that I shouldn't bother him again.''

Hurt hovered around her like fire. He could see it burning away her self-control. He ached *for* her. ''I'm sorry.''

''Don't be.'' She shrugged. ''It's no big deal. I didn't care on my behalf. I was worried about my mom. I didn't want her to know I'd gone there or that he'd turned me down.''

Jordan glanced at his lap and was surprised to see his hands curled into tight fists. Consciously he relaxed.

Holly's father was a first-class bastard, and he would like nothing more than to teach him the price of hurting his own daughter. Holly might claim not to feel pain, but he could see it and feel it radiating from her. She raised her chin slightly and blinked. He realized she was fighting tears.

"I suppose it's silly," she said, her voice thickening. "But he never said anything about being my father. I thought he would. I guess I wanted him to acknowledge me. But he didn't say a word."

Jordan stood up and crossed the linoleum floor. When he was in front of her, he held out his arms, inviting her to find comfort with him. He didn't touch her, somehow sensing the decision had to be hers.

She hesitated for a moment, then threw herself against him. Her hands clawed at his sweatshirt, and her face pressed against his chest. A sob shook her, then another. He held her close.

"It was so h-horrible," she said, the words muffled and broken. "I just stood there staring at him. I could s-see we even sort of looked alike. But he didn't say anything. He didn't care about her, and he d-didn't care about me. I thought fathers were supposed to love their children."

Jordan thought about his father. "They are, but not all of them do."

He cupped the back of her head and ran his other hand up and down her spine, all the while murmuring soothingly. He ached for her. It wasn't a physical pain like he had from his injuries. This was down to his soul and into the blackness. It was a hungry pain of loss and emptiness, of forgotten promises and broken dreams. The depth and intensity stunned him. Most of the time he was able to disconnect from everyone else. He was used to not feeling much at all.

When her sobs lessened, he kissed her cheek and brushed

the tears from her skin. She continued to cling to him, and he continued to hold her. He knew he was supposed to be comforting her, but there was something soothing and welcoming in her warmth. He tried to ignore the way her breasts flattened against his chest and her thighs brushed his.

She sniffed a couple of times. "I must look horrible," she murmured. "I always do when I cry. My eyes get puffy, and my nose gets red."

"I think it's cute."

She laughed, then stepped away from him. "Thanks, Jordan. I appreciate it." She cleared her throat. "I want to go take a shower. Would you mind if we put off dinner for a half hour or so?"

"That's fine."

She nodded, then started for the door. He called after her, "Holly, your secret is safe with me."

She glanced at him. "I know. You're a good friend." Then she left the room.

He stared after her in equal parts of pleasure and annoyance. He was pleased that she trusted him to hold her and keep her secrets safe. After all, he was a master at keeping secrets. But he didn't like her thinking of him as a friend.

How else should she think of you? a voice in his head asked mockingly.

Jordan didn't have an answer for that. He didn't want a relationship; at least, that was the story he always told himself. He knew firsthand the dangers involved. But a flicker of need inside warned him letting Holly go wasn't going to be as easy as he'd first thought.

Chapter Nine

Holly smoothed the oversize sweater, then reached for the towel on her head. When she pulled it loose, her wet hair tumbled onto her shoulders. She stared at herself in the mirror, then shook her head.

It didn't matter that she'd spent several minutes splashing cold water on her face. She still looked puffy and red eyed. It was obvious she'd been crying.

She should have changed the subject, she told herself. She could talk about her mother and their holiday traditions, and she could talk about that ill-fated trip to visit her father, but she couldn't talk about them together. Every time she thought about what that man had said, how cruel he'd been, she got so mad and so hurt for her mother that she…

Tears burned, but this time she blinked them away. She wasn't going to cry any more. She was supposed to be here looking after Jordan, but every time she turned around, he was taking care of her.

She reached for her brush and began the slow process of untangling her hair. When that was done, she plugged in the blow dryer, then bent over at the waist and started drying her hair. The low, steady roar of the machine was soothingly familiar. She cleared her mind of unpleasant thoughts and resolved only to think about nice things for the rest of the evening.

That was easy, she thought with a smile. She would focus on Jordan. A delicious, sensual shiver went through her as she remembered what it had been like when he'd held her. She knew he'd meant it as a comforting gesture. But she'd liked the feel of his arms around her. She'd felt safe and comforted at the same time. He was strong yet gentle. Usually she didn't show a lot of herself to other people. She didn't have much experience with relationships, even friendship, and her awkwardness made her wary. But around him, she forgot to be afraid.

Very out of character, she told herself as she straightened and began to dry the front of her hair. But then several family members had told her that Jordan was a brooding loner, and she'd never seen that part of him. Maybe they were different with each other than they were with the rest of the world. Maybe the odd circumstances allowed them to let go of the barriers normally in place. She would like to believe Jordan thought of her as special, even though she knew she was fooling herself. He probably had dozens of women in his life. He wouldn't have time for her.

Then why aren't any of those women here? a voice in her head asked.

Holly didn't have an answer for that. She didn't want to think about it, either. If she allowed herself to hope, she would end up being disappointed, or worse, hurt. She didn't want to do that. Besides, there was no point in wishing for a romantic relationship when she wasn't willing to commit to one.

Something warm rubbed against her leg. She glanced down and saw Mistletoe.

"We always want what we can't have," she said, then turned the blow dryer to warm and patted the counter.

Mistletoe was huge, with her wide belly hanging low. The cat couldn't make the jump to the counter easily, so she jumped onto the toilet, then stepped across. When she stretched out by the sink, Holly petted her soft fur.

"How's my pretty girl? Are you enjoying this big house?"

Mistletoe purred. Her wide, flat face and green irises made her look wise. Her eyes closed in pleasure as Holly pointed the blow dryer at the cat's coat.

Mistletoe loved the heat of the machine. She could lie there for hours being warmed and petted. Her purr rumbled as low as the motor. Holly felt the vibrations through her fingers. She turned the dryer off after a few minutes. Mistletoe bumped her fingers with her damp nose as if asking for more.

"Wait until you have your babies," Holly said.

Mistletoe stretched, then rested her head on her front paws, as if she intended to nap on the counter.

"Fine by me," Holly said. She glanced in the mirror. Her nose was still red, but some of the puffiness had gone down around her eyes. Her hair wasn't completely dry, but that always took forever. She pulled it back into a loose ponytail and walked out of the bathroom. First she would check on Jordan, then she would finish dinner.

As she approached the study, she heard a muffled curse. When she walked in the room, Jordan was pacing shirtless.

He held his right arm close to his chest. Lines of pain stretched from his nose to his mouth.

"What's wrong?" she asked as she hurried to his side.

"I painted the baseboards. At least, I started to. Then this muscle seized up in my back." He tried to straighten his arm, then grimaced.

Holly walked behind him. She touched him by his shoulder blade and felt the large knot of muscles. "I used to massage my mother," she said. "Do you want me to try and do you?"

He turned so he was facing her. "I'm in too much pain to be done," he said, then grimaced.

She stared at him blankly. "You don't want me to rub your back?"

"Yeah, that would be great."

"Then why did you say—"

He cut her off with a shake of his head. "Joke. Bad timing. Forget it." He glanced around the room. "Where do you want me?"

"Lie down on the bed." As soon as she said the words, she started to get embarrassed. Thankfully he did as she asked without looking at her first.

She went into the bathroom by his room and found a bottle of body lotion. As she returned, she tried not to notice how he looked wearing jeans and nothing else, stretched out on clean white sheets. Her insides felt funny, as if they were being jolted by a slight electric shock. She wore socks but not shoes, and she couldn't stop her toes from curling.

He was hurt, she reminded herself. He was in pain and he needed help. This was medicinal. She wanted to heal, not indulge in some bizarre fantasy.

She approached the bed slowly. His eyes were closed,

and a dark lock of hair fell across his forehead. A twitch by his mouth was the only indication of his pain.

She sat on the edge of the bed and uncapped the lotion. After pouring some in her palm, she shifted so she was facing his back and touched her hands to his skin.

He was hotter than she'd expected. While she worked at the knotted muscles, part of her mind stood back and noted differences. Her mother's skin had been thin, her back more narrow, her muscles easily manipulated. Jordan was pure male in his prime. Lean ropes of strength challenged her trained fingers. She pressed her palms against the tightness, trying to force the lactic acid out, and with it, the pain.

She leaned toward him, using her body weight to increase the pressure. Her conscience split in two. One side was the nurse, noting the slight relaxing of tension in his body. That portion of her allowed her to straddle his narrow hips so she was able to put more pressure into her massage. The other part of her, the shy, inexperienced woman, was shrieking at what was going on. She couldn't believe she was doing this, on his bed, in his room, with nothing but a few layers of clothing between them.

As she worked, moving slowly, starting her strokes low at the small of his back and sliding up, she tried to ignore the curve of his rear pressing intimately against her. She tried to ignore the dryness of her throat and the nearly uncontrollable urge to giggle. She wanted to stand up and scream, *Look at me. I'm touching a man's bare back.* But she doubted Jordan would understand.

She rubbed the knot and found it was much smaller. Jordan groaned. "If I pay you a million dollars, will you promise to never stop?" he asked.

"Do you have a million dollars?"

"Not with me."

"Too bad. I would have promised."

She stretched up until she reached his shoulders and neck. She squeezed the muscles there.

"This is heaven," he murmured. "I haven't felt this good in weeks."

"I aim to please."

"You're doing a damn fine job." He raised his head. "You're also probably getting a cramp in your hands."

She shook out her fingers. They were a little sore. "I'm fine."

"Stop for now," he said. "You can do more later."

"Sure."

She slid off him. Now that she wasn't massaging him, the nurse inside her faded away and she was left with just the woman. Awkwardness returned, and with it a feeling of self-consciousness. She needed to get away from this bed.

But before she could leave, Jordan turned toward her and grabbed her hand. "Don't go."

It wasn't what he said; it was the way he said it. Holly stared at him. The low, throaty sound of his voice vibrated in her ears. Something about the tone or the pitch sparked an answering resonance deep in her soul. *Don't go.* He said it the way she'd always imagined men said it to women. She was immobilized. She felt as if she'd forgotten how to breathe.

A dark light flared in his eyes. Some forbidden spark that tempted her. She wasn't sure what she was being tempted for or with. Their gazes locked. She thought about looking away, but he held her in his spell. The room faded around them. There was nothing in the world but the man in front of her.

"Holly."

He spoke her name as if the sound were precious to him. She tried to swallow, but nothing was working. It was then that she noticed he was circling her palm with his thumb. Sensations skittered up her arm, diffusing in her chest, then refocusing in her oddly sensitized breasts.

"I want to kiss you," he said, his gaze never leaving hers. "And touch you. If that frightens you, then you can go, now or later. I'm not going to make love to you, though. Not because I don't want to, but because—" He paused, then gave a rueful grin. "I couldn't handle the pressure right now. Maybe when I'm stronger."

She blinked several times, sure she couldn't have heard him correctly. He announced he was going to kiss her and touch her? Just like that? He was talking about sex? And it wasn't even seven o'clock? Was he crazy?

But curiosity and anticipation were stronger than terror. The thought of leaving was quickly pushed aside. She remembered Jordan's last kiss, and definitely wanted to repeat the experience. Most women experimented with the opposite sex while they were still in high school, or at least in college. Holly knew she was backward when it came to the man-woman thing. Even if Jordan hadn't made her blood race and her heart pound, she still would have been tempted to kiss him again.

If nothing else, she trusted him not to hurt her or do something that would make her uncomfortable.

"You're not leaving," he said. "So the idea of kissing me doesn't horrify you?"

Embarrassment forced her to look away. How long were they going to *talk* about it? Couldn't they just do it? She shook her head.

"Good."

He tugged her closer. She resisted and sat straighter.

One corner of his mouth curved up in a smile. "I'm in a weakened condition. You're going to have to come to me."

She stared at him uncomprehending.

"I can't sit up," he said.

"Oh." Then she got it. The muscles in his back. His pain. *"Oh!"* He needed her help. She could do that.

But when she went to lean toward him, she found she *couldn't* do that. It was too bold, too beyond her comfort level. She didn't know what to do.

"Jordan, I can't."

"Yeah, you can. Kiss me, Holly."

She stared into his eyes, then allowed herself to get lost in the dark depths. She leaned forward and touched her lips to his.

The hand he was still holding got caught between them, and her wrist bent back. Sharp pain shot up her arm, and she pulled back. It wasn't going to work.

"I'm just not good at this," she muttered, and turned away.

"Sure, you are." He raised the bed a little, then patted his belly. "Straddle me like you did when you were giving me a back rub." He grinned. "I'm pretty sure I can stand it."

She eyed him doubtfully. She might not have ever seen a man naked before, but she knew where all the parts went. If she straddled him, then his…his…she-knew-what would be pressed awfully close to her private parts, and she wasn't sure that was right or even legal. Although the statement about him being able to stand it was confusing. Would it hurt him?

"Never mind," Jordan said suddenly. "Bad idea. Why don't you let me get some rest?"

Now Holly was really confused. What was going on? One minute he wanted to kiss her, the next he was dismissing her?

Then she looked at him closely and recognized the tension around his mouth. He was embarrassed. She wasn't sure by what, if it was his weakened condition or the fact that he thought she wasn't interested. It didn't matter. Holly's already soft heart melted. She grabbed his hand in both of hers.

"Don't be mad," she said quietly. "I don't mean to be shy, but this is all new to me."

He gazed at her for a minute, then relaxed perceptibly. "Yeah?"

"I swear. Tell me what to do."

His eyes narrowed. "Is this some sort of new-tech nursing technique?"

"I'm sure kissing is considered a breach of professional ethics." Her voice was prim. "I've never heard of it being prescribed for medicinal purposes."

"A guy can always hope."

He smiled and she relaxed. "Tell me what to do."

"Straddle my stomach."

Feeling as coordinated and elegant as a newborn giraffe, she did as he requested. Thank goodness her sweater was loose so he couldn't get a good look at her body. That would be too embarrassing to stand.

"Lean forward," he instructed. "Rest your forearms on the bed."

"But then my—" She glanced down at her breasts. "Then I'll be touching you with my chest."

His smile broadened. "That's the point."

"Oh. Are you sure?"

"Trust me."

She did as he requested. Their faces were inches apart. She could feel his sweet breath fanning her face. Her breasts nestled against his lean strength as if they'd spent their whole lives looking for this one spot to rest.

Holly wasn't quite as comfortable. She didn't know what

to do with her hands. She felt as if her butt was sticking up in the air. To make matters worse, every inch of her was tingling and trembling, and she couldn't catch her breath.

"This would have been a whole lot easier when I was sixteen," she murmured.

"Not for me. Back then I was more interested in results than the process itself."

She didn't know what that meant, but before she could ask, he raised his head slightly and kissed her.

It was better than she remembered. His lips were firm and warm as they caressed hers. He brushed against her sensitive skin, awakening the nerve endings and reminding them why they'd been put there.

He opened his mouth. She didn't need urging to follow suit. The anticipation of those few seconds waiting for his tongue to touch hers nearly made her swoon. Suddenly she knew what to do with her hands. She cupped his face and urged him closer. She buried her fingers in his thick dark hair and tried to communicate her need.

He got the message. He invaded her mouth, touching, stroking, tasting, leaving wickedly wonderful sensations in his path. He stole her breath, made her relax against him, made her want more. She squirmed in delight when he drew her lower lip into his mouth and suckled it. The gentle tugging started a chain reaction that coiled all the way to that waiting place between her thighs. Tremors rippled through her.

This wasn't a kiss; it was a life-changing event. She felt herself being pulled under, drowning, and she didn't care. She followed his retreat, invading his mouth, assaulting him as he'd assaulted her. She felt answering shudders in his muscles.

His hands stroked down her back. One played with her

hair, while the other discovered the sweet spot where her derriere curved into her legs. He touched that place over and over again. It tickled yet sent hot rivers of feeling through her legs and up her chest.

She wanted to kiss him forever. She liked the hard breadth of his body below hers. She'd been denied physical passion so long, she wasn't sure she would ever get enough.

He reached for the hem of her sweater and tugged it up. Holly broke their kiss. "What are you doing?"

"Nothing."

When the sweater was bunched around her waist, he slipped his fingers under it and began to touch her bare skin.

"You're doing something. I can feel it."

Lines deepened by the corners of his eyes as he smiled faintly. "I don't know what you're talking about."

She wasn't sure she did, either. He traced her spine up to her neck. His soft touch sucked away her strength. She couldn't even protest, not that she wanted to.

He touched her shoulders, then down her sides and over her ribs. Without planning the action, she raised herself slightly. She didn't even know what she'd done until his hands slipped under her, circling around and coming to rest on her breasts.

Large hands cupped her full curves. He didn't move, but just supported their weight against his palms. She closed her eyes and concentrated on the sensations. No man had ever touched her there. Everything was new. The whisper of embarrassment, the tingling, the way her nipples puckered and ached for more of his caress.

Then he began to stroke her. His thumbs swept across the taut peaks. She felt the jolt clear down to her toes. Her arms trembled violently, then strength faded and she collapsed against him.

' He didn't give her time to have regrets. He claimed her mouth, sweeping inside, taunting her, tempting her, teasing her until all she could do was cling to him.

She didn't recognize herself anymore. She was painfully alive and aware of her body. She'd never thought about physical pleasure before, and now she couldn't think about anything else.

His hands stroked her back. She was vaguely aware of a slight tugging on her bra, but she ignored it. Jordan could do whatever he wanted. She was never going to protest again.

"Sit up," he said, then kissed her cheek and her jaw.

She did as he asked. She swayed for a moment, finding balance, then glanced down at him. His bare chest was in reach. Not sure where she gathered the courage, she placed her hand on top of his breastbone. His eyes closed slowly, and he breathed her name.

"Touch me," he said.

She wasn't sure where or how, but figured she couldn't really hurt him. She brushed her hands against the sprinkling of hair between his flat nipples. She traced the shape of his ribs and the width of his shoulders. She wondered what he would taste like, but couldn't bring herself to test his skin to find out.

After several minutes he stilled her hands. "Take off your sweater."

"Why?" she asked, her voice squeaking on the single syllable.

When he didn't answer, she swallowed hard. Okay, take off her sweater. No big deal. Hadn't she just promised herself she was going to do whatever he asked? Besides, if she took it off he might touch her breasts again, and wouldn't that be lovely?

She did as he requested and in the process realized he'd

unfastened her bra. She didn't want to think about how awkward it must look as she tried to pull one piece of clothing off while attempting to keep another firmly plastered against her chest.

Finally she was able to pull her sweater over her head with one hand while the other held the bra against her breasts. She tossed the sweater on the floor.

"That, too," he said, tugging on the hook end of the undergarment.

"I can't," she said miserably.

"Why?"

She looked away. "They're too big. It's ugly. I always wanted those little perky breasts like you see in the magazine ads."

"Everything about you is beautiful."

She glared at him. "Oh yeah, right. Including the extra fifteen pounds. I'm stunning. Modeling agencies are pounding at the door to get me to work for them."

He studied her for a moment, then nodded as if he'd come to some conclusion. "Scoot up."

That she could do. She scooted a little closer.

"Close your eyes."

That request made her suspicious, but she did as he asked. Still, she didn't release her death grip on her bra. Fortunately he didn't try to take it away from her.

Instead, he placed his hands on her thighs. He stroked her from knee to hip bone. With each back-and-forth, his hands slipped closer and closer to the insides of her legs until at last his thumbs brushed over private places. She jumped.

"Keep your eyes closed," he said.

She found it difficult to breathe, but it was easy to not look. He kept his thumbs there, touching, pressing more than moving. He seemed to be looking for something. She was about to tell him there wasn't anything there when he found it.

He rubbed a tiny spot. A shudder raced through her, and goose bumps broke out on her skin. What was that? Would he do it again? He would and he did. Several times he touched that magical place, caressing her until she was weak. Then he moved away and stroked her bare arms and shoulders.

Her breasts ached. There was no other word to describe the heavy sensation that filled them. Her nipples were tight. She needed relief, but didn't know what to do. She suspected Jordan had the answer. But that would mean letting him look at her. The battle was lost the moment he traced a single finger over the outside curve of her left breast. The soft touch was so sweet, she wanted to weep. Instead, she relaxed and let him pull the bra away.

Within fifteen seconds she wondered what she'd been fussing about. After a minute she decided she'd been a stupid fool.

He touched her breasts as if they were precious and objects of worship. Long fingers caressed every curve, every inch of sensitized skin. His thumbs teased her nipples, circling the tight peaks until she could think of nothing else but having him touch her like that for always.

"If I give you a million dollars, will you promise never to stop?" she asked.

"I'll promise without the million dollars," he whispered. "Why would I want to stop?"

She opened her eyes and glanced down. His tanned fingers contrasted with her pale skin. Somehow, with him touching her, she could believe she wasn't ugly there. When his thumbs and forefingers gently pinched her nipples and she saw, as well as felt, the delicious tug, her hips arched involuntarily.

Her breathing increased, and she didn't know why. Her skin was hot; her panties felt damp. Everything confused her, but it was wonderful.

When he urged her to stretch out next to him, she didn't protest. She lowered the bed so it was flat as he used a couple of pillows to support his back. He turned on his side so he faced her. Then he did the most amazing thing. He bent his head and took one of her nipples into his mouth.

The moist heat overwhelmed her. She whispered his name, then buried her hand in his hair to hold him in place. Unbelievable heat and longing filled her.

He suckled her breast, then moved to the other side and repeated the wondrous event. She barely noticed his hands slipping under her leggings and brushing against her bare skin. It was only when one of his fingers touched that magic spot between her legs that she realized what he was doing.

But then it was too late. He'd begun to move back and forth, then around. Speech was impossible. She half expected her heart to stop beating.

"Relax," Jordan whispered, then stuck his tongue in her ear. "I'm not going to hurt you. I'm going to make you feel good."

He was. Absolutely. She tried to tell him, but she couldn't.

He nibbled on her lobe. "Do you feel the pressure building?"

She nodded. It was incredible. Every fiber, every cell, focused on his fingers and what he was doing there.

"Have you ever felt anything like this before?"

"No," she gasped.

"Good. Just go with it." A spasm jerked her body. He chuckled. "It's not going to take very long."

She wasn't sure if that was good or bad, but decided it didn't matter. He bent over her and kissed her. Their tongues danced. He drew her into his mouth and sucked. The quick spasm matched the rhythm between her legs. She thought she would die of the pleasure.

Then his hand shifted slightly. She became aware of an insistent, pleasurable pressure. She focused on it. Something she didn't understand swam just out of reach. Jordan broke the kiss, then bent over her breast. He stroked his tongue against her nipple. That was all she needed.

For a moment the world stopped, suspended on a point of pleasure so intense, she finally understood why lovers were willing to risk everything for this moment. Then time resumed, and the release crashed through her body. She gave herself up to it, riding it, feeling it, becoming one with the man at her side, knowing nothing would ever be the same again.

Jordan watched Holly's face, the flush that climbed from her chest to her cheeks, the way her lips parted as if she needed to draw in more air. At last her eyes fluttered open.

"Wow," she said reverently.

"Pretty amazing, huh?"

Her hand fluttered for a moment. "I need a new set of words to describe that."

He kissed her forehead. "I'm glad."

He was. Except for the intense, throbbing pressure in his groin, he felt great. He couldn't give Holly everything she deserved, but he had opened a door for her. He was pleased that she'd found pleasure in his arms.

He kissed her gently. "What about my dinner?"

She stirred. "Hmm, I'm hungry, too. Steak and baked potato. Give me fifteen minutes."

She sat up slowly, then stretched. Her long hair tumbled down her back. As she raised her arms, he saw her left breast and the rosy-tipped nipple. His erection flexed against the fly of his jeans, but he ignored the signal. He'd promised not to make love with her, and he intended to keep his word. Holly was innocent enough not to realize he was aroused and suffering. Better for both of them if she didn't offer to take care of him.

She stood up and reached for her bra. He had a brief view of her bare chest before she turned quickly and dressed. Surprising him, and probably herself, she bent over and gave him a quick, hot kiss before she left to start dinner.

Jordan stared after her. Holly Garrett was deadly. He could feel the danger all the way down to his soul. There was something about her that appealed to him. Was it her innocence or her sweet spirit? He wasn't sure. All he knew was she made him want things he could never have. He treated her differently than he'd ever treated another woman. In the past he'd always held back. With her, he wanted to give.

But he couldn't get involved. He knew the price love required. His parents, Travis and his first wife, Craig and Krystal. Everyone he knew and cared about had paid a high, ugly price for the privilege of love. He was going to play it safe. That's why he'd always held himself at arm's length from relationships.

So how had Holly slipped inside his barriers? Was it because they'd never officially dated? She'd just been around, and he'd grown to like her.

He drew in a breath. For the first time in his life he wanted more. He wanted to be with her, make love with her, hold her, confess his darkest secrets. For the first time he was tempted. He wanted to believe it was possible, that this time was different. But he'd learned his lesson too well for that. This time was exactly the same. If he risked getting involved, both he and Holly were going to get burned.

Chapter Ten

It was early afternoon on Sunday when Louise and Holly pulled the last cookie sheet from the oven. They'd finished decorating the sugar cookies while the batch of chocolate-chip cookies had been baking. The delicious smells filled the house. Vanilla and chocolate, sweet icing, cinnamon, all surrounded by the homey scent of fresh-brewed coffee for the expected guests.

Louise expertly transferred cooled cookies to a large plate then handed it to Holly. "Take these into the living room," she said.

"But there are three plates in there already."

Louise winked. "I know how these girls eat. The cookies will disappear. Trust me."

Holly did as she requested. Once in the living room, she rearranged the plates of treats, then glanced around at the open area. Jordan's contribution to furniture had been a single sofa and a rather ratty-looking recliner. The dimensions of the room were substantial. In honor of the events of the day, Holly had loaned a few antique sofas, some tables and floor lamps. Nothing matched, but at least everyone would have a place to sit.

She stared at the plain white walls and thought about how beautiful the house could be. They'd finished the dining room yesterday. Kyle and Travis had come over to help move in the furniture Jordan had ordered. With some time and effort the rest of the house would be just as lovely. She wanted to be a part of the project.

As she ran her fingers along the stiff back of a Victorian-influenced blue settee, she imagined the house filled with laughter. She'd been happy here. Others could be, too. She wondered what it would be like to live here permanently, to know she was going to raise a family here. She'd thought about having children, of course, had wanted to, but didn't think it was likely. She wasn't sure she was prepared to be a single parent. The thought of raising a child on her own terrified her, and she admired those who were able to keep it all together without someone else to depend upon.

She'd thought of family, but she'd shied away from marriage. She knew she would never trust anyone enough to be able to commit to forever.

She heard voices in the kitchen. Louise's higher pitch followed by Jordan's low rumble. Her heart began to beat faster. Funny, after all they'd been through, working on the house every day, talking about nearly every aspect of their lives, he still had the power to make her knees weak.

A restlessness swept over her, propelling her to walk faster through the room. Energy she didn't understand filled her, spilling out, making her want something, if only she could figure out what that something was.

Jordan?

The thought came unbidden, but once it arrived, she couldn't let it go.

Heat coiled low in her belly as she remembered how he'd touched her and what wonderful pleasure he'd brought her. There hadn't been a repeat of that incredible time together, but the aftereffects lingered.

He touched her more now. He stole kisses in the hallway. She'd even kissed him once, although the thought of it still brought a flush to her cheeks. If asked, she wouldn't be able to define their relationship. They weren't dating or lovers. They seemed to be more than friends, although she wasn't sure. Most frightening of all, she was starting to sense she might be able to trust Jordan. If she did, if she allowed herself to fall for him, that would ruin everything. No matter how nice he was to her, in her heart she knew she wasn't his type. When he was healed and able to get on with his life, he would go back to the kind of women he was used to.

The sound of cars in the driveway broke through her musings. She walked to the front window and stared out. A gleaming Mercedes pulled up first, followed by a mini-van and two sport-utility vehicles. One had a small open trailer hitched to the back bumper.

Adults and children spilled out onto the driveway. Holly stared in amazement. She'd met most of the adults of the family, but not many of the children. It was one thing to know intellectually that Craig had three boys and Sandy and Kyle had four children, counting the baby. It was quite another to see all of them running around.

She watched as the adults called to each other and laughed. The women hugged, and the men shook hands. It was as if they hadn't seen each other in months instead of just a few days. Holly fought a tightness in her throat. She envied Jordan his beautiful Victorian house, but even more than that, she envied him his close, loving family. While she appreciated that they drew her in and made her feel welcome, she wished she was there because she belonged instead of on a temporary basis by virtue of living in Jordan's house.

She wondered if Louise fought these feelings. She and the housekeeper had talked about their solitary lives. The Haynes family offered a refuge.

"Are they here?" Jordan asked as he walked into the room. He moved easily with a natural elegance that only added to the temptation he already provided. Late last week he'd started physical therapy, and the exercises and treatments seemed to be easing his pain.

"They just pulled up." She looked at him, then at the jacket he was holding. "Are you going to be all right?"

"I swear I won't cut down a single tree." He made an X over his heart. "My brothers will take care of that." He moved next to her and tugged on her long braid. "Don't worry, I'll be fine. I'll see you later this afternoon."

He started for the front door. Out of nowhere Mistletoe materialized and sauntered in front of him. He had to sidestep suddenly to avoid tripping on her. Jordan swore under his breath. Mistletoe gave him a long, unblinking stare, then turned away and began washing her face.

"Mistletoe, that's rude," Holly said. The cat ignored her.

Jordan opened the front door and moved out onto the porch. Holly followed. She watched as he walked down the steps and greeted his family. His sisters-in-law fussed over him, while his brothers teased him about being a slacker. Holly smiled and knew even though it was temporary, she was going to enjoy every minute she had with this family.

Elizabeth, Rebecca, Jill and Sandy started up the stairs toward the house. As they did, Louise came out onto the porch and shrugged into her coat.

"Everything is set up," the housekeeper said. "The coffee is in a carafe, and I've started a second pot. You know where everything else is."

Holly stared at her disbelievingly. "You're not leaving."

"Sure. I always go with the guys. Someone has to be around to keep track of the little ones. Take the girls to the bathroom, that sort of thing."

Holly glanced from Louise to the four women she didn't really know. "But I can't be the hostess." It wasn't right. Besides, she was terrified.

"You'll be fine." Louise gave her a wink. "If there's a lull in conversation, ask them how they met their husbands. That will keep them talking for hours."

With that, she walked down the stairs and approached the minivan. Holly looked at the four women now standing in front of her. "Hi," she said awkwardly, and stepped back to let them in.

Elizabeth led the way. She paused and gave Holly a hug. "Thanks for having us."

"My pleasure," Holly muttered, not wanting to say it hadn't been her idea to entertain these women alone. She'd thought Louise was going to be here. Whatever were they going to say to each other?

They all walked into the living room and found seats. Holly busied herself taking coats and bringing in the coffee. How long would the men and children be gone? Two hours? Three? It was only one in the afternoon. What if they were gone until dark? How would she survive? She couldn't think of a single thing to talk about.

When there was nothing else to keep her in the kitchen, she reluctantly made her way toward the living room. The four women there were chatting easily, as if they'd known each other for years. They had, Holly reminded herself.

She hovered by the entrance to the living room until

Elizabeth saw her and patted the sofa where she was sitting. "Come sit with me," she said.

Holly crossed the room and perched on the edge of the seat. She forced her lips into a smile, hoping it looked more natural than it felt.

Jill, her pregnant belly rounding the front of her flannel maternity top, reclined on a chaise by the fireplace. Rebecca and Sandy shared a sofa across from the one Elizabeth and Holly sat in. Holly felt everyone staring at her.

"I've got it," Rebecca said as she snapped her fingers. "I know what's different. You're blond."

Holly touched her head self-consciously. "I know."

"None of us are. The Haynes brothers generally prefer brunettes."

"Excuse me?" Jill said, pointing to her own red hair. "That's not completely true."

Elizabeth laughed. "Craig always has been his own man." She nodded slowly. "You're right, Rebecca. Holly is our first blonde."

Holly held up her hands. "We're just friends. Jordan and I don't date."

Knowing looks were exchanged. Holly felt herself flush.

"Sandy, throw me a pillow, please," Jill said. She grabbed the pillow as it flew toward her, then tucked it under her back. "Everything hurts. Little people like me aren't supposed to puff up this much. It's fine for you tall types."

Rebecca tossed her long, dark, curly hair over her shoulder. "Jill is our poor little troll."

"I'm not a troll, I'm short. Something people like you can't appreciate. Do you know what it's like to never be able to reach the top shelf at the grocery store? I have to stand there waiting until a tall person walks down the aisle. It's humiliating."

Sandy leaned back against the sofa and sighed. "I can't believe you've already got Craig's three boys and you're going to have another child."

Rebecca, Elizabeth and Jill stared at her, then laughed.

"You had three kids, then had a fourth with Kyle," Elizabeth said.

Sandy nodded slowly. "I know. I can't believe Jill was as foolish as I was. Four children. Do you know how much laundry that is?"

"I refuse to think about it. Anyway, Louise will come to help." Jill touched her belly. "I know it's going to be a lot of work, but it will be worth it."

Rebecca leaned forward and grabbed a plate of cookies. She took two, then passed it on to Sandy. "You don't regret the baby for a minute," she said.

"You're right," Sandy said. "Although four is a handful. That's why this afternoon is so wonderful. In fact—" she glanced at Holly "—you might never get rid of me."

"At first I thought the men taking their children to get Christmas trees and not taking the wives was a bad idea," Jill said. "I thought I might feel left out."

"Don't," Elizabeth told her. "It's cold out. The children constantly have to go to the bathroom, although not at the same time. They argue, they whine, they can't agree on the tree they want. Oh, and the men will come home with huge monstrosities that won't even begin to fit in the house." She took the plate from Sandy and picked out a couple of cookies, then handed it to Holly. "It's much better to stay in here and be warm. We have witty conversation, no husbands, no children. Gee, Holly, Sandy's right. None of us will want to leave."

"You're welcome to stay as long as you like."

Elizabeth winked. "Oh, sure. We believe that."

Sandy started to prop her feet up on the coffee table,

then froze and looked at Holly. "Is this a valuable antique?"

"No, it's Jordan's."

"Whew! Okay then, let's trash the place."

Everyone laughed. Holly joined in and felt some of her tension ease away. These women were nice to her, and she appreciated that. She enjoyed their company. By the end of the day she would probably be able to figure out who was married to whom. Except for Rebecca, who wore a dark wool jumper over a cream turtleneck, they were dressed in jeans and sweatshirts. No one had on a lot of makeup or expensive jewelry. They were friends, and they obviously welcomed Holly into their circle. She wished she could tell them how much that meant.

Elizabeth looked at Jill. "How are you feeling?"

"Tired, even though I've been sleeping well."

"It gets worse."

Jill grimaced. "I sort of figured that. When are you going to have another one?"

Elizabeth poured herself a cup of coffee. "We've been talking about it. Little Jessica is nearly two. If we're going to do it, now's the time. I want another baby. Of course, that would mean three girls." She shook her head. "You know what they say."

Holly stared at her. "About having girls?"

Elizabeth nodded. "With boys you just have to worry about one—" she pointed to her lap "—you know. But with girls you have to worry about all of them."

Laughter exploded in the room. When they had quieted, Jill said, "I think you should have another baby."

"We're thinking about it, too," Rebecca said. "Of course, not being married to an official Haynes brother, I have the option of either a boy or a girl."

Jill glanced at Holly. "How long have you known Jordan?"

Holly cleared her throat. She reached for her coffee, then changed her mind. Better to not have something to spill. "A few weeks. After my apartment was destroyed in that last big storm, he offered to let me live here for a while. I'm helping him restore the house in return for room and board."

Jill stared at her. "You're *living* with him?"

Holly felt color flare on her cheeks. "No," she said quickly, then realized she was.

"They're not living together," Rebecca said.

"What would you call it?" Jill asked.

"Louise is here," Elizabeth said. "I'm sure everything is very circumspect."

For the second time in ten minutes, laughter broke out in the room. "A Haynes brother behaving himself," Sandy said. "Oh, that's new." Her smile faded. "I suppose out of all of them, Jordan is the most likely to be a gentleman."

"The first time I met Travis, he picked me up and carried me," Elizabeth said. "It was very romantic."

"Fine for you," Sandy grumbled. "The first time I met Kyle after I moved back here, he came riding up on his motorcycle, all tanned and muscled. I couldn't even speak. There I was, a grown woman with three children, and I couldn't form entire sentences. I didn't know whether to throw myself at him or run away screaming."

"I was naked," Jill said brightly. Everyone turned to stare at her. "Okay, maybe not naked, but I was just wearing a skimpy little robe. I thought it covered me just fine. Craig later told me it didn't. He spent our whole first conversation in a very uncomfortable state."

Elizabeth raised her eyebrows. "I believe Rebecca has the best story of all."

"It's silly," Rebecca said, and nibbled on a cookie.

Jill brushed her short red hair off her forehead. "I don't think I ever heard this story. What happened?"

Rebecca waved her hand. "Nothing."

"Not nothing." Elizabeth picked up her coffee and gestured with the cup. "Rebecca had a crush on Austin. It was very tragic. She couldn't even be in the same room with him without knocking something over or spilling. So one day she went to see him."

Rebecca drew in a deep breath. "If the story has to be told, I'll tell it. Although I don't know what purpose it serves."

"Entertainment," Elizabeth said.

"I went to see him at his house. It was raining, and my car got stuck. When the storm got worse, he lost his phone, so we couldn't call for a tow truck." She folded her hands primly in her lap. "There. Are you happy?"

Elizabeth grinned. Her brown eyes danced with amusement. "That's not the whole story. Tell us the good part."

"I had to spend the night."

"And?"

Rebecca rolled her eyes. "We made mad, passionate love. All right? Can we drop this now?"

Holly was surprised. "The first night you went over to his house?"

"It was an accident."

Jill sat up. "Honey, there are no accidents."

Rebecca smiled. "You're right. I seduced him. Although he denies it. He says he was the one doing the seducing."

"They all do," Sandy said. "It's better to let them think that. At least they've all grown up. You should have been here in high school. They were dangerous heartbreakers then. No female was safe."

"Did your heart get broken?" Holly asked.

"Not really. Jordan and I went out for a while, but we didn't have chemistry, so we ended up being friends. Good thing for all of us. It would have been so awkward to face him as my brother-in-law if we'd gone at it hot and heavy in the back of his car."

At first Holly didn't recognize the tight feeling inside her belly. Then she realized it was annoyance. She didn't want any of these women to have a past with Jordan. It was illogical and unfair, but it was how she felt.

Then Sandy's smile faded. "All teasing aside, I think we're very lucky women. The Haynes brothers, including Austin, are about the best men I've ever met."

"You're right," Elizabeth said. "I never thought I'd be willing to risk caring about anyone again. Travis taught me differently."

"I agree," Jill said, then sniffed. "But can we please not talk about this. I'm pregnant, and it doesn't take very much to make me cry."

Sandy leaned over the sofa and took her hand. "Don't cry. We'll tell funny stories instead."

Holly reached for the carafe of coffee. It was empty. "I'll go get some more," she said, and stood up.

"I'll help," Rebecca said, and followed her.

When they were in the kitchen, Rebecca shut the door. "I don't mean to intrude. I just wanted to make sure that you're all right. This is new to you, and sometimes the teasing can be a little overwhelming. For what it's worth, if we didn't like you, we wouldn't be telling these wild stories."

Holly felt her eyes tear, and she didn't have the excuse of being pregnant. "Thank you for that. All this is very different for me, but I like having everyone here. You're all so nice and you barely know me."

Rebecca touched her arm lightly. "We heard good things

about you. Jordan has talked to his brothers and to Austin. Word gets out. Jordan mentioned your mom died a couple of years ago and you're all alone. We're happy to share our holidays with you.''

"Thanks."

Rebecca leaned against the counter. "Austin and Jordan are a lot alike. They're both loners."

"I don't understand. Everyone says that to me, but Jordan's not a loner. He's friendly and open. He's got a great sense of humor. Sometimes I feel as if you're talking about someone else."

Rebecca's delicate eyebrows rose slightly. "Interesting. You're seeing a side of him he keeps hidden from most people. I wonder what that means."

"Nothing," Holly said quickly.

"You know what they say about people who protest too much."

"We're just friends." She ignored the image of the evening she'd spent in his bed. Nothing had happened, she reminded herself. They had both been fully dressed. Well, she didn't have her shirt and bra on, but aside from that...

He'd touched her, though. Touched her in the most intimate way a man can touch a woman. And he'd made her feel wonderful things. He'd shown her the possibilities.

"Why isn't Jordan married?" Holly asked.

Rebecca reached for the pot of brewed coffee and began to pour it into the carafe. "Probably because he doesn't date."

"How could he not? He's so good-looking and fun. There must be women crawling all over him."

"Maybe, but he manages to ignore most of them." Rebecca looked at her. "You're the first woman I've seen him with since I moved to Glenwood, and that's been nearly four years."

Holly couldn't take in that thought. It didn't make sense.

"Jordan holds a lot of himself inside. He doesn't open up easily or share what he's thinking."

"I agree with that," Holly said. Jordan rarely talked about personal things. She didn't have a clue as to what he was thinking about her, or their situation.

"The Haynes brothers don't make it easy," Rebecca continued, "but they're worth the trouble. Just one warning. Once you fall in love, there's no getting over it."

Holly took a step back. "You don't have to worry about me. I'm not going to fall in love with Jordan. I know I'm not his type."

Rebecca picked up the full carafe. "Of course you're his type. But that's not what's at issue. As for not falling in love, we don't always get a choice. I'll go ahead and take this back to the living room."

Holly stayed in the kitchen for a few more minutes. Love? The concept startled her. She'd never thought of her feelings in that context. She didn't love Jordan. She barely knew the man. But the word had a nice ring to it. Love. She would like to love someone and have him love her back. But that required trust, and she'd been let down too many times.

She shook her head. Everything was too confusing. This time last month she'd been living a solitary, albeit happy, life. It had been just her and Mistletoe. Her business had been growing steadily, and she was content. Now her life was upside down. Still, she wouldn't trade it away for anything. Looking at the world from a new point of view showed her things she'd never seen before.

She glanced at the clock and saw it was nearly two-thirty. Then she hurried back to the living room. She hoped the men and children didn't return too quickly. She wanted to spend some time with her new friends.

* * *

The crowd returned a little after seven. They'd called at five to say they were stopping for dinner. The "hunt" had been successful, but everyone was hungry. The women had ordered pizza and continued the fun until the cars had pulled up in front of the house.

They grabbed coats and walked onto the porch. Holly saw the small trailer was now filled with several cut trees. Children circled the cars, calling out for their fathers to make sure they put each tree on the correct car.

Jordan headed for the stairs. Holly could see he was limping.

"Are you all right?" she asked as she hurried to the edge of the porch.

He looked up. The light by the door illuminated his face. There were shadows under his eyes and lines of strain around his mouth. "I'm tired," he said.

"You're hurting." She tucked her arm under his and helped him inside. He collapsed on one of the sofas.

When she would have settled next to him, he waved her away. "Go be social," he said. "I'll be fine here. Oh, and make sure Kyle brings in the tree."

Holly hesitated, not wanting to leave him alone but knowing she should see everyone off. Reluctantly she returned to the porch. Elizabeth pulled her to one side.

"I have a favor to ask," the woman said. "May I bring over several presents? They're for the children. I'm afraid they're going to find them. I know it will be okay with Jordan, but I don't want him to be responsible for them. Men don't remember things like bringing presents back in time for Christmas morning."

"Sure," Holly said. "There are plenty of closets here. Do you want me to wrap them?"

"They're already wrapped. But thanks for the offer." Elizabeth squeezed her hand. "I know there isn't a romance between you and Jordan. Speaking for all the Haynes wives, I wanted to tell you, we would love it if you two got together. You're good for him, and I think he's good for you, too." Elizabeth's brown eyes danced. "If he's anything like his brother, I promise you won't be disappointed when the lights go out."

Holly already suspected that. "You've all been so nice to me. I don't know how to thank you."

"You don't have to."

Impulsively Holly gave her a hug.

"Hey, if there's hugging going on, I want to be included," Kyle said as he carried one end of a huge fir tree up toward the open front door.

"Talk to your wife," Elizabeth said.

Travis came up the stairs, holding the thick end of the tree. "Wife," he said.

Elizabeth laughed.

Holly led the way inside. Austin followed behind with a tree stand. In about ten minutes the tree was up in the living room's bay window. Five minutes after that the appropriate trees had been tied onto car roofs and everyone had left.

Holly checked on Jordan. He pulled himself to his feet and grimaced. "I'm tired," he said. "Would you mind if we decorated the tree tomorrow?"

"Not at all. I'm worried about you."

He gave her a half smile. "I'll be fine. I just need to rest."

The front door opened, and Louise stepped inside. "What a day," she said. "Those little ones about ran me into the ground."

Jordan's jaw tightened. Had something happened to upset him?

"I have a few ornaments I brought from the store,"

Holly said. "I want to bring them down before I forget."
She waved at Louise and headed for the stairs.

"The tree looks nice in here," Louise said.

Jordan grunted.

Holly started up the stairs. Some premonition made her
slow her step. Something was going to happen. She could
feel it.

"Do you want me to hang the lights tonight?" Louise
asked, her voice slightly muffled as she walked into the
living room.

"No," Jordan roared. "Haven't you done enough today?
Just stay the hell out of my life."

Chapter Eleven

As soon as he said the words, Jordan wanted to call them back. It would be a big mistake to get into this now. They were both tired, and nothing would be accomplished.

But watching Louise with his nieces and nephews had been more than he could stand. She'd held the little ones, played with the older ones. All the kids adored her. He hated knowing she'd wormed her way into his family under false pretenses.

Louise tossed her coat over a chair by the entrance to the living room, then she walked toward him. Her cheeks were flushed, her blue eyes bright with anger. In her purple slacks and fuchsia shirt, she didn't look like anyone's idea of a dangerous person, but he knew the truth...and her secrets.

She came to a stop about three feet in front of him. After planting her hands on her hips, she glared at him. "I've had it with you, Jordan. I've been here nearly a month. I'm tired of the rude comments, the innuendos and hostile looks. Your attitude stinks. If you've got something to say, then be man enough to say it.''

He stared at her for a long time. ''You don't want to hear this,'' he said at last, his voice low.

''Try me. Or are you only good at being a bully?''

The taunt did what it was supposed to. The heat of his anger increased. He made one last effort to maintain self-control, then let it go. ''I don't like you, Louise. I haven't for a long time.''

''Why?'' she asked, her confusion obviously genuine. ''What did I ever do to you?''

''You destroyed my family.''

She stared at him as if he were crazy. ''I don't know what you're talking about.''

He focused his attention on her face. He wanted to see her admit the truth. ''I know about your affair with my father.''

His expectations were fulfilled. Louise paled to the color of chalk, then sank onto the sofa behind her.

''Oh, Lord,'' she murmured. ''After all these years.'' She raised her head and looked at him. ''How did you find out?''

''That's not important. The point is I know what you did.''

She tried to smile, but her lips were trembling too much. ''What I did? You make it sound like I planned the affair. I didn't. I was just seventeen. Still in high school.'' She turned away. ''A virgin.''

He saw the flush of color on her cheeks. Jordan steeled himself against any hint of softer emotion. After what she'd done, she deserved to suffer.

She drew in a deep breath. ''He came to the high school and talked about drunk driving. I was sitting in the front row. Your father was older, of course, but a handsome, charming man. He smiled at me and—''

''Spare me the details.''

Her spine straightened. ''All right. Have it your way. I was seventeen, and Earl Haynes seduced me. There, I confess my crime. Are you happy? What I did was wrong, I admit that. I knew he was married.'' She was silent for several seconds. ''I'm not proud of what I did. My only defense is that I was naive.''

''He had a wife and four sons. Did you ever think about what your so-called innocent affair would mean to us?''

She flinched.

Jordan fought to keep his anger flowing. He didn't want to feel anything for the woman in front of him. Not compassion or empathy.

''He said no one would ever know.''

''There's an excuse.''

''I'm not excusing, I'm explaining. I was so young.''

He folded his arms over his chest. ''That's it, then? You were young? Don't you want to declare undying love for my father?''

Her blue eyes darkened with regret. ''I didn't love him, Jordan. I don't know if that makes it worse or better, but it's the truth. You can say whatever you want, but none of it will be more ugly than what I've already said to myself.'' She drew in a deep breath. ''It was twenty-nine years ago. Maybe it's time to let it go.''

''You'd like that, wouldn't you?'' he said. ''But there's so much more to the story.''

For the first time she looked frightened. ''What do you mean?''

''I told you I knew everything. I know that you left town nearly thirty years ago. I know you were pregnant and that you had a child.''

Louise's eyes fluttered closed. He suspected if she hadn't been sitting, she would have swooned. As it was, she swayed on the sofa.

"No," she murmured. "No. Not now. Not after all this time." She covered her face with her hands.

"What happened to the child?"

"Adoption."

He'd expected as much. Even so, the single word shocked him. There was another Haynes in the world. A half sibling he didn't know.

He glanced at Louise. Her shoulders shook, and she rocked back and forth, but she was silent in her pain. Jordan found he had to turn away.

He'd expected to enjoy this conversation. He'd rehearsed it a thousand times in his mind. Louise had always been broken and crying, begging forgiveness. But he didn't feel any satisfaction. Lives had been destroyed, and it was too late to bring back the past.

"I've been punished enough," she said. "You have no right to discuss this with me. What happened between your father and me was a mistake, but no one ever knew. I'm not responsible for the destruction of your family. Earl Haynes did that all on his own."

He turned back toward her. There were tears on her cheeks, and for the first time she looked every day of her forty-six years. "That's where you're wrong. Seventeen years ago you came back to Glenwood, and my father got in touch with you."

Her mouth opened. "No," she breathed.

"Yes."

"No. I mean, Earl contacted me, but I wouldn't have anything to do with him. I was older. I'd learned from my mistakes. Jordan, I swear, I refused to even talk to him. I wasn't interested in having a relationship. He was married, and even if he hadn't been, I would never have trusted him.''

"Too bad you didn't make that clear."

"What?"

"You should have told him you wouldn't be interested even if he were single.''

"I did."

"He didn't believe you."

She frowned. "What are you talking about?"

This time Jordan didn't have to search for the anger and pain. It swelled up inside him, fueled by ugly wounds left over from a childhood fraught with hurt.

"My father was convinced you would want him if he wasn't married. Because of you, he asked my mother for a divorce.''

"That's crazy."

Jordan curled his hands into fists. "After twenty-five years of screwing everything in a skirt in a fifty-mile radius, after twenty-five years of being a complete bastard to my mother and beating the crap out of his kids, my father wanted a divorce. So he would be with *you*.''

Louise stared at him wide-eyed. "I don't believe you."

"You damn well better. I was there. I heard everything."

She shook her head. He didn't know if she still didn't believe him or if she didn't want him to continue. He didn't care which; he was determined to finish his story.

"After he asked for the divorce, he left. My mother stood in the kitchen, her home for the last twenty-five years, and she started to laugh." He shuddered. "I still remember the sound," he added softly.

It had been horrible. He'd been sixteen, just old enough to believe he couldn't cry anymore or ask for comfort.

"Jordan, I—"

He cut her off. "She left. She packed her bags that afternoon and left. I begged her not to go, but she wouldn't listen. She said we were all old enough to take care of ourselves, then she was gone.'' He glared at the woman sitting on the sofa. "She never contacted us again. Not a phone call or even a letter.''

"I'm sorry," Louise said as a tear rolled down her cheek. "I'm so sorry. I never meant to hurt any of you.''

"That's not good enough.''

He walked over to the fireplace and stared at the unlit logs. He was filled with conflicting emotions. In a small corner of his mind, he felt compassion for Louise. She *had* been young, and she'd gotten in over her head.

She should have known better, he reminded himself. If she hadn't slept with a married man, none of this would have happened. He poked and prodded his anger until it flared back to life.

So many lives ruined. Hers, his mother's, his brothers'. "What happened to the child?" he asked.

"I don't know. I never saw her again.''

Jordan froze. For one intensely agonizing second every cell in his body screamed in pain. Then he sucked in a breath, and the moment passed. But it left him weak and shaking.

"Her? You had a girl?''

"Yes. Why is that surprising? Oh, Lord. You can't really believe that family curse, can you?''

The Haynes curse. No female child had been born in four generations. Until Travis had fallen in love with Elizabeth. Until Kyle had fallen in love with Sandy. Haynes men who love their wives have girls. Haynes men who love the one they're with have girl children. Louise had a girl.

The son of a bitch had loved her. Really loved her. He'd never loved his wife. Jordan doubted his father had cared about his sons, either.

His chest tightened, and it was hard to breathe. He turned on his heel and left the room. Once in the foyer, he didn't know where to go, so he stepped outside, onto the porch.

The night air nipped at his skin, but he didn't care about the cold. At last he could draw in a breath. He exhaled a steamy cloud of air. The front door closed, and he heard Louise's footsteps on the wooden floor.

"I'll pack my bags and be out of here by morning," she said.

He wanted her gone but it wasn't an option. "No. You can't go. I've kept this secret for seventeen years. If you go, I'll have to explain. I'm not going to ruin everyone's holiday by confessing all now. Besides, if you left, Holly wouldn't be comfortable staying here with me alone. I want her to have one good Christmas. I want you to stay until after the first of the year."

"Fine."

He couldn't tell her emotional state from that single word, but he didn't care what she was thinking. Even though having a daughter wasn't her fault, he blamed her for that final insult.

He heard the front door open, then Louise spoke. "I was only seventeen," she said. "I made a mistake. I didn't know what I was doing."

"You knew enough to destroy my family."

She sucked in a breath. "You're never going to forgive me, are you?"

"No."

"As quickly as that? You don't even have to think about it?"

He didn't answer.

After a moment she said, "It must be nice to always be right. You obviously get a lot of satisfaction from that. I've been wrong lots of times, but then you already know that.

Tell me something. What's it like never to make a mistake? What is it like to know there isn't one single thing you're ashamed of?''

Louise didn't wait for an answer. Instead she went into the house and closed the door behind her.

Jordan stood alone in the cold. Somewhere out there was his half sister. He didn't know anything about her, and she didn't know anything about him. She didn't know that she was a Haynes, and that was a lucky break for her.

He tried to imagine what she would look like. She must be—he did some quick calculations—twenty-eight. Only a couple years younger than Kyle. They had a little sister. He hoped she'd had a better life growing up than the Haynes brothers. He hoped there had been parents who had cared about her.

He held on to the porch railing and wondered what he was supposed to do now. After the New Year, Louise would leave. She probably expected him to tell his brothers all he knew, but he wouldn't. It was her secret to keep or give away. He didn't care what she did as long as she got the hell out of his life.

Holly stared into the darkness, but sleep would not come. She glanced at the clock. It was after midnight. Finally she gave up and threw back the covers.

The corner of the blanket hit Mistletoe's butt, and the cat murmured a sleepy protest. Holly petted her in apology, then pulled on her robe and slippers. If she couldn't sleep, maybe some milk or an hour of pacing would help.

She crossed the room and opened the door, then stepped into the hallway. The house was silent, a contrast to the noisy thoughts swirling through her brain. It had been wrong of her to listen to Jordan's conversation with Louise, but she hadn't been able to help herself. She'd been heading upstairs when Jordan had told Louise to stay the hell out of his life. Holly had climbed to the top of the stairs, then sunk down on the landing and eavesdropped. She'd heard everything, except whatever they'd said when they went outside.

She didn't know what to think. At last Jordan's anger made sense. He'd been sixteen when he'd found out the housekeeper had had an affair with his father, and that the affair had led to the birth of a child.

A baby. Holly pulled her robe tightly around her and hugged her arms to her chest. Fierce longing filled her. It was probably the result of the afternoon spent with Jordan's sisters-in-law, all of whom had children.

When Holly reached the bottom of the stairs, she saw a light coming from the study where Jordan slept. She hesitated, not wanting to intrude but wondering if he was in pain from his strenuous day.

She crossed through the library, then stopped at the open door to the study. Jordan was sitting up in bed. He was holding a book but staring off into space rather than at the pages. He didn't notice her at first, and she took the opportunity to study him.

He wore sweats, and the loose-fitting clothing merely hinted at the strength concealed beneath the soft fabric. Lines of tension straightened his mouth. Undiluted pain filled his eyes.

"Jordan?"

He glanced up at her. Instantly his expression shuttered. A second before, she'd been able to read his soul; now she didn't even know what he was thinking. She recalled Rebecca's claims that Jordan was a loner, always on the outside looking in. For the first time she believed that might be true.

"You're up late," he said, putting the book on the bed.

"I couldn't sleep." She stuffed her hands into the pockets of her robe. "I wanted to make sure you were okay."

He turned his dark stare on her. "Why wouldn't I be?"

He was a cool stranger, and that frightened her. "You were gone a long time today, and I was concerned you might have overdone things physically. Are you in pain?"

He closed his eyes briefly. "No."

She wondered if she should leave or risk staying. The cowardly part of her said running wasn't a bad idea, but her compassionate nature won out. She settled on the overstuffed chair next to the bed.

There wasn't an easy way to say it, so she just blurted it out. "I was standing on the stairs. I heard everything."

He opened his eyes, but he didn't look at her. Instead, he stared at a place behind her left shoulder. Not a single twitch of a muscle gave his thoughts away.

"Jordan?"

"It doesn't matter," he said. "It was a long time ago."

"Of course it matters. There are so many unresolved issues. I'm sorry you had to carry this around for so long. It must have been hard for you."

He didn't respond.

She drew in a slow breath. "You know, it's not all Louise's fault."

He grimaced. "Being female, you *would* take her side."

"That has nothing to do with anything."

"If it's not her fault, then whose fault is it?"

"Louise deserves some of the blame, just not all of it."

"How convenient of you to take care of assigning blame," he said sarcastically. "Why don't you divide it all up, then let me know how much is mine, how much hers and how much belongs to everyone else? After all, you're such an expert on relationships."

His words pelted her like sharp stones. She felt the individual blows, even though she would bear no physical scars. This Jordan was hard and ugly. She didn't like him or trust him. But she still cared about him, so she stayed in her seat.

As if he read her mind, he looked at her and gave her a weak smile. "Sorry. I don't mean to be such a bastard. There's a lot going on, and it's tough to talk about. You can't understand this situation, Holly. You're too innocent."

"As innocent as Louise was when this first happened to her?"

The smile faded. "One point for your side."

She felt his pain and tried to ignore her own. "Jordan, this isn't about points, or winning and losing. It's about life. You've got to come to grips with this. Not for Louise, but for yourself."

"You don't know what the hell you're talking about. If she'd just slept with the old man, I could have understood that. He was a first-class bastard, and he would have enjoyed seducing schoolgirls. I doubt Louise was the first or the last. But that's not all she did. She should have just stayed away. Instead, she had to come back. She returned to town and destroyed my family."

His rage was a tangible creature, living and breathing in the room with them. Holly gathered her courage. "It sounds to me like your family was destroyed long before Louise came back to town."

"We had problems. Everyone does. But if she hadn't come back, my mother wouldn't have left. Now Louise is here, in everybody's lives. I hate that. Every time I turn around, she's at another family function."

"She's not hurting anyone. She takes good care of the family. What's wrong with that?"

"She's playing us for fools."

"No." Holly leaned forward and clasped her hands together. "She cares about everyone in the family, even you. She loves the children."

"Love." Jordan laughed harshly. "It will be the death of us."

A coldness swept over her. "What do you mean?"

"This love you're so proud of only destroys. If you'd asked my father, he would have said he loved his sons. The beatings were just to keep them on the right track. He loved his wife. So what if he fooled around? He slept in his own bed every night. That made things okay. His father and uncles, his brothers, even his grandfather had done the same thing before him."

He paused for a moment and leaned back against the hospital bed. "You want to hear about love? Craig loved his first wife, Krystal. She was an alley cat, but he didn't know for years. She was just like our father. She came on to each of his brothers. It scared us, and we never told him. Krystal claimed she loved Craig. Supposedly she loved her boys, although she managed to leave them and never once visit them after the divorce. Love destroys everything it touches."

Holly didn't know what to say to him. Her first instinct was to tell him he was wrong. Love didn't hurt. But it had hurt people in her life. Her mother had loved her father, and he'd let her down. Even when she was dying, he couldn't be bothered to help.

Holly knew love sometimes did hurt. Like when her mother had died. But there were good sides to love. She'd had wonderful times with her mother.

"Sometimes love is worth the risk of hurting," she said.

"You really believe that?"

"Yes," she said. "What about your family? You care about them."

"One exception in a long, ugly list of rules."

She studied his face. He was tired. She could see that in the shadows under his eyes. She wished she could make him feel better. "We're quite a pair," she said. "You believe love hurts, and I'm afraid to trust anyone."

Like love, trust was a risky business, but when it worked, it was worth the potential for heartbreak. Did she believe it enough to convince him of that?

"I wish I had the right words to make you feel better," she said miserably.

"That's not your job. I'll be fine."

She thought about the sixteen-year-old boy who had learned ugly family secrets. He'd said he'd kept them to himself, and she believed him. He'd carried this burden for a long time. She didn't agree with his need to blame Louise, but she understood where the impulse came from.

"You're exhausted," he said. "Go to bed. I'll be fine."

She shook her head. "In a minute." She rose, then perched on the edge of his mattress. "I'm sorry," she whispered.

"You have nothing to be sorry about."

She didn't tell him she was sorry for him. He wouldn't want her pity or her understanding. Instead, she told him without words. She leaned forward and rested her head in the crook of his neck, then wrapped her arms around him.

He didn't respond in any way. She continued to hold on to him, willing him to accept her comfort. Bits of the evening's conversation filled her mind. He'd carried dark secrets for too long. She wanted to help him, but he wouldn't let her.

Her eyes burned, and she tried to force back the tears. One escaped. Before she could brush it away, it fell on his neck.

Jordan grabbed her arms and set her away from him. He

studied her face, then reached up and touched a tear. "I'm not worth even one of these," he said gruffly.

"You're wrong. You're worth so much more."

He muttered a curse, then hauled her against him. She settled against his strength and held him tight. How alone he must be, this man who refused to believe in love. How alone she was, a woman who refused to trust. Would they ever be able to take that leap of faith, or were they destined to spend their lives searching for the one thing they feared to claim?

Holly knew she didn't want that to be her destiny. She wanted more out of life. But she was afraid.

Another time she would wrestle with the demons that kept her alone. Another time she would search her heart and try to find the key to escape her solitary world. For tonight it was enough to hold and be held in Jordan's comforting arms.

Chapter Twelve

When Holly came down to breakfast the next morning, she found Louise already up and making coffee. If she hadn't known what had happened the previous night, she might not have noticed the slightly puffy eyes and shadows from sleeplessness, but she still would have known something was wrong. It took her a moment to figure out why, then she realized it was Louise's clothes.

Instead of her normally, bright, barely matching colors, Louise wore black jeans and a plain white long-sleeved shirt. Also missing were her frequently zany earrings. Plain gold studs gleamed in each earlobe.

Before Holly could say anything, she heard Jordan behind her. She turned and gave him a tentative smile. He didn't respond, but as he walked past her, he squeezed her hand.

She'd spent most of last night in his bed. They'd held each other silently. Finally, when his breathing had slowed and she'd known he'd fallen asleep, she'd made her way upstairs to her room. She hadn't been able to sleep much, instead replaying the events of the previous evening over and over in her head. Mistletoe had cuddled close, and the cat's warmth and gentle purring had been a great source of comfort as she'd wrestled with all that she'd learned.

Questions of right and wrong, who had hurt whom and why had dominated her thoughts. At last she understood why Jordan was always angry with Louise. She wished there was an easy solution for everyone, but there wasn't. She felt badly for both him and for the housekeeper.

Jordan stepped into the kitchen. Louise didn't turn around, but her shoulders stiffened.

"The coffee's not ready," she said. "It'll be a few minutes. I'll bring you a cup." The housekeeper's hands shook as she measured out the coffee grounds.

Jordan stared at her for a moment. Holly watched him. Emotions flashed through his eyes. She recognized compassion and a flicker of regret, but anything else disappeared before it could be identified. He paused in the kitchen, then turned and left.

Louise filled the pot with water. "Talk about tension," she said, then tried to smile. The corners of her mouth trembled.

"I'm sorry," Holly said, then crossed to the other woman.

Louise blinked several times. "He told you."

It wasn't a question. "No. I overheard. I didn't mean to, but…" Her voice trailed off.

Louise's blue eyes filled with tears. "Everything is going to come out eventually. I suppose you think I'm a horrible person."

"The thought never crossed my mind." Impulsively

Holly reached toward her and gave her a hug. Louise hugged her back, then quickly straightened.

"All this emotion before I've even had my morning coffee. I'm not sure my old heart can stand it."

Louise turned back to the coffeepot and flipped on the switch. Then she settled at the small kitchen table by the window.

It was a cool, crisp winter day. The clear sky provided a perfect backdrop for the bright sunlight. Holly took the seat next to her.

"Everything he said is true," Louise said, resting her hands on the table. "I knew it was wrong to fall in love with Earl Haynes, so I'm not sure why I did it." She shrugged. "There are the usual excuses. I didn't feel that anyone cared about me, and Earl made me feel special. Pretty, even. I never meant to hurt anyone."

A tear trickled from the corner of her eye. She wiped it away impatiently. "I was a fool."

"You were very young." Holly leaned toward her. "I don't understand everything that happened. I agree that you made a mistake, but you were only seventeen years old. He was an adult. He should have known better."

"Maybe."

"Not maybe. He was a mature man with a wife and four children. He took advantage of you."

Louise sniffed. "You sound so sure of everything."

"I am. He was the sheriff in town, too. He used his position and authority to his advantage. You never had a chance, Louise. Stop blaming yourself."

"It's hard to let go of the guilt," the older woman admitted. "I've carried this secret around for so long. I probably should have realized why Jordan didn't like me, but I never thought he knew." She shook her head. "Now everything makes sense. He blames me for destroying his family." She looked at Holly. "I swear I wouldn't have come back to town all those years later if I'd thought it was going to make trouble. I had no idea what Earl was going to do."

"That's not your fault, either," Holly said.

"Maybe not, but Jordan won't forgive me. Having the baby was bad enough, but forcing his mother to leave is so much worse."

Holly hated how Louise was taking all the blame on herself. Maybe because she was new to the situation, she could see more clearly. There were misunderstandings on both sides.

"Jordan's mother didn't leave because of you," she said. "She left because her husband asked for a divorce."

"To marry me."

"But you didn't want him to get a divorce. You didn't want to have anything to do with him. It's not your fault."

Louise drew in a deep breath. "In my head I know what you're saying makes sense. In my heart that's a different matter. I feel so guilty. It's not all about the Haynes family, either. Some of it is about my little girl. I think about her all the time. I want her to be happy and s-safe." Her voice broke, and she had to turn away to hide her emotions.

Holly tried to imagine what it must be like to have to give a child up for adoption. She couldn't think of anything more tragic.

"Did you get to see her when she was born?"

"Just for a minute." This time Louise managed a full smile. "She looked just like a Haynes. Big eyes, lots of dark hair. She was so pretty. And then they took her away."

"You've never tried to get in touch with her?"

"No." The tears returned. Louise brushed them away. "What would I say to her?"

"How about the truth? You were young and frightened, and giving her to a loving couple seemed to be the best thing to do."

"That sounds so nice. The truth is not seeing her is my punishment for what I did. I don't deserve to have her in my life."

Her friend's pain cut through Holly, too. She knew what that kind of emptiness and longing felt like. She understood about being alone.

"It's too bad your daughter has to be punished, too," she said softly. "Look at all she's missing. A wonderful mother and four half brothers. Have you considered the fact that she might *want* to be in your life?"

Louise stared at her. "I hadn't thought of it that way. But what if she likes her world the way it is?"

"What if she doesn't? The worst that will happen is that she won't want to see you. I know it's scary and a risk, but what if she's been waiting her whole life for you?"

"What if?" Louise echoed softly.

This year the family had chosen to go caroling on Travis's street. They bundled up against the cold, passed out sheet music and flashlights, then started down the block.

"We have to rotate where we sing," Jordan explained to Holly. "We're really bad, so we give the neighbors a break by not coming back for a couple of years."

She leaned against him and grinned. "I don't believe that."

"Most of the Haynes family is tone-deaf. Trust me, it's awful."

It had been nearly a week since Jordan's confrontation with Louise. Christmas was in three days. A sort of armed truce had settled over the house. Louise avoided him whenever possible, and he avoided her. He'd heard the housekeeper talking with Holly several times. Snatches of conversation had carried to him. He knew they were talking about the past and the child Louise had given up for adoption.

A girl. A Haynes daughter. Once again the rage filled him as he remembered his father had cared for Louise as he had never cared for his wife and family.

It wasn't fair, but then so little in life was.

They came to a stop in front of the first home. The porch light was on, and there was a lit plastic Santa on the front lawn. The Haynes family was loud and filled with laughter as they prepared to share their Christmas spirit. The smaller children were already asleep, and had been left behind with Louise to watch over them. The older ones were more interested in playing than singing.

Someone called out the name of the first song. There was a brief moment of shuffling as everyone found the right page, followed by a single note from a pitch pipe. As if that would help.

"'Hark, the herald angels sing.'"

The words were clear, but the key was wrong and the voices didn't blend at all. The neighbors came out onto the porch and tried to act pleased, but they were obviously pained by the discord.

Holly actually had a very nice voice. She sang softly, but he could hear the clear tones and perfect melody. Maybe there was hope.

Kyle heard, too. "This one can sing," he said, and grabbed her arm. "Come up front where they can hear you. Maybe they won't throw things at us."

Holly gave Jordan a quick glance. "It's okay," he told her. "You do sound better than the rest of us."

She wore a thick blue sweater that matched the color of her eyes. The cold night air brought out the pink in her cheeks. In the light of the overhead lamp he saw her smile, and something deep inside him responded.

He liked her. The knowledge should have scared him into bolting, but all he could do was stand there and be grateful for her presence. Everything about her was wrong for him. Her decency, her innocence, her trust. But until the holidays were over, he was going to enjoy every stolen minute with her. When their time together was over, he would retreat to the darkness of his world and survive there.

His longing for her was about more than sex, he thought as she turned and went with Kyle to the front of the group. Even as the thought passed through his mind, his gaze dropped to her round hips and generous behind. He adored her lush feminine form. He knew that she agonized about an extra couple of pounds, but he didn't want her to change. He'd spent hours reliving the evening when he'd pleasured her. He could still see, taste and feel her full breasts. He wanted to feast on them forever.

But more than wanting a physical relationship, he enjoyed his time just being with Holly. He liked talking with her and working with her. He liked the care she took as she completed a task on his house. He liked her views of the world and her unflagging enthusiasm. Despite the blows the world had delivered, she still believed everything could work out for the best.

They began a second song. Jordan dropped behind Austin and Rebecca, who were absorbed only in each other. Lindsay, Sandy's oldest from a previous marriage, had brought a girlfriend with her, and they were doing more giggling than singing. Neither teenager noticed as he slipped behind them to the rear of the group.

Jordan cast a longing glance at the house to their left. Travis's house. Would anyone notice if he went back?

Before he could decide, Elizabeth moved next to him and slipped her arm through his.

"I thought Holly had cured you of this," she said, glancing up at him.

"Of what?"

"For a while you were actually like the rest of us. Smiling, participating in conversations. Once again you're brooding. Want to talk about it?"

He shrugged. He didn't have anything to say to her. He wasn't prepared to expose Louise's secret, and he didn't want to discuss their argument.

"Is it a guy thing?" Elizabeth asked.

"It's a family thing."

She stared at him for a long time. He realized she was a part of the Haynes family. He dropped a kiss on the top of her head. "Sorry. I didn't mean that the way it came out."

Her brown eyes saw more than they should. She continued to study him, then she nodded and disappeared into the crowd. A couple of minutes later Travis walked over to him.

"Elizabeth sent me to talk to you," Travis said. "What's going on?"

Jordan didn't want to talk about it, but the look on his brother's face told him he wasn't getting a choice. He shifted on the walkway and pulled his coat closer against the evening chill.

"I've been thinking a lot about Dad," he said, which was, in a way, the truth.

Travis grimaced. "Why bother? I'm glad the old man lives on the other side of the country. I wouldn't send him a Christmas card if Elizabeth didn't make me. You want to get in touch with him?"

"No," Jordan said shortly.

"I didn't think so. He's a bastard down to his bones."

Travis's expression hardened. "I'll never forgive him for what he did to all of us."

Craig was standing nearby and overheard the conversation. As the group moved on to the next house, he dropped back to join them.

Travis spoke. "You ever call Dad?"

"Why would I?" Craig asked. "I don't have anything to say to him. Nothing I've done has ever been good enough for him. I quit caring about him and his opinion a long time ago." Bitterness darkened his voice.

Jordan stared at his oldest brother. He'd never thought about what Craig must have gone through because he was the firstborn. He had endured the brunt of Earl Haynes's rage. Jordan remembered Craig had often taken the blame for things he hadn't done. When Travis had asked why, Craig had said he was bigger, so the beatings didn't hurt him as much. With the hindsight of an adult, Jordan knew Craig had just been looking out for his brothers.

Around them another song began. The words of peace and hope contrasted with the mood of the conversation. They paused to listen.

"You guys okay?" Elizabeth asked when the song ended.

Travis looked at her. "We're fine." But he stayed on the sidewalk with his brothers. By now Kyle and Austin had joined them. Only the women and children walked up to the next house. In the back of his mind Jordan noticed that the group sounded slightly more in key.

"I blame the old man for a lot," Travis said. "I never knew how to be a husband or a father."

"None of us did," Craig said. "I knew I was supposed to be the leader, but I never knew what I was doing. Obviously, or I wouldn't have married Krystal."

"I nearly lost Sandy because of him," Kyle said. The

night air was cold, and he pulled his leather jacket closer.
"I was afraid I wasn't good enough for her and her kids."

"I nearly lost Elizabeth," Travis said.

"We all made mistakes," Craig said. "Everybody does,
but I know we would have done better without him and his
brothers around."

"I remember not wanting to be like them," Travis said.
He shoved his hands into his coat pockets.

They nodded. Jordan had made that vow, too. He didn't
want to be like his father or uncles, using women, then
tossing them aside. He'd wanted more. Then he'd learned
how much it hurt to love someone, and he'd decided to
avoid relationships altogether.

Austin cleared his throat. "For a while I thought you
guys were lucky. You still had a family. Folks who cared
about you. Then I figured out sometimes it was better to
be alone."

"We've come a long way," Craig said, and slapped Kyle
on the back. "Even you, baby brother."

"Gee, thanks."

Craig was right. They had grown and changed. None of
them had turned out like their father. Jordan wondered what
his brothers would say if he told them the truth about the
past. No one had ever figured out why their mother had
left. At first he hadn't said anything because he was too
stunned. In his heart he'd hoped she would come back.
He'd hated Louise and the tragedy she'd brought to their
lives. Then he hadn't mentioned the truth because he'd
been afraid.

In his young, sixteen-year-old mind he'd worried that if
he brought everything out in the open, Earl would marry
Louise. Jordan couldn't bear the thought of her being his
stepmother and a part of the family.

Conversation flowed around him. He was caught up in a

dilemma. He believed Louise's affair was her secret to keep, but what about the child? Should he tell his brothers they had a half sister? She was grown up now and living her life somewhere. Did they have the right to get in touch with her? Did she want her life disrupted, or would she welcome the addition of four half brothers?

It wasn't until Holly rested her fingers on his arm that he realized that the caroling party had broken up.

"Are you feeling all right?" she asked, then touched his face. She was in her nurse mode, fussing over him.

"I'm fine." He captured her hand and brought it to his mouth, where he kissed her palm.

He heard her breath catch in her throat. "You're thinking about Louise," she said, and there was only a slight tremor in her voice.

"A little," he admitted. He put his arm around her and headed back to Travis's house.

"You haven't told them, have you?"

He shrugged. "I don't know what to say."

She snuggled close. "You're a very complex man, Jordan Haynes. On the one hand you're angry and resentful toward Louise for all that happened, but on the other hand you won't expose her secret. What does that say about you?"

"That I'm a fool."

"I prefer to think of you as a gentle soul."

"Thanks. That's what every guy likes to hear."

She laughed softly, then sighed. "Are you going to tell them about the baby?"

"I don't know. It was a long time ago. Wherever she is, she's not a baby anymore, she's a woman. Would she want to be a part of this?" What he didn't say was that he *did* want to find his half sister. The reason he held back was Louise. By admitting the truth, he would be giving Louise a permanent place in the family. He still blamed her for everything that had happened. He didn't want to reward that by welcoming her as one of them.

"I always wanted a sister," Holly said. "You're lucky to have such a close family."

"You wouldn't say that if you'd met my father."

"I heard a little about him from Louise and from what you've told me. He sounds difficult."

"That's a nice way of putting it." He thought about the past. "If I'd figured the truth out sooner, about my father and Louise, I mean—"

"What would you have done? You were too young to have made any changes."

"You're probably right." They paused by the front steps of Travis's Victorian home. Everyone else had gone inside.

Holly stood on the first step so they were nearly at eye level. She placed her hands on his shoulders. "So you admit you were young and didn't know what to do?"

"Sure, if it makes you happy."

Her gaze locked on to his. "Louise was young, too."

Jordan tried to turn away and she tightened her hold on him. He could have broken away easily, but he didn't want to hurt her feelings.

"It's not going to work, Holly."

"Why not? It's true. She was seventeen years old. She made a mistake. You've just admitted you could have made mistakes, too. Why does it have to be all her fault? Your father was the adult. If anyone deserves blame, it's him."

He didn't want to argue about this, and he didn't want to listen to her words. "What's your point?"

"I'm saying that it might be easier to blame Louise than to blame your father, but that doesn't change the truth."

He stared at her a long time. He didn't want to believe

what she was saying, but he wasn't sure he could continue to ignore it.

She studied him, her pretty face solemn. Then she smiled and took his hand. "Come inside where it's warm," she said, tugging him along with her.

As her words sank in and he took a step closer, he had a flash of longing so intense, it took his breath away. He knew she was talking about going into the house and out of the cold, but for that single heartbeat he wanted her to be talking about more. He wanted her to be inviting him into her heart.

Chapter Thirteen

They arrived home close to midnight. Holly knew she should be tired. She'd been up most of the previous night talking with Jordan, then had put in a full day at the store. Customers had been waiting when she'd first opened the doors, and she'd had to stay late to take care of everyone's requests. It seemed many people had saved their Christmas shopping for the last minute.

Instead of exhaustion, however, she felt a strange restlessness. The caroling had been great fun. The more time she spent with Jordan's family, the more she adored them. He was lucky to have so many people to care about him. For the first time in years she understood the meaning of security. Although it was only a temporary situation, she trusted Jordan to look out for her. She hadn't trusted anyone in so long. The sensation was unfamiliar, but she was willing to risk getting used to it.

Jordan held the door open for her, then stepped into the house behind her. He flipped on the lights in the foyer.

"It's so quiet," she whispered, then giggled. "I guess I can talk in a normal voice. There's no one here to wake up."

"Except the damn cat."

He took her coat and hung it up in the hall closet. Holly looked in the living room, but didn't see a sign of Mistletoe. She frowned. Her cat didn't like Jordan, but she always came out to spit at him. Mistletoe also came to greet Holly and get her cuddling.

"Mistletoe?" she called.

Jordan glanced at her. "What's the problem?"

"She's usually waiting for us by the door." A seed of worry planted low in her belly. "I hope she didn't get out."

"Unlikely. You saw her right before we left, right?"

Holly nodded.

"I was the last one out, and I know I closed the door. I had to unlock it to get back in. Louise was baby-sitting the children all evening, so she wasn't here to accidentally let Mistletoe out. She's probably sleeping upstairs."

"You're right. She's been a little tired lately. Maybe she didn't hear us come in." Holly started for the stairs.

"I'll check the downstairs," Jordan said.

"Thanks."

She sighed softly. She knew he didn't care much for her cat. And she couldn't really blame him, given that Mistletoe had taken an instant dislike to Jordan.

The old house was silent. Holly went from room to room switching on lights. Some of the second-story bedrooms had furniture, but most were bare.

Louise had a room right by the stairs. The housekeeper had fallen asleep in Travis and Elizabeth's guest room, and they'd left her there. Travis had promised to bring her back in the morning. Now Holly got on her knees and checked under the four-poster bed. Nothing. She checked the closet and even the small space behind the dresser.

"Mistletoe? Where are you?" she called as she entered the hallway.

She was halfway to her room when she heard Jordan's voice from the first floor.

"I found her," he said. "In my room."

She headed toward him. He was waiting for her at the bottom of the stairs. There was an odd light in his eyes and a half smile tugging at the corners of his mouth.

"What is it?" she asked.

He took her hand. "Congratulations. You're a grand-mother."

"Mistletoe gave birth? Is she okay?"

"She looks great. There are four kittens."

Elation followed on the heels of relief. She quickened her step. "I thought she was acting a little odd these last couple of days. I should have realized."

They entered Jordan's makeshift room. The closet door was open. Clothes had been pulled off hangers to create a nest. Mistletoe lay in the center, curled protectively around four tiny kittens.

Three were gray like their mother, and one was black. Mistletoe blinked sleepily, then gave a throaty purr.

Holly crouched down next to her and stroked her head. "What a clever girl you are. Four wonderful babies." She petted her cat but didn't disturb the kittens. They were so tiny, with thin, slick fur.

"Are you hungry?" Holly asked, then glanced at Jordan. "Do you think we should move her food in here along with her litter box? Then she wouldn't have to go so far."

"Sure." He rose to his feet and left.

While he was gone, Holly continued to speak softly to

her cat. Mistletoe savored the attention, as if she knew she'd done a wonderful thing.

"She's not even spitting at you," Holly said when he returned with the cat's food and water.

"Oh, I think she got back at me already tonight." He pointed to the makeshift bed.

For the first time Holly realized Mistletoe had given birth on a pile of Jordan's clothes. On top was his favorite sweater.

"Oh, no." She covered her mouth with her hand and stared at him. "Jordan, I'm so sorry."

"It's not your fault."

She dropped her hand to her side. "You're not mad?"

"It's just some clothes, Holly. If they can't be cleaned, then they can be replaced."

"But Mistletoe has been so mean to you, and it's her fault you were injured in the first place."

He touched her arm. "It's okay. I swear."

She looked into his dark eyes, then studied the shape of his mouth. Her own father hadn't been willing to help her mother when she was dying. Through her life many people had let her down. But this man had opened his home to her, introduced her to his family and generally made her feel as if she finally belonged somewhere.

Deep in her heart, in a place that had been empty and cold for so long, a tiny flicker of hope burned brightly. She didn't understand the tingling she felt when Jordan was near or the pleasure she took in his company or the way his kisses and touches had made her feel. She didn't understand anything. She only knew that he was the most wonderful man she'd ever met in her life, and she would have done anything for him.

Jordan reached past her. Mistletoe eyed him mistrustfully, then sniffed his fingers. When she was done, he gently stroked the top of her head. The cat didn't purr, but she didn't pull away, either. After a couple of minutes he rose to his feet.

"Maybe we should let them be," he said, holding out his hand.

She took it and he pulled her up. "You're right. I'm sure she needs to rest."

As they walked through the library, he continued to hold her hand. Holly thought about pointing out the fact, but she liked the feel of him so close to her. When they reached the living room, he paused in front of the fireplace.

"Maybe we should celebrate," he said. "I've got some champagne in the refrigerator."

The only light came from the Christmas tree. She could see the planes of his face, the shape of his body, but the rest of the room disappeared into shadow. They were alone in the house, and she felt as if they were in fact alone in the world. Her stomach tightened nervously.

"I'd like that," she said, and sank down on the thick carpet.

Jordan moved to the fireplace, where he touched a match to the kindling and logs stacked there. The dry tinder caught instantly. By the time he returned with two half-full glasses, the scent of wood smoke mingled with the piney fragrance of the tree.

He detoured around the back of the sofa and hit a button on the CD player. After a couple of seconds she heard the opening bars to a familiar Christmas carol. He settled on the floor next to her and held out one of the glasses.

As she took it, she noticed her fingers trembled. She could barely touch her glass to his when he proposed a toast. Her throat was tight, her skin both hot and cold, her gaze unable to hold his. The urge to bolt for safety battled with the need to stay and be close to him.

She glanced at the tall tree they had decorated last week, then at the fire. Anywhere but at the handsome man sitting next to her.

"You're so beautiful," he murmured.

She rolled her eyes. "Yeah, right." She shifted until she was sitting cross-legged, then set her champagne on a nearby coffee table.

Jordan frowned. "You don't think you're attractive?"

The question confused her. "I don't think I have to wear a paper bag over my head, if that's what you're asking. But beautiful?" She shook her head. "I'm not like those actresses on television—skinny and sophisticated with perfect makeup."

"I wouldn't think you were beautiful if you were like them." He set his champagne next to hers, then leaned closer. He fingered a strand of her hair. "Soft. Just like I thought it would be." He cupped the back of her head and held her still. "Amazing."

She blinked. He was kidding, right? Or she was dreaming. She wasn't really having this conversation with him. Jordan Haynes, single hunk, didn't really think she was attractive, did he?

"But I have to lose fifteen pounds," she blurted out, then felt herself flush with embarrassment. "I don't have skinny thighs."

He pressed his lips against the side of her neck. "I don't want skinny thighs. You're perfect the way you are."

"But everything is too big." His lips were making her skin tingle, and she was having trouble forming words.

He moved to her earlobe and nibbled on the sensitive skin. "Trust me, Holly. You're built to drive men wild."

She jerked her head back and stared at him. "You're kidding, right?"

But he wasn't smiling. His eyes were dark, his expression intense. If she hadn't known him so well, he might have frightened her.

"Jordan?"

"Trust me. Men want you."

He might well have been speaking Russian. "Even you?" she asked without thinking, then could have cheerfully died. Right there on the rug. Instant death. She wouldn't have complained at all.

Unfortunately she continued to live. "Sorry," she mumbled. "Stupid question. I'll just head up to my room and bury my head under the pillows."

But before she could stand, he had his arms around her and was lowering her onto the rug. The fire in his eyes burned hotter and brighter than the one in the hearth.

"Especially me," he said, his voice thick with an emotion she couldn't identify. Then he kissed her.

This time she was prepared for the sensations he evoked. At the first brush of his mouth, her body filled with heat. By the time he got around to testing the seam of her mouth with his lips, she was already weak with longing.

She wrapped her arms around him and pulled him close. He was hard muscle and angles to her curves. His long legs brushed against hers.

He tasted her, explored her mouth, teased her until she couldn't catch her breath. She laced her fingers through his hair, feeling the silky strands. With her other hand she traced a line down his spine. She could feel the heat of him through his shirt.

Unexpectedly Jordan pulled away. He rolled onto his back and covered his eyes with his forearm. "Damn, this is going to hurt."

Holly stared at him. "What's wrong? I thought your back was doing better. Did you overdo it at physical therapy today?"

He gave a weak laugh. "My back is great," he said. "I don't feel a thing…there."

Then what was hurting? "I don't understand."

"Do you remember the last time we did this?" He dropped his hand to his chest.

She nodded slowly. She remembered every detail of the magic she'd felt in his arms. Some nights she couldn't sleep because she was remembering. Her body got hot, and she felt an odd restlessness.

"When a man wants to make love, his body changes."

She knew enough about the process to have figured that part out, but she didn't say anything. She also didn't dare lower her gaze from his face. Was he…like that? Would she be able to tell?

Jordan sat up and rubbed his hand over his face. "Arousal brings a certain amount of pleasure, which later turns to pain if it's not followed by release. Last time—"

She shot into a sitting position as if she'd been jolted with electricity. Humiliation flooded her. Last time he'd touched her and made her feel those wonderful things, but he'd done nothing for himself.

"I'm sorry," she said softly. "You must think I'm a thoughtless, selfish…" Her voice trailed off. She didn't have any words. She'd been a jerk. Or worse.

"Just innocent," he told her. "You didn't know."

"You should have told me. I would have done, well, *something!*"

"I'm intrigued to imagine what."

She risked glancing at him and saw that he was teasing her. Then his smile faded.

"Holly, you've never seen a man naked. You can't be expected to understand the workings of male anatomy or the details involved in making love."

He had a point. "What if I want to?" she asked without

thinking. She flinched in anticipation of his rejection, but didn't take the words back.

"See me naked or make love?"

She glanced at him out of the corner of her eye. She couldn't tell what he was thinking, but he didn't look mad. "B-both."

The silence made her nervous. Oh, there were Christmas carols in the background, and the snapping of the logs on the fire, but Jordan didn't speak. Of course he wouldn't want her. She wasn't like his other women. She wasn't attractive enough or experienced. He wouldn't want to bother with her.

"I'm sorry," she said, and started to stand up. "My mistake." She had to get out of here before she started to cry.

He grabbed her hand and held her fast. "Don't go," he said. "Please." He gave her a half smile. "I want to make love with you, Holly. I'm stunned that you would pick me to be your first. Stunned and honored."

"Yeah?" She wanted to believe him.

He kissed her gently. "Yeah."

They stared at each other for a moment. She swallowed nervously. "What do you want me to do?"

"Just sit there. I'll be right back."

He headed for the stairs and took them two at a time. At least he wasn't acting as if this was going to be hideous. A small but comforting thought. She pressed a hand against her now-fluttering tummy and wondered if she was making a mistake.

She laughed softly. No. She'd chosen wisely. Jordan was tender and considerate. He would make her first time wonderful. With him, she wouldn't mind being awkward and asking questions. He had a way of easing her discomfort, even when she was embarrassed.

He returned with a thick quilt and a small box. She got

up and helped him spread the quilt in front of the Christmas tree. Then she shifted her weight from foot to foot. "Are you sure it's okay to do it here?"

He kissed her forehead. "We can do it anywhere you like. I thought this would be romantic."

She glanced around at the tree and the flickering fire. It *was* romantic. "Okay."

He set the box next to the champagne glasses. "I'll take care of protection."

"P-protection?" She took a step back. Oh my gosh. They were going to have sex. Sex as in they needed protection. She stared at the box as if it contained live snakes.

"Holly, are you all right?"

"Ah, fine."

He stood in front of her and took both her hands in his. His dark gaze met hers. "I know this is strange and you're scared. I wish I had the right words, but I don't. I'm just as scared as you are."

Somehow that was comforting. "But you've done this before."

"Not with you."

Interesting logic. She liked it. "I'm afraid I'm going to say or do something stupid."

"I'll promise not to laugh if you will."

"Why would I laugh?"

He smiled. "Sex is pretty silly. Have a seat." He settled next to her, then reached for the box. "These are condoms. Have you seen one before?"

She shook her head.

He opened the box and dumped the contents onto the quilt. Before she could pick one up, he was undoing the box and smoothing it flat. She glanced down and was stunned to see detailed instructions along with some odd-looking illustrations.

"They tell you how to use them?" she asked, her voice rising into a shriek.

"How else would you learn?"

"I thought guys just sort of knew."

"Sorry. At the beginning we're just as nervous and ignorant as everyone else."

She scanned the instructions. Involuntarily her gaze dropped to Jordan's lap. He was wearing jeans, and she couldn't tell if he was "erect" as they mentioned in step one. If she couldn't even tell that, how on earth was she going to figure anything else out?

Before she could panic even more, he reached for one of the packages and ripped it open.

"W-what are you doing?" she asked, terrified the next step was undoing his pants and pulling "it" out.

"Trying to show you it's not scary." He handed her the open package. "Take it out."

She assumed he meant "it" as in the condom and not "it" as in, well, his "it." She cleared her throat, then dumped the contents onto her palm.

The condom was flat and round, sort of an ivory color. She inhaled the faint odor of latex.

"You can unroll it," he said.

She held it between her thumbs and forefingers, then did as he suggested. When it was completely unrolled, she stared at it. The condom hung limply from her fingers.

"Somehow I was expecting more," she said.

"Still scared?" he asked.

She wiggled it slightly. "Not of this."

"Good." He rose to his feet. "I'm going to get more champagne. I'll be right back."

Holly stared at the condom. It looked like a weird little balloon. An idea formed in the back of her mind. She tried to ignore it, but once there, the idea demanded attention.

She glanced toward the kitchen, but didn't see Jordan. After taking a deep breath, she cupped the open end of the condom, then brought it to her mouth.

It blew up perfectly. With three deep breaths she had it nearly as big as a loaf of bread. Behind her glass clinked against the wood table. Jordan had returned.

He crouched in front of her, took the blown-up condom from her now-shaking fingers and grinned. "Ah, I'm afraid I'm not going to meet your expectations."

"Oh, no." She buried her face in her hands and heard a whistle of air as he deflated the protection.

"My brothers and I found out they also make great water balloons."

She risked a quick glance through her parted fingers. He was sitting next to her on the quilt. Firelight made his dark hair shine. His face was in shadows, but she could see the hint of a smile tugging at his lips.

When he saw her looking at him, the smile faded. "I want to make love with you," he said slowly. "But I'm not going to rush you. I want your first time to be perfect."

She didn't care about perfection. She only wanted to be with him. "Tell me what to do."

"Trust me."

"I do."

Chapter Fourteen

Jordan touched her face, then trailed his fingers down to her shoulders. Holly remembered the last time he had stroked her and the feelings he'd evoked. Could she do the same to him?

She frowned. "Would you like me to touch you? I mean would you enjoy it?"

"'Enjoy' isn't the word I'd use." He must have caught her confusion. He smiled. "I was thinking more of ecstasy."

She wasn't sure she could do ecstasy, but she was willing to try. She shifted until she was kneeling in front of him, then leaned forward. He didn't move as she got closer. Instead of touching his mouth with hers, she pressed her lips against his neck, in that sensitive spot just below his left ear.

His warm skin appealed to her. After several chaste kisses she risked touching him with her tongue. He tasted of himself, a combination of masculinity and temptation. A faint tremor rippled through him.

She continued her exploration, tracing the curve of his ear, then trailing a damp path to his mouth. As she kissed him, he held her arms and lowered them both to the quilt.

Bodies touched, tongues stroked, breath mingled. Their slow dance of arousal left her weak and shaking, but she didn't want to stop. She figured that she'd gotten lucky with Jordan. He was a kind, gentle man who made her heart beat faster and her thighs tremble. For some reason he liked her, even wanted her. Men like him weren't usually interested in women like her, and she didn't understand what combination of circumstances had allowed him to find her appealing. Whatever it was, she was grateful. She wanted her first time to be with him because she knew he would make it wonderful. She didn't even mind being afraid.

She lay half on top of him. He shifted her so one of her legs slid between his. She braced one arm on the floor. Her free hand rested on his chest. As he tilted his head and explored her mouth, she wondered if it was all right to touch him as he'd touched her.

Tentatively, almost hoping he wouldn't notice, she spread her fingers and began moving across his chest. He moaned low in his throat. He'd laced his fingers in her hair, and now he urged her closer. The rate of his breathing increased, as did hers.

"Unbutton my shirt," he whispered, then drew her lower lip into his mouth. The sucking sensation forced all conscious thought from her mind, and it was several seconds before she could respond to his request.

Unbutton his shirt. Easy enough, she thought, reminding herself she'd unbuttoned her own shirt countless times. Surely this couldn't be harder. Could it?

She slid her hand to the center of his chest, then followed

the line to the slight V below his collar. The first button came undone easily. As did the second. Then she noticed the combination of hot skin and soft, crinkly hair brushing against her knuckles. How was she supposed to concentrate while that was going on? When combined with the delicious things Jordan was doing to her lips and tongue, she didn't have a prayer.

She broke the kiss, then pushed herself into a sitting position. "I want to see what I'm doing," she said.

He raised his arms and tucked his hands behind his head. "Be my guest."

It was both easier and harder to work this way. Although she wasn't distracted by his magical touch, she was aware of him watching her. She forced herself to ignore his dark gaze and instead pay attention to his shirt.

The rest of the buttons opened easily. She worked quickly until she reached the waistband of his jeans. Now what?

"Pull out the shirt," he said helpfully.

She could do that. She tugged until the fabric came free. The cotton was warm from his body, and wrinkled. She unfastened the last three buttons, then drew the center of his shirt apart.

His chest was bare to her gaze. She stared at him. She'd seen men's chests on television and in magazines. She'd even seen Jordan's, but this time she was responsible for baring his skin to her gaze.

She could feel the heat of him, inhale his scent. He was alive and real and right in front of her. Tentatively, half-afraid he would protest, she placed her hand on his flat belly.

His muscles rippled under her touch. She glanced at him, but his face gave nothing away. His eyes were closed as if he were completely focused on what she was doing.

She moved her hand up slowly, delighting in the way his chest hair felt against her palm. When she reached his collarbone, she brushed the shirt off his shoulders. He half sat up and shrugged out of the garment, then sank back onto the quilt.

Now his eyes were open. He placed his hands on her hips. "Straddle me," he said.

She shifted over him, but this time when she came down, she wasn't on his belly. She could feel his hips between her thighs and something else. Something hard and long. Something that made her insides feel funny and that place between her legs tighten.

He held out his hands. She laced her fingers with his. Slowly he began to draw her closer. She had to lean toward him, then allow him to lower her to his chest. The action required cooperation and trust.

He met her halfway, touching her mouth with his. They kissed. She felt herself slipping into a world she didn't understand. A world of sensation and desire. She wanted and needed, but the specifics required eluded her. Her body strained toward the release he'd offered her once before. She wanted to feel his hands on her, his mouth touching her breasts.

She broke the kiss and lowered her head until she could kiss his chest. She tasted him there, then trailed through the dark hair to his belly button. She nipped his skin, delighting in his involuntary reactions. He groaned when she suckled his flat nipples. He sighed when she ran her hands from his shoulders to the waistband of his jeans. He gave a half laugh, half strangled moan when she kissed the sweet spot under his ear.

Still straddling him, she leaned close and whispered, "I want to see you."

His hands moved to his belt. As she moved off him, he

unbuttoned his jeans. When he sat up, he removed his boots and socks, then put his hands on the waistband.

"You sure?" he asked.

She nodded. Somehow still being fully dressed made her feel safer.

He pushed off the rest of his clothing, then lay back down.

Holly stared intently at his feet. Her courage had momentarily deserted her.

"Scared?" he asked.

"Uh-huh. But you have nice feet."

"Thanks. Check out the knees. They aren't too bad, either."

Knees? Well, okay, that would be safe.

"Give me your hand," he said.

"What? Are you crazy? You want me to touch it?"

Involuntarily her gaze shifted to his face. Now she was in the same trouble, but only from the other end.

"Are all virgins this much work?" he asked, his voice teasing.

"Gosh, I really hope so. I'd hate to be the only one."

She was sitting next to him, her hip pressed against his. It would be so simple to just look down, but she couldn't.

"Give me your hand," he said again.

She drew in a deep breath and did as he requested.

"Now close your eyes."

That was harder, but slowly she lowered her lids.

Surprisingly the darkness comforted her. What she couldn't see couldn't hurt her. Not perfect logic, but it worked for the situation.

He drew her hand across his belly. She felt his skin and the crisp hairs. Then her hand bumped into something else. Something so soft it made her think of velvet and satin blended together.

She relaxed her fingers and let him guide her. She found herself holding him. He was long and hard, a steel sheath encased in whisper-smooth skin. From top to bottom she let her fingers discover him.

At last she opened her eyes and stared at him. Her pale fingers gripped him confidently, as if she'd done this a hundred times before. Okay, maybe not a hundred, but at least ten. She touched the thick hair protecting his maleness, then slipped lower to the soft, tender sacs between his legs.

The contrast of shapes and textures amazed her. He was so different from herself. Male to her female. She studied his long, lean legs, then brushed the tops of his thighs.

"This is nice," she said, amazed that it was.

"I'm glad you approve."

She continued touching him, then moved her hand up and down in the motion he'd shown her. "Do you like this?"

A muscle tightened in his jaw. "Oh, yeah."

She glanced from him to the deflated condom resting on the rug by the leg of the coffee table. "It's good that those things stretch. Otherwise, it would never fit."

He gave a strangled laugh, then grabbed her shoulders and lowered her to the floor. "Enough," he said. "You're driving me crazy."

"What did I do wrong?" she asked, suddenly panicked. "Did I hurt you?"

"Nothing's wrong," he said, looming over her. The fire burned bright in his eyes. "Everything is right, Holly. That's part of the problem. When you're touching me, I start to lose control."

"And that's bad?"

He smiled slowly. "That's very good."

"Then why—"

He cut off her words with a kiss. His tongue plunged inside and circled her own. He tasted her thoroughly.

She reveled in the feel of him on top of her. When he reached for the hem of her sweater, she helped him pull it over her head. The last time he'd done that, she had been shy, afraid to show herself to him. Now she wanted him to touch her bare skin and take her to that place she'd been before.

Her bra followed her sweater onto the growing pile of clothing. Jordan cupped her full breasts, stroking them gently, teasing her nipples into tautness, then drawing the tight points into his mouth. His fingers traced patterns on her ribs before reaching for the snap on her jeans. She didn't want him to stop kissing her breasts, but she did want his hands between her legs, so she raised her hips enough to push off the rest of her clothing.

And then she was naked before him. For a moment she worried about those extra pounds and the fact that no man had ever seen her completely bare. Then he ran his hands from her ankles to her thighs, and she didn't care about anything but being with him.

His mouth settled on her breast. She held his head in her hands and urged him to suckle deeper. His bare legs brushed against hers. His hair tickled. She felt his hardness pressing into her hip, and wondered what it would feel like when he entered her. Would it hurt? Would it feel wonderful?

Then his fingers slipped between her thighs, and she forgot to worry about anything. The tension she remembered from the last time they'd done this returned, only faster. Her muscles tightened as her whole body prepared itself for release.

Then his fingers were gone, and his mouth moved away from her breasts. She wanted to sob in protest. Why was he stopping? But he didn't stop completely. He trailed kisses down her ribs to the slight mound of her belly. He paused long enough to dip into her belly button and make her squirm.

Had she known what he was going to do, she would have tried to stop him. Had she known how good it was going to feel, she would have begged him to do it sooner.

He kissed her lower and lower on her belly, then moved down to kiss her thighs. When she would have closed her legs against him, he nudged to keep her knees apart. Fighting embarrassment and embracing the hopeful belief that anything this wonderful couldn't possibly be bad, she did as he requested.

Then he kissed her there. A slow kiss, tasting her, teasing her, making her want to scream and faint and beg him to never, ever stop.

Tension returned and with it the promise of a release beyond anything she'd ever imagined. In just a few minutes she was panting and ready, poised yet caught in pleasure too wonderful to end.

The intimacy of the act delighted her. That he would want to touch her that way, there. She felt her body begin to collect itself. Pleasure spiraled, circling higher and higher as the pitch increased.

He flicked his tongue faster, and she was his. Drawn up and out, ripped apart, then put back together. Disassembled with every beat of her heart, assembled by the touch of his tongue.

When her body stopped shaking, she found herself in his arms. He held her close and brushed the hair from her face.

"Jordan?" Her voice shook.

He smiled gently. "How was it?"

She laughed. "I know you don't have to ask. I vaguely recall mumbling something, and I'm sure you heard."

"You weren't mumbling, you were screaming." The twinkle in his eyes told her he was teasing.

"I'm not the screaming type."

"I could change that."

She sighed. "I think you could." Something flexed against her hip. She wiggled closer. "Now, please."

He looked into her face as if trying to judge her true feelings on the subject, then he pushed up and reached for one of the condoms.

She'd been afraid that watching him put it on would be awkward, but instead she found herself fighting tears. His willingness to protect her, his genuine concern, touched her down to her heart. Emotions filled her chest. She didn't want to identify them now. Later, when she was alone, she would figure out what they meant.

He knelt between her legs. Their gazes locked. This was a moment of no return. Once the act had been completed, she would no longer be a virgin.

"Yes," she said.

He pressed into her. At first she felt a slight pressure. He was large and she was untried, so her body had to stretch to accommodate him.

He leaned forward and kissed her right breast. The slow tug as he drew her nipple into his mouth sparked an answering response deep inside. He suckled again, then pushed in.

The brief pain surprised her. She stiffened and he stopped.

"It's okay," she said. "I guess now you know I wasn't kidding about being a virgin."

"Holly, I—"

"No." She flexed her hips, urging him in deeper. "I want this. I want you."

With one steady thrust he buried himself in her. When

she had adjusted to his width and length, he withdrew and plunged inside again. She closed her eyes and found herself caught up in the rhythm of their erotic dance. The low stirring became tension, followed quickly by the urge to press on to a release.

She arched toward him. He moved in and out of her more quickly, then reached a hand between them and touched her most sensitive place.

His fingers brought her to the edge, then she found herself calling his name. Once again she was caught up in the spiraling magic. This time he followed her, straining against her, his muscles hard, his face a mask of intense pleasure. Together they completed the ancient dance of male and female, afterward settling into the safety and warmth of each other's arms.

When Jordan rolled over and opened his eyes, the room was dark. His internal clock told him dawn was still a couple of hours away. At first he didn't recognize the shadowy shapes in the room, then Holly shifted, cuddling against him, and he remembered everything.

They'd made love. He smiled slowly and reached out to stroke her smooth skin. Her heat warmed him to his soul.

After exhausting themselves in front of the Christmas tree, they'd come upstairs to her room. Not only was her bed bigger, but neither of them wanted to disturb Mistletoe, who was in Jordan's closet.

Once in bed, Holly had gotten shy, wanting to put on a nightgown instead of sleeping naked. When words hadn't worked to persuade her, he'd tried kisses. He wasn't sure who had persuaded whom, because they'd ended up making love again, slowly, erotically.

He could still see her body beneath his, feel her passion and taste her sweet skin. She'd been all he'd imagined her to be, and more. He'd wanted to take her again and again, but sleep had claimed them before he could act on his fantasy.

Now, listening to the steady rhythm of her breathing and fingering the silky hair he admired, he wondered how he'd gotten so damn lucky. He'd never met a woman like Holly, and he doubted he would again. She was honest and open, loving, generous, pretty and sexy enough to make him hard in less than five seconds. In short, she was perfect, and that scared him to death.

He slipped out of bed and made his way down the stairs. Once in his makeshift bedroom, he flipped on the lamp by the bed, then checked on Mistletoe. She was curled up on his sweater, dozing. He reached above her and collected his robe, then put it on. After tying the belt, he crouched in front of the cat. Mistletoe glared at him, then spit softly.

"I'm not impressed," he murmured.

Mistletoe stood up. Her babies made soft mewing sounds, then settled back to sleep. After stretching, Mistletoe stepped out of the closet and wound her way around Jordan's legs. When he reached down to pet her, she hissed at him, then bumped her head against his hand as if asking to be scratched there.

"Make up your mind," he told her.

She ignored him and continued to growl and hiss between bouts of purring. Then she ate some food and drank a little water.

Jordan moved to the bed and stretched out on top of the blankets. Mistletoe followed, then climbed on his chest and stood there. They were practically nose to nose, and he could smell the cat food on her breath. She flattened her gray ears, then began to knead. Sharp claws dug in through the terry-cloth robe. He winced with each press of her paw. She seemed to delight in causing him discomfort, because she kneaded deeper, then sank down on top of him and breathed in his face.

He reached up and scratched under her chin. Mistletoe arched her head. When he stopped, she licked his fingers, then nibbled as if warning him to continue or suffer the consequences. He continued.

As he stroked her soft fur, he found himself thinking about Holly and their night together.

She'd been a virgin. He'd known that fact; they'd even discussed it. But knowing it and actually being the first man to make love to her were two different things. He'd felt the tightness, the protective barrier that, once broken, could not be repaired. The act of making love with her had been different from making love with anyone else.

In a primitive male way, he felt a connection and sense of responsibility. She'd marked him with her innocence, and he'd claimed her with his seed. If he were a different kind of man, he would want to hold on to her forever.

If he were a different kind of man, she would be safe with him.

But he wasn't different. He was stuck in a world where he could not escape the truth. Because he respected her and cared about her, he would not try to destroy her by loving her. As he stroked Mistletoe and listened to her purring, he swore he would treat Holly right. He wouldn't betray her or let her down. Others had done that before him, but he was going to be different. He was going to give her the best gift of all. He wasn't going to hurt her. If the price of that was not loving her, then so be it.

Holly woke to the smell of coffee. She opened her eyes and saw sunlight streaming into her bedroom. Despite the familiar furniture, something was different. She blinked as she tried to figure it out. Then she remembered last night.

In the same instant she realized she was naked beneath the covers and that Jordan was entering the room.

She stared at him and felt her heartbeat increase. His hair was tousled, his face unshaven. He wore a white terry-cloth robe loosely knotted around his waist. Bare legs led to bare feet. He was gorgeous and smiling at her.

"I brought you breakfast," he said, holding out a tray. "Are you hungry?"

"Starved." After pushing her hair out of her eyes, she started to sit up. The sheet chose not to cooperate, and there was a quick tug-of-war as she tried to get into a sitting position without flashing Jordan.

He set the tray over her lap, then leaned toward her. "You don't have to work so hard to cover up. I've seen it all, and it's lovely."

Before she could recover enough to speak, he settled on the bed next to her and poured them both a cup of coffee. There was also toast and fruit.

"I checked on Mistletoe," he said. "She ate breakfast, and the kittens seem fine. They don't have their eyes open, though."

"That takes a little while," Holly commented automatically, not able to believe they were practically naked, eating breakfast in bed after making love. As if this were *normal.* She wanted to shriek. It wasn't normal, at least not in her world. Normal was living alone and being lonely, not passion in front of a Christmas tree and a man who threatened to steal her heart.

"How do you feel?" he asked.

She took a quick sip of coffee and nearly burned her tongue. "Fine," she said, her voice a high-pitched squeak.

"No repercussions?"

"Like what?"

He smiled. "Are you sore?"

Sore? "From what?"

He reached toward her and pulled at the sheet until the top of her breast was exposed. Then he touched the curve. Nerve endings caught on fire and burned all the way down to her feminine center.

"Making love. Different muscles get used. You were very tight when I was inside you. Are you tender today?"

Oh, my. Heat flared on her cheeks. He wanted to talk about it? About doing that? About making love?

She swallowed, then set her coffee on the tray. "I feel fine."

"Let me know if that changes."

She wanted to ask what he would do about it if she was sore, but then she wasn't sure she wanted to know.

He leaned forward and kissed the top of her breast, then her neck, then the sensitive skin below her ear. "You're feeling a little awkward," he said, making the sentence a statement, not a question. "I'm going to leave you to shower and dress in private. But you owe me one."

"A shower? There are four more bathrooms in this house."

He stood up. "But you're going to be in this one."

Men and women showering together? Was that even legal? Her confusion must have shown on her face, because he was laughing as he left the room.

Holly moved the tray and got out of bed. Now that Jordan had mentioned it, she was sore. Her thigh muscles ached as if they'd been stretched a couple of inches too far, and the place between her legs was a little raw. She wanted a long, hot shower. Things would be clearer when she was done.

But as Holly wiped away the steam and stared at her reflection in the mirror, things weren't better. If anything, they were more confusing.

She tucked the towel around her body and wondered if making love had really changed her. This time yesterday she hadn't known about the intimacy that joined a man and a woman. While she didn't regret what she'd done, she was beginning to realize that there was a lot more to sex than just the act itself.

She reached for a wide-tooth comb and began drawing it through her wet hair.

"I'm all grown-up," she murmured. She had a business that was more successful than she had imagined, and she was taking care of herself. She was smart, capable and she'd finally joined the mainstream. She had a lover. All she needed was a beeper or a cellular phone.

Holly sank down on the edge of the tub and sighed. On the outside she might be just like everyone else, but on the inside she was different. She'd always been a little out of step. Having a lover wasn't her style. She could say and do all she wanted, but in her heart she was an old-fashioned woman.

She wanted to love the man she gave her body to, and Jordan didn't love her. Worse, he believed that love caused pain. In his mind it created more problems than it solved. So where did that leave her?

There was nothing to be solved right now, Holly decided. She finished with her hair, then dressed and headed downstairs. Jordan was in the living room, sitting on the sofa in front of the Christmas tree. The quilt was gone, as were the fire and the empty bottle of champagne. Even so, her gaze was drawn to the place where they had made love.

She remembered the beautiful lights on the tree and the scent of the fire. She remembered Jordan touching her with his hands and his mouth, loving her until the world disappeared and they were alone in the universe.

He stood up as she entered the room. He'd showered,

too, and his dark hair was brushed away from his face. A worn sweatshirt hugged his shoulders, and faded jeans clung to his thighs with the familiarity of an old lover. She'd seen him dressed that way countless times before. It didn't matter. Once their gazes met, her heart rate increased and her legs started to tremble.

He stepped toward her and pulled her into his embrace. His arms were strong and sure. She felt comfortable next to him. As his mouth brushed hers, she parted for him. Her body began to heat in anticipation.

He cupped her behind and pulled her hips toward him. Something hard pressed into her belly. Now she knew what his arousal meant. He wanted to make love, and she did, too.

She broke their kiss. "Jordan, I—"

He silenced her by placing a finger on her lips. "This is all going too fast for you."

She stared at him. "How did you know?"

He touched her face, then reached down and took her hand. "I can see it in your eyes. You're confused and afraid. Last night was great, but reality is difficult to deal with. You've got to be at the shop in—" he glanced at his watch "—an hour. You've got other things to do. I'm a complication you don't need."

Her eyes burned, and it took her a second to figure out she was fighting tears. "I'm sorry," she whispered.

He hugged her. "Don't cry, Holly. Please don't be upset. I understand. You need time to think about everything that happened."

"I know." She rested her forehead on his shoulder. "I'm not crying because I'm upset, I'm crying because you're being so nice."

"I thought being nice was a good thing."

"It is." She raised her head and smiled at him. "Thank you."

"You're welcome." His eyes darkened. "I do have one request."

"Which is?"

"Don't leave me until after the holidays."

She thought about what he was asking. The store was doing so well, she had the money to get another apartment. But the thought of leaving hadn't occurred to her.

"I'll stay," she said. "To be perfectly honest, the thought of leaving never crossed my mind."

"Good." He winked. "Let's try breakfast again. This time in the kitchen."

"Sounds great."

He headed that way. Holly started after him, then stopped in her tracks. Why *wasn't* she thinking of leaving? There was no future for her here, and even if there was, she didn't want a future with Jordan or any man. She didn't trust people.

But she did trust Jordan. She cared about him and enjoyed being with him. She wasn't sure how or when it had happened, but she'd come to trust him…and care about him.

She wasn't sure when she'd started to trust him and let him inside. Maybe that first day when he'd gone back into her apartment and saved Mistletoe. Maybe the first time he'd kissed her. Jordan Haynes was everything she'd ever wanted in a man. How was she supposed to resist him?

She loved him. With all her heart.

She closed her eyes as emotions overwhelmed her. She loved Jordan. Loved him, loved a man who was terrified of love. She must never let him know. She would have to be strong. She could continue to be his friend, and he would never know the truth.

An odd combination of joy and sadness filled her. She was finally ready to trust someone enough to fall in love, and he wasn't going to want her. In his own way Jordan was letting her down just like everyone else, but that didn't make her love him less. She couldn't help her feelings. It wasn't fair, but she didn't want to take her heart back. Jordan would have it forever, whether he wanted it or not.

Chapter Fifteen

Nine-year-old Mandy shrieked in delight when she unwrapped the huge box. The Victorian dollhouse had been built by hand from a kit, then painstakingly painted and decorated. Her big eyes got bigger, then filled with tears. She leapt to her feet, ran to the sofa where her parents sat and threw herself at Travis and Elizabeth.

Jordan watched his brother hug her close.

"I'm glad you like it," Travis said, his voice thick with emotion. "All your uncles worked on it with me."

Mandy sniffed, then faced the rest of the adults. "Thank you so much. It's the best dollhouse I've ever seen."

Holly shifted on the floor where she was sitting and glanced up at him. "When did you guys build it?" she asked.

"At the end of summer." He grinned, remembering the complicated directions and short tempers. "We used to build model airplanes together, but that was a long time ago.''

She raised her eyebrows and smiled. "Did some of you forget how to play well with others?"

"I think so. But it was fun." He leaned toward her and lowered his voice. "With everyone having girls, we figured we'd better learn how to build dollhouses, or we were going to be in a lot of trouble."

She glanced around the room. Jordan followed her gaze. Most of the children had already gone outside to play with new toys, bikes and in-line skates. Torn pieces of wrapping paper littered the floor. There were piles of bows, empty boxes and discarded directions everywhere he looked.

Did Holly see the mess, or did she see the happiness in the room? Jordan touched the top of her head, earning himself a quick smile. He knew what she saw. She had a gentle heart and a sweet spirit. She would see the good in the situation.

Travis carried the dollhouse up to the playroom. Mandy ran and got her cousin Nichole, who was her age, and both girls went upstairs with their new dolls. When Travis returned, he settled next to his wife and sighed.

"So what did *I* get for Christmas? I know I was good all year."

"How do you figure that?" Elizabeth asked.

He grinned. "You kept telling me."

She swatted his arm. Everyone laughed.

"I've been good, too," Kyle said. "So what has Santa brought me?"

"Wallpaper for the dining room," Sandy told him, then grinned when he groaned.

Jordan saw Holly smile at the conversation. Although she had been a little shy at first, she seemed to enjoy spending time with his family. He liked watching her interact with them. His brothers were protective and caring, and his sisters-in-law had claimed her as one of their own. He'd seen her whispering with the other women. They all had secrets, and he hoped she was comfortable enough to share hers. A part of him was curious as to what the females were always talking about, but then he figured he was probably better off not knowing.

Sandy said something, and Holly responded. As she spoke, she rested her head against his knee. He leaned back in the sofa and enjoyed her closeness.

He wanted her. Making love hadn't decreased his attraction. Instead, he could now picture her naked and beneath him. He knew what she felt like when he was inside her, and he wanted to be with her again. But he understood her caution. Relationships were new to her, and she didn't want to mess up.

Hell, he was hardly an expert at relationships, either, he reminded himself. He'd never had one that worked. In his heart he still believed that love was destructive. It would be safer for everyone if they just stayed friends. Friendship he understood and trusted.

The only problem was he didn't know if he and Holly *were* going to stay friends. She filled his life with joy. Even more, she filled the empty hole in his soul. He'd only known her a short time, yet he couldn't imagine his world without her. That would be trouble for both of them. He didn't want to hurt her; he didn't want to be hurt himself.

So where did that leave them? He had no answer to the question. He would simply have to take each day as it arrived and hope for the best. For today Holly was with him, and that was enough.

"Oh, my. These can't be for me," Holly said, drawing him back into the conversation.

He glanced up and saw Elizabeth and Sandy passing out presents. There were several boxes stacked in front of Holly.

She looked up at him. "Jordan?"

He shrugged. "Don't ask me. I'm always the last to know."

She counted. "Fourteen boxes? This is crazy."

Elizabeth paused by her and touched her hand. "It's not crazy. They're gifts. We all wanted to get you something."

"But I can't accept. It's too much."

"You don't even know what it is yet," Craig said, and pointed. "At least open a couple so we can all see." He glanced at his wife. "I bet you already know what it is."

"Of course," Jill said, then rested her hand on her belly. "The women always know everything."

"Don't you hate that?" Craig said.

"Yeah," Travis grumbled. "We need to think up some secrets to keep from them."

Elizabeth kissed him briefly on the mouth. "It would never happen, but it's sweet of you to want to try." She returned her attention to Holly. "Please open one of the boxes. If you really don't want the gift, you can tell us then."

Jordan understood Holly's confusion. She hadn't known everyone was going to get her a gift. He hadn't known, either, or he would have warned her. She'd baked cookies and passed them out, but he knew she wouldn't think that was equitable.

He leaned forward and put his hand on her shoulder. "They're trying to be nice. It means they like you."

She nodded, then reached for one of the packages. When

it was unwrapped, she opened the plain brown box and removed a white china cup and saucer. The old-fashioned design reminded him of some of the dishes he'd seen in catalogs she'd brought home from the store.

Sandy pointed. "We know you lost everything when your apartment was wrecked," she said. "So we got together and bought you new china. Each box is a place setting, and the other two are the completer set and some serving pieces. Please say you like them."

"They're beautiful," Holly said, sounding a little shell-shocked. She held the cup up to him.

He took it and touched the soft, cool piece. He could see this cup in Holly's capable hands. His mind filled with the image of her in bed, dressed in satin and lace, sipping her morning coffee. Even more terrifying, he could see himself there, too.

Longing twisted his gut until he couldn't think about anything else. He wanted her. He needed her. If only there was a safe way to keep her in his life.

"Just be polite and say thank you," he told her. "You'll make my family happy, and you'll get some plates out of it, too. Not a bad deal."

Elizabeth drew her eyebrows together. "We were trying to help. I hope you understand."

Holly nodded. "You're all so wonderful. Thank you. I love my gift." She leaned over and hugged Elizabeth.

"I think it's great," Kyle said, "but twelve place settings seems like a lot for one person. Of course, if she marries—"

He stopped talking suddenly as Sandy jabbed him in the ribs.

"What'd I say?"

Jill and Elizabeth started talking at once. Craig and

Travis exchanged knowing looks. Holly blushed. Jordan knew Kyle had simply voiced what everyone else was thinking. It was obvious something was going on between Holly and himself, and they wanted to know what.

Sandy and Elizabeth got busy passing out the rest of the presents. Jordan's brothers had given him some tools for his new garage. Kyle was disgusted to find out he really was getting wallpaper, then his good humor returned when he opened a box containing tickets for a Caribbean cruise.

Sandy placed a large, flat package in front of Jordan. He looked at the tag. It was from Holly. She scooted over on the carpet to give him room to open it. He tore away the paper and exposed a stunning Impressionist painting.

"Holly, you can't give me this."

She shrugged. "It's not by anyone really famous, so don't get too excited."

She'd mentioned a find of lesser-known artists at an estate sale about six months ago. She'd sold most of the paintings, but had admitted to keeping a couple of favorites for herself.

Her blue eyes were dark with a warm and welcoming emotion. "I wanted to give you something special," she said softly so the others couldn't hear. A smile tugged at the corner of her mouth. "Just be polite and say thank you. Isn't that what you told me?"

"Thank you," he said.

"I thought it would look nice in the dining room."

He grinned. "That's the only room that's finished, so I suppose it makes sense."

There was a second box wrapped in gaudy red-and-silver paper. The gift tag had a paw print on it. "It's from Mistletoe," she told him.

"I figured that." He shook the box. "What do you think

she put inside? Something that explodes, or at the very least smells bad?''

"Jordan, Mistletoe is a wonderful cat. I'm not sure why she hasn't taken to you, but as she likes everyone else, maybe this is your problem and not hers."

He grinned. "Great. I've been judged and found wanting by a cat."

He tore the paper. When he opened the oversize shirt box, he found a thick pullover sweater in black, gray and midnight blue.

"Mistletoe is sorry she used your favorite sweater for a bed," Holly said.

"No, she's not."

One corner of Holly's mouth curved up. "Even if she isn't, I am."

Around them the other adults were opening packages. Happy comments were exchanged, along with hugs and kisses. If a few of the embraces went on a little long, it only added to the festivity of the morning.

Jordan wanted to haul Holly into his arms and show her exactly how happy she made him. Instead, he forced himself to give her a quick kiss on the forehead. Even as he reminded himself he respected her need to come to terms with their odd relationship, he wanted to claim her as his. He wanted everyone to know that they were lovers and that he cared about her. He wanted her to be comfortable touching him in public.

"Oh, look what I just found under the tree," Elizabeth said, and handed Holly a small, square, jewelry-size box. His sister-in-law raised her eyebrows. "I've always been curious about your taste, Jordan. Guess I finally get to see what it's like."

"Guess so," he said mildly, but his heart started pounding hard against his ribs.

He'd wanted to get Holly something special. Something that would remind her of him without being threatening. His condition hadn't helped matters. For a while he'd been afraid he wouldn't be able to get out and around in time. But the physical therapy had done wonders, and he'd been able to find exactly what he wanted.

Holly stared at the small gold-wrapped package. "You shouldn't have."

"How do you know? You haven't looked at it yet."

She nodded, then fumbled with the wrapping. The black velvet box opened silently, exposing pearl earrings surrounded by a circle of diamonds. Holly stared at the jewelry, but didn't say a word.

Jordan found himself in the unfamiliar situation of feeling unsure of a gift. "The diamonds are earring jackets," he said quickly. "You can wear them with other things, and you can wear the pearls alone." He paused, then added lamely, "I thought they would look nice with your long dresses and fancy blouses for work."

Holly raised her head and stared at him. Light reflected off the moisture in her eyes. "They're so beautiful. You spent far too much money."

"He can afford it," Kyle said from across the room.

Jordan glanced around and saw they were the center of attention.

"That's right," Craig added. "The last dividend check was impressive."

Holly frowned. "What are they talking about?"

Jordan leaned back on the sofa and grinned. "Didn't I tell you? When Austin was starting his company, my brothers and I threw in with him. None of us had much money, but we gave him all of it. We now own a chunk of his very successful firm. In addition to being heartbreaking charmers, the Haynes brothers are well-off.''

"I guess that explains the Victorian mansions. I wondered how you did that on a fire fighter's salary.''

"Now you know.''

She stared at the earrings, then unfastened them and tried to put them in her ears. Her hands were shaking. When the task was accomplished, she sat up on her knees, then leaned forward and kissed him on the mouth.

It wasn't a passionate kiss. Even as she brushed her lips against his, color flared on her cheeks. But for Holly it was a bold, public move.

Before she could pull away, he touched her cheek and smiled at her. Her warm and welcome expression made him want…something. He couldn't explain it or define it. The need grew, pressing against his heart. If he had to put words to it, the closest he could come was that he wanted what his brothers had. Not the love. That still terrified him. But the secure relationship with someone who cared.

When all the presents had been opened, Elizabeth assigned tasks. Holly was in charge of piling up the gifts so there was room to walk around, while Jordan was sent to help in the kitchen. He was supposed to be fixing coffee, but instead, he found himself remembering Christmases past.

In the recent past he'd been the odd man out. Even before his brothers were married, they usually each brought a woman around during the holidays. He never had. Somehow sharing that part of his life had been too personal. He hadn't wanted to deal with a stranger. Better to be alone than with the wrong person.

"What do you look so serious about?" Elizabeth asked.

He glanced up and saw her leaning against the door frame. He shrugged. "Other holidays. This one is better."

She moved toward him. Elizabeth had a heart-shaped face and wide eyes. When she'd married Travis, she'd made his brothers her responsibility, too. Once she was part of the family, birthdays were remembered and celebrated, and family dinners became a part of everyone's lives.

She planted her hands on her hips and glared at him. "I swear, if I could have just one wish, it would be to spend five minutes alone with Earl Haynes."

"My father? Why?"

"That...that *bastard* doesn't deserve to live. He hurt you four so much. I want him punished for his crimes, and I want to be there to watch."

Her fierceness startled him. Although he hadn't been thinking about his childhood, Elizabeth's words brought it back to him. His father leaving to be with another woman. His mother crying softly in her room. The four Haynes brothers not sure what they were supposed to feel, only knowing that all the toys in the world couldn't make their home an easier place to live.

"That was a long time ago," he said.

"Maybe, but you're all still suffering because of it. You think I don't see what he did to you? All of you? Sometimes Travis can't sleep because of the memories. He's a wonderful man, yet he was terrified he didn't know how to be a good husband and father." She drew in a deep breath, then smiled. "I do love to go on, don't I?"

"You can be a little intense."

"That's because I care." She stepped closer and placed her hand on his arm. "Jordan, you've got to deal with the past. Your chance at a happy present is going to slip away if you don't get a grip on this."

He moved back. ''I don't know what you're talking about.''

''Yes, you do. I wish there was a way to erase everything and start over, but there isn't. Your parents—'' She shrugged. ''I don't agree with what your mother did, but I almost understand it. After all that time, she just snapped. Still, I wish she'd stayed in contact with the four of you.''

Jordan thought about what had really happened that last day. ''I don't blame her, I blame the other women. They could have said no to my father.''

Elizabeth stared at him oddly. ''Of course they are at fault, but they aren't the only ones. They said yes, but Earl was the one doing the asking. He spent his whole life trying to seduce anything in a skirt. Maybe it's easier to blame the women, but the real culprit is your father.''

She crossed the short distance between them. ''I know what you're thinking, Jordan, but it's not like that. You don't have to be like him. You are your own man.'' She smiled. ''If I wasn't so happily married, I might just make a play for you myself. Except I'd be too late.'' She hugged him. ''Holly is very special. Don't let her get away. If you do, you'll regret it for the rest of your life.''

She left the kitchen, and he was alone. As he made coffee, he thought about what his sister-in-law had said. That it was easier to blame the women than to blame his father. She was right. He did blame Louise. He blamed her for everything. Yet how much of it was really her fault? What about his father's part in the events? And his mother? In that, he agreed with Elizabeth. He understood his mother's need to leave Earl, but he resented her walking away from him without once looking back.

The Haynes family was in a hell of a mess. He shook his head. That wasn't true. His brothers had figured out how to fix things. He was the only one still fighting the past. Maybe it was time to let it go.

Holly snuggled closer to Jordan. They were sitting on the sofa in front of their Christmas tree. To her right a fire snapped, and the scent of wood smoke filled the room.

"Dinner was great," she said, then touched her earlobes and the beautiful earrings he'd given her. "Everything about the day was perfect. Thank you for a wonderful Christmas."

His arms tightened around her. "You're welcome."

She closed her eyes and held on to the happiness flooding her body. She wanted this day to last forever. She wanted to always be a part of him, of his world. She wanted to be able to confess her feelings and have them returned. She wanted him to love her.

A small sigh escaped her lips. There was no point in wishing for the moon. Jordan wasn't going to love her, because he wasn't going to love anyone. He feared love as she had once feared trust. He and his family had shown her otherwise, but who was there to show him?

Still, if she could have one more Christmas wish, it would be to have him want to be with her always.

"Holly, there's something I want to ask you," he said.

"What?"

He straightened slightly, shifting so he could see her face. His dark eyes were alive with emotions she couldn't read. She felt his tension, but didn't know the cause. Before she could ask what was wrong, he spoke.

"Holly, will you marry me?"

His question left her stunned and speechless. She could only stare. Marry him? He wanted her to marry him?

"I know this is sudden," he said. "But I've given it a

lot of thought. I enjoy everything about you. Being with you, talking to you, making love.''

The joy was so bright and so intense, she thought she might die right there. He wanted to marry her. *Her!*

"We want the same things," he continued. "A home and a family. I have the house.'' He motioned to the room. "Together we can be a family. I've always wanted kids. I'll take care of you, respect you." He touched her face, then kissed her lips. "I think we could make it work.''

She searched his face, waiting, but he was finished. The joy faded slowly, like a rainbow disappearing into the mist. At first you weren't sure it was going, then the edges blurred and it was gone. In the end there was only the memory of how beautiful it had been.

He wanted to marry her, but he hadn't said a word about his feelings for her.

"Commitment without love?" she asked, pleased that her voice sounded steady.

"I would honor you," he said, cupping her face in his hands. "I would be a faithful and giving husband.''

Almost, she thought sadly. Almost like love, but not exactly the same thing.

"I care about you," he told her.

She nodded. Caring. "I appreciate that. You like me and I'm glad. I like you, too.'' She pulled away from him, then slowly got to her feet. Her mind was spinning. She didn't know what to think. It had happened too fast.

Marriage to Jordan. She'd been dreaming of it since the moment she realized she loved him. He was offering her everything she wanted…almost. She could make love with him, share his bed, his life, have his children. She could be accepted by the loving embrace of his family. She could belong.

But he wouldn't love her. He would never know the down-to-the-bone, heart-filling emotion of love. He would never dream about her the way she dreamed about him.

"Holly?"

She laughed softly, wondering if the sound covered her pain. "You're right," she said. "About everything. We would do well together. Mutual affection and respect. Many marriages survive on less. There's only one problem." She looked at him and shrugged. "I changed the rules."

"What are you saying?"

"I'm not sure. I—" She broke off, not sure how much to confess. "I was so afraid to trust anyone. Everyone had let me down. Then you came along with your good looks and your smile. You drew me in, and I never had a chance. You offered me everything I'd ever wanted. I found myself trusting you."

His expression didn't change, but suddenly she didn't know what he was thinking. It was probably better that way, she told herself. Better for both of them.

"I've only ever asked for three things in my life," she said. "First, when I was fifteen, I asked my boyfriend to understand when I couldn't go with him to the dance because my mother was sick."

"He dumped you," Jordan said flatly. His hands tightened into fists.

She nodded. "Then I asked my father for money to help with my mom's medical expenses. You know what happened there."

"What's the third?"

"I asked my mother not to die and leave me. She did." Tears threatened, but she fought them back. "Now I want a fourth thing. I want a miracle." She drew in a steadying breath. She was probably only going to get to say this once in her life. She wasn't going to chicken out and miss the opportunity.

"I love you, Jordan. You're honorable and kind, loving, smart, funny. You're a good man. You make my knees weak and my heart beat faster. I love you, but I won't marry you. Not unless you can honestly say you love me back."

Chapter Sixteen

Holly sipped her coffee and tried to hold back her tears. She'd been up most of the night crying, and she felt as attractive and puffy as a wet sponge. If she held her head up and blinked steadily, she could get a little control, although the pain in her chest wasn't going away. At first she hadn't been able to identify the sharp ache, but she'd finally figured it out.

Jordan had broken her heart.

Oh, he hadn't meant to. His proposal had been genuine and sincere. He thought they could have a good life together. Maybe that's what made it worse. If he didn't care at all, then she could tell herself it was just a crush and she would get over it. But he did have feelings for her. Unfortunately he didn't love her. She felt as if she'd made the finals in one of life's most important events only to be told she didn't have whatever it took to win. There she was, Holly Garrett, first runner-up in the game of love.

Louise came into the kitchen. She'd reverted to her brightly colored clothes. In honor of the holiday season, she wore scarlet fitted trousers and a green patterned shirt. Three-inch plastic Christmas trees dangled from each ear.

She walked to the coffeepot and poured herself a cup. "You want to talk about it, or do you want me to leave and pretend I didn't see you?" she asked without turning around.

Holly rested her elbows on the kitchen table in front of her. "You can ignore me," she said.

Louise turned and glanced at her. "I don't think so, honey. You look a little too miserable to be left alone." She crossed the room and pulled out the chair next to Holly's. "Tell me what happened."

"I—" Fresh tears started down her cheeks. She swept them away, then tried to smile. "Christmas is supposed to be a happy time, yet here I am crying. Pretty silly, huh?"

Louise patted her hand. "Not at all. Life goes on, even if it is the holidays. Sometimes I think all the celebrating makes it worse. We're dealing with old memories, childhood dreams. You've got every right to be a little weepy."

Holly nodded. She appreciated the other woman's counsel. At times like this she missed her mother even more than usual. She, Holly, didn't understand life and men. She wasn't sure she understood all the questions, let alone had any answers.

"Jordan asked me to marry him," she said softly.

"Congratulations, child. He's not the Haynes brother I would have picked, but I know you have a soft spot for him." She looked closer at Holly and frowned. "You don't look very happy, though. Didn't you accept?"

"I couldn't. I—" She cleared her throat, then stared into her cup of coffee. "He doesn't love me."

"What?" Louise sounded outraged.

The tears started again. This time Holly let them fall down her cheeks. "He doesn't love me. He said he likes me and cares about me, that we get along well together and that we could have a happy marriage." She paused to swallow a sob. "I want more. I want him to love me with all his heart. Am I crazy, Louise? I tell myself I'm a child wishing for the moon. Jordan is a good man. He treats me like a princess." She pressed her lips tightly together and fought the tears.

"Oh, honey." Louise shifted her chair closer, then hugged Holly and drew her close. "I understand."

"I l-love him."

"I know. You've loved him from the beginning, haven't you? You came in here all innocent and lost your heart to him. I'm so sorry."

Holly leaned against Louise. The housekeeper wasn't her mother, but it felt nice to be comforted. "It's not your fault," she whispered. "It's no one's fault."

"It's mine. He knows what his father did, what he wanted, and that changed him."

Holly raised her head. "That was a long time ago."

"Jordan hasn't forgotten."

"Louise, you didn't ask Earl Haynes to divorce his wife."

"The result is the same, as if I did."

"You're blaming yourself for something that isn't your fault."

Louise was quiet for a minute. Her blue eyes darkened, and the lines around her eyes and mouth deepened. "I wish I could believe you were right, but in my heart I know the truth. Jordan was scarred that day. You forget I've known the Haynes brothers for years. I know that Craig was too responsible, that Travis worried about not being a good father, and Kyle wondered if he would ever grow up enough to care about someone else. I even know that Austin believed himself to be unlovable. And Jordan…'' She drew in a deep breath. ''Jordan is the most difficult of all.''

''Jordan believes love hurts,'' Holly whispered.

''Yes, he does. He's wrong, of course. All he has to do is look around his family and see all the good that love has brought them. But he's stubborn, like most men.''

Holly straightened and wiped her fingers across her face. ''Am I wrong not to marry him?''

''Only you can answer that.''

Holly nodded. She already knew the truth. Hearing it from Louise confirmed everything she knew. ''Since I was fifteen years old, I've been scared to trust anyone. My world wasn't secure at all. I've made my peace with that. I've learned to trust again. I trust Jordan and I love him. But if he can't trust and love me back, then I can't be with him.''

''You're very brave,'' Louise said. ''I wish I could be like you.''

Holly frowned. ''I don't understand.''

Louise wrapped her hands around her coffee mug and squeezed until her knuckles turned white. ''I keep thinking about what you said about my daughter. I want to get in touch with her. I want to give her a choice.''

For the first time since the proposal, Holly smiled. ''Do it, Louise. You've lost so much time with her already. If she doesn't want to see you, then you'll have the answer to your question. I know that would be painful to hear, but at least then you'll know. I suspect she's going to be thrilled to hear from you. Wait until she finds out she has four half brothers.''

Louise shrugged. "I might not tell her that all at once. I wouldn't want to scare her away." She thought for a minute. "You're right. I'll do it. We've lost twenty-eight years already. I don't want to lose another minute."

Holly was pleased. At least one of them had a chance at happiness.

Jordan opened the front door and stepped inside his house. He knew right away that something was wrong. He wasn't sure if it was the absence of sound or movement, or just a sixth sense kicking in.

He started to take the stairs two at a time, then turned back and headed for the study that had been his makeshift bedroom. The closet door was partially closed. He flung it open and stared at the clean, bare floor. He didn't have to look any further. Mistletoe was gone, and with her, Holly.

He walked to the chair next to the rented hospital bed that was being returned in the morning. He sank down, rested his elbows on his knees and his head in his hands.

Gone. Just like that. Without warning. Without saying goodbye.

As soon as she'd refused his proposal, he knew he'd done everything all wrong. He should have planned his words better. But the truth was, he hadn't thought he would be proposing. He'd been thinking about not wanting to lose her when he'd blurted everything out.

He'd been a fool. Worse, he'd hurt her. Now she was gone and he didn't know what he was going to do.

"She left a note."

He glanced up. Louise had silently entered the room. She stood in front of him and held out an envelope. He took it, then opened it and glanced at the contents.

Jordan,

I'm sorry to leave this way. It seems so cowardly, but I'm the first to confess I don't have the courage to face you right now. I'm leaving because I can't stay. Before it was easy to pretend I didn't love you. I can't do that anymore. I know this doesn't make sense. After all, if I really loved you why wouldn't I jump at your proposal? Maybe I'm being foolish and wishing for the moon. I don't know. The only thing I am sure of is that I want a man who can love me back. One who trusts me enough to give his heart. I don't blame you for not being able to do that. I wish it could have been different.

Much love,
Holly.

He read the paper over and over until he'd memorized every word. Until he couldn't breathe past the pain or focus on anything but the ripping hole in his chest. Then he crumpled the note in his hand.

"She's gone," he said, too stunned to realize he'd spoken the words out loud.

"This morning." Louise took a step closer to him. "I know you don't want to hear this from me, and you're not going to believe me, but I'm sorry, Jordan. Sorry for both of you." She paused. "I'm leaving, too. You're back on your feet, and with Holly gone you don't really need me."

He nodded without saying anything. She started from the room.

"Wait!" he called, springing to his feet and hurrying after her. "Where did she go?"

Louise's gaze saw far too much. "Does it matter?"

"Yes."

"She's rented the gate house on Kyle and Sandy's property." She touched his forearm. "You have your reasons for hating me," she said. "I don't agree with them, but I understand. Even so, I'm going to give you a piece of advice. You're a fool if you let her go."

He tightened his fist around the small ball of paper. "It's none of your business."

She laughed. "You're right, it isn't. So what? Are you going to get mad at me? Jordan, you've carried a chip on your shoulder for nearly twenty years. I don't care what you think anymore. You can continue to act like a bastard, but I don't give a damn."

Maybe it was the rawness of the pain, or the shock. For once Jordan wasn't able to hide behind a mask of indifference. For the first time since that afternoon so many years ago, he allowed himself to really look at Louise.

Her plastic Christmas-tree earrings caught the light and twinkled. There were lines around her eyes, and her skin wasn't as tight as it had been, but other than that, she was the same woman she'd always been. She had a good heart. Her willingness to put up with him proved that.

Jordan thought about how empty his world was going to be now that Holly was gone. If his father had felt a tenth of the same feelings for Louise, then maybe Jordan could understand some of his actions. He still didn't excuse them, but he could almost understand.

If he was willing to go that far for his father, the truly guilty party, then what did he owe the woman in front of him? She had made a mistake. One she'd paid for every day of the past twenty-nine years. She'd only been seventeen. He'd hated her for destroying his family, when the truth was his family had never been more than a collection of unrelated parts. Earl Haynes had made sure there was nothing left to destroy.

"I'm sorry," he said.

Her gaze narrowed. "What'd you say?"

"I'm sorry. I blamed you for everything, and it was never your fault."

She planted her hands on her hips. "Dammit, Jordan, I just got this thing figured out. Don't you go confusing me again."

He shook his head. "I wanted to blame you because it was safer than blaming my father. It's been a whole lot easier to be angry with you. I've made your life hell. An apology can't change that or the past, but it's all I have."

She pursed her lips, then wiped at the corner of her eye. "I can't believe this. Now you've got me all weepy. Apology accepted."

He didn't believe her. "Just like that?"

"Would you feel better if I punished you first?"

"Yes."

"It's not my style. I have a big heart, Jordan. I can forgive. I'm not saying I won't be snippy a time or two when I remember how mean you've been, but I understand why you did it. If you're sincere, then I'm willing to forgive."

He reached out and drew her next to him. She was stiff at first, then she relaxed against him. "Now I know why my father fell in love with you."

She swatted his arm and stepped back. "You Haynes boys were always sweet-talkers. Stop wasting time with me. Go find Holly and bring her back."

Now it was his turn to be uncomfortable. "I can't."

"Figures you couldn't be good-looking *and* smart. Tell me why not."

"She needs me to love her."

"You do."

He shook his head. "No, I don't. I won't love her."

"Didn't you learn anything? You don't get a choice about loving someone, Jordan. It just happens, then you have to deal with it. Can't you see you've loved her from the first moment you set eyes on the girl?"

"No." He turned away. Not love. Never love. He knew the danger, the price love extracted. He'd felt the cold blade of love, and knew the damage inherent in the emotion.

"There's no fool like an old fool," Louise muttered, and left the room.

Jordan was alone in the silence. He listened to it and wondered how long it would take for him to forget the woman he'd lost.

Jordan felt like a fifth-grader being called to the principal's office. He stood in front of the fireplace, facing his three brothers and Austin.

Kyle threw himself on the sofa and raised his hands toward the heavens. "You talk to him," he said in disgust. "He's not listening to a word I'm saying."

"I'm listening," Jordan explained patiently. "I agree with your point. However, nothing has changed."

Travis paced from the Christmas tree to the far wall. "Everything has changed, Jordan. That's the point. We're all different. Ten years ago—hell, five years ago—I would have agreed with you. Loving someone was a terrifying thought. None of us knew how to have a relationship. Dad really screwed us up inside. But we've all learned to take a chance. That's what this is about. When you find someone special, you have to be willing to take risks."

Jordan frowned. He appreciated what they were trying to

do, but they didn't understand the situation. They didn't know the real truth. It had been easier for them.

Yet a small voice in the back of his mind reminded him that he *wanted* his brothers to convince him. He wanted to believe. In the seven days Holly had been gone, he'd learned that surviving without her was nearly impossible. He couldn't stop thinking about her. He needed to hear her voice, her laughter. He needed to hold her and touch her; he needed to explain how empty his world was without her. He even missed the damn cat.

"We've all let the past go," Travis said. "You've got to do the same."

"It's not that simple," a woman said.

Jordan glanced up at the newcomer. Louise entered the living room and looked at him.

"You didn't tell them, did you?" she asked.

He shook his head.

"Why not?"

"It's your secret," he said. "It wasn't mine to share."

She wore a cobalt blue blouse that brought out the color in her eyes. But her face was pale, and her mouth pulled into a straight line.

"The time for secrets is over," she said. "Travis, have a seat." She motioned to the sofas.

Austin and Craig sat in one. Travis joined Kyle in the other. Louise stood in front of the men and clasped her hands loosely together. Jordan moved behind her and squeezed her shoulders. She gave him a brief smile that didn't quite take, then drew in a breath.

"Twenty-nine years ago, when I was seventeen, I had an affair with Earl Haynes."

As she told the story, Jordan walked over and stared at the Christmas tree. There were ornaments from his childhood and several Victorian decorations that Holly had brought. He touched an old-fashioned Santa and remembered her laughing as she'd placed it on the tree. Somehow in a few short weeks she'd woven herself into the fabric of his life. Short of unraveling everything into a pile of string, he didn't know how he was going to let her go.

His brothers listened quietly. Jordan watched the different emotions play across their faces. Confusion, surprise, concern. He didn't see any anger. None of them blamed Louise.

"You're saying we have a sister?" Craig asked when she was finished.

"Half sister."

Travis grinned. "Hot damn."

Kyle bounced to his feet. "Hey, I'm not the youngest anymore."

"Where is she?" Craig asked, also getting to his feet.

"Have you been in touch with her?" Kyle asked.

Louise held up her hands. "One at a time. No, I haven't been in touch with her. I gave her up for adoption. I don't know where she is."

Travis glanced at his brothers. "We have to find her. I know a good private detective. Let's go down to the station and give him a call."

Kyle linked his arm through Louise's and headed for the door. "Do you know her name? Maybe we can trace her through the computer."

Craig joined them. "I have a couple of friends with federal agencies. They can help, too. We'll find her, Louise. Then you can invite her home."

They were still talking when the front door closed behind them.

"How do you feel about having a half sister?" Austin asked.

Jordan turned. His friend still sat on the sofa. "I thought you left with the rest of them."

Austin shrugged. "Your problem never got resolved."

"Maybe there isn't a solution."

"Maybe." The other man wore his hair long, and he had an earring in one ear. Compared to the clean-cut Haynes brothers, he was an outlaw. But he was family, so they teased him about his wild ways and accepted him into the fold.

Austin stretched his long legs out in front of him and stared at his black cowboy boots. "You're afraid," he said flatly. "That's what this is all about."

"Bull."

"Deny it all you want, it doesn't change the truth. I know, Jordan. I recognize the symptoms." Austin glanced up. His dark eyes didn't give anything away. "I never wanted to care about Rebecca. Sure, I knew who she was. I even knew she had a crush on me. But I wasn't going to get involved. Not with an innocent like her."

Jordan thought about Holly's innocence. She'd been a virgin. Now that was gone. He couldn't replace what he'd taken.

"Then one day she was in my life," Austin continued. "Soaking wet and dripping in my garage. I couldn't turn her away and in the end I couldn't resist her."

"Do you have a point?" Jordan asked, perching on the far end of the sofa.

"Yeah, I do." Austin shifted, leaning forward and resting his elbows on his knees. He laced his fingers together. "The worst part is the unknown. The pain of being alone, the loneliness, is familiar. You've dealt with that. You understand it. But loving someone, risking everything, is unknown. There's no way to know how bad it's going to be. You barely survive the pain of being alone, so how can you deal with anything worse? So you don't bother to try."

"You don't know what the hell you're talking about," Jordan said, but he was bluffing. Everything Austin said made sense.

Fortunately Austin ignored him. "I nearly lost Rebecca because I was a fool. You're doing the same thing." He rose to his feet. "Don't. Don't let pride and fear stand in the way. Even if we'd only had one day together, I still would have risked it. Knowing what I know now, my only regret is that I held back so long. I hate to think of the time I wasted being foolish. Don't you do the same thing. You're never going to find another Holly. If you let her go, you'll spend the rest of your life waiting for the pain to stop. And it never will."

With that, he left.

Once again Jordan was alone in the silence. He sat in front of the Christmas tree and tried to figure out what he was going to do.

Austin had made sense, but he didn't know all the facts. Jordan knew loving someone was more than a risk. It was a promise for disaster. He'd seen the consequences of love and what it had done to his family. He'd seen the pain and suffering.

A thin shaft of sunlight danced off the ornaments. He remembered last year when he'd spent the day at Kyle and Sandy's while the kids decorated the tree. He remembered the laughter and joy in the house.

As he closed his eyes, he could see and hear conversations and incidents from the past few years. Husbands and wives, nieces and nephews, births, holidays, celebrations.

Hundreds of disconnected events, thousands of happy moments, with one constant emotion.

Love.

For the first thirty years something had destroyed the Haynes family, but it hadn't been love. Travis and Craig had chosen poorly the first time they'd married, but then they'd figured out their mistakes.

Love hadn't torn apart his family. Love had made them whole.

Holly had offered her heart to him, and he'd turned her down. What the hell was wrong with him?

He raced toward the front door, pausing only long enough to grab his leather jacket, then hurried down the porch stairs and to his car.

Fifteen minutes later he stood in front of the small gatehouse she had rented. He raised his hand to knock, then paused. What was he going to say to her? How could he convince her to believe him and give him a second chance?

He figured the words would come or not, then rapped sharply. The door opened, and she stood in front of him.

Her long blond hair was loose around her face, the way he liked it. The silky strands hung almost to her waist. Wide blue eyes stared at him. Her mouth parted slightly, but she didn't speak. She wore a rose sweater over dark leggings. Her feet were bare. She was the most beautiful creature he'd ever seen. He wanted her as he'd never wanted any woman before. He needed her.

"Jordan?" The soft sound of her voice washed over him, healing him and giving him courage.

She stepped back and motioned for him to come inside. He did as she requested, then shrugged out of his jacket and tossed it on the sofa in the small but neat living room.

"Holly, I—" He wasn't sure what to say. He took her hands in his and gripped them tightly.

"Marry me," he said. "Not because it's sensible or because we'd be good together. Marry me because you are the best part of my world. Marry me because without you my soul is cold and dark and my heart doesn't know how to love. Marry me because I need you more than I need to draw breath. Marry me because..."

He searched her face. She glowed with happiness, and her mouth curved up at the corners.

"Marry me because I finally understand that love isn't something to be feared. Love makes us whole. Marry me because I love you."

A single tear trembled on her lower lashes. She blinked, and it slipped to her cheek. She brushed it away impatiently. "Are you sure?"

"That I love you?"

She nodded.

"Yes," he said. "About anything else? No. Not for a minute. I'm terrified of what's going to happen. But I'm more terrified of being without you."

She pulled her hands free and flung herself at him. He held her close and knew that this was where they both belonged. In each other's arms.

"I love you, too," she said.

"So you'll marry me?"

"Yes." She raised her head and kissed him.

As their lips touched, he knew he'd found where he belonged. Somehow this kind, gentle spirit had seen past his protective barriers. She'd made a place for herself in the dark recesses of his being, and stubbornly insisted he let her chase the shadows away.

As her mouth parted and he dipped inside to taste her,

he was vaguely aware of something brushing against his leg. He broke the kiss and glanced down. Mistletoe had bitten into his leather jacket and was dragging it across the room.

"Probably going to take it to her kittens to use as a chew toy," he muttered.

"What?" Holly said as she ran her hands across his chest, then reached for his shirt buttons.

He didn't answer, because he was doing his own exploration, reaching under her sweater to cup her behind and urge her against him.

"When we get married, I want a dog," he murmured, then nibbled on her neck. "I'm going to need some protection against that damn cat."

"I like dogs," she said as she unfastened two buttons and pressed her lips on his bare chest. He sucked in his breath. "Maybe a baby," she continued. "Then it can be three against one. That should be about right."

He bent over and picked her up in his arms. She wrapped her arms about his neck as he carried her toward the bedroom. He kissed her again. He wanted to have children with her. Lots of golden-haired daughters who looked just like their mother. He wasn't sure he deserved that much happiness, but he wasn't about to refuse it. With Holly, anything was possible. They'd found a miracle together and learned firsthand about the magical healing powers of love.

Epilogue

Red roses and poinsettias filled the church. Wreaths of evergreen, trimmed with red velvet ribbons, hung below the stained glass windows.

The guests were seated by the Haynes brothers and Austin, who were acting as ushers. Since Holly was new in town and didn't have any family, there was no division by bride or groom. Just as well, Jordan thought, watching the church fill up. They were going to have enough trouble fitting everyone in as it was.

What had started out to be a small wedding for just family had ballooned into an extravagant occasion that included most of the town.

Organ music filled the church, accompanied by the quiet rumble of conversation. Perhaps there were those in the crowd who questioned having a Christmas theme wedding in late January, but he didn't mind. The holiday had brought them together and would always be special to them. There hadn't been enough time to prepare a wedding for New Year's Eve, and neither he nor Holly had wanted to wait until the following Christmas to be joined as husband and wife.

As it was, her decision to stay at Kyle and Sandy's gatehouse until the wedding had sorely tried his patience. He'd barely had a taste of her lush body in his bed, then he was forced to do without. At least all the waiting would end tonight. They would spend the weekend in San Francisco, at an expensive hotel with excellent room service. Then Monday morning they would fly to Hawaii for their honeymoon.

The organ music changed to a classical piece. His brothers and Austin took their places beside him, while his sisters-in-law began their slow march down the aisle. Louise had already been seated in the front row, accepting her due as honorary mother of the bride.

The doors at the rear of the church closed briefly, the wedding march began, and the doors opened.

Holly stood at the end of the long aisle, a beautiful vision in white. Her pale gown clung to her torso before flaring out to the ground. A long veil trailed behind her. She wore her hair piled on top of her head, circled by a wreath of white roses.

Love, still a new and wondrous emotion, filled him. He wanted to go to her and draw her into his arms. Instead he waited, willing her to come to him, knowing that he'd spent his whole life preparing for this moment.

She moved slowly and confidently, her gaze never leaving his. When she reached his side, he held out his hand. She placed her palm on his. At last he was where he belonged. They both were. They smiled, then faced the minister.

"Dearly beloved," the man began.

"Wait," Holly interrupted. She looked at Jordan. "Before we say the vows, I want you to know that I love you."

He searched her face, noting the sincerity in her blue eyes, knowing his expression reflected the same earnestness. "I love you, too."

The minister chuckled. "I was going to scold you two and tell you that the loving-each-other part comes later in the ceremony, but you're right. Everything begins with love. As it should."

They exchanged vows and rings; they kissed and accepted the congratulations of their friends and family. Holly and Jordan had begun their new life with the promise of love, and that promise would last a lifetime.

* * * * *

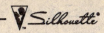

SPECIAL EDITION™

Don't miss this emotional journey from

MARIE FERRARELLA

HER SPECIAL CHARM
(SE #1726)

The last book in her miniseries

The Cameo

**Available December 2005
from Silhouette Special Edition**

Schoolteacher Constance Beaulieu loved a challenge,
and charming gruff detective James Munro was
a task she had to undertake. As he reluctantly
accepted her drop-ins and dinner offers, he began
to realize the depth of his feelings for her. Suddenly
he had a task of his own: heal from the past and
surrender to this woman's special allure.

Available at your favorite retail outlet.

Visit Silhouette Books at www.eHarlequin.com   SSEHSC1205

▼ *Silhouette*®

SPECIAL EDITION™

HOLIDAY HEARTS

Because there's no place
like home for the holidays…

UNDER THE MISTLETOE
(SE #1725)
On-sale December 2005

by
KRISTIN HARDY

No-nonsense businesswoman Hadley Stone had work to
do—modernize the Hotel Mount Eisenhower and increase
profits. But hotel manager Gabe Trask stood in her way,
jealously guarding the Victorian landmark's legacy. Would
the beautiful Vermont Christmas—and meetings under
the mistletoe—soften the adversaries' hearts?

Also in the series…
WHERE THERE'S SMOKE, November 2005
VERMONT VALENTINE, February 2006

If you enjoyed what you just read,
then we've got an offer you can't resist!

Take 2 bestselling love stories FREE!

Plus get a FREE surprise gift!

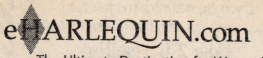

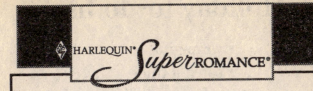

HARLEQUIN *Super*ROMANCE

Critically acclaimed author

Tara Taylor Quinn

brings you

The Promise of Christmas

Harlequin Superromance #1309
On sale November 2005

In this deeply emotional story, a woman
unexpectedly becomes the guardian of her
brother's child. Shortly before Christmas,
Leslie Sanderson finds herself coping with
grief, with lingering and fearful memories and
with unforseen motherhood. She also
rediscovers a man from her past who could
help her move toward the promise
of a new future....

Available wherever Harlequin books are sold.

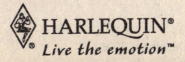

HARLEQUIN®
Live the emotion™

Holiday to-do list:

- wrap gifts
- catch a thief
- solve a murder
- deal with Mom

Well-respected Florida detective Maggie Skerritt
is finally getting her life on track when a
suspicious crime shakes up her holiday plans.

Holidays Are Murder
Charlotte Douglas

Kate Austin makes
a captivating debut
in this luminous tale
of an unconventional
road trip…and one
woman's metamorphosis.

dragonflies AND dinosaurs

KATE AUSTIN

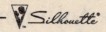